I struggled awake and sat up in bed to listen. Someone or something was rapping on the tower door. I reached in alarm for the cord of my bed lamp and blinked in the resulting brightness of the room.

There was no further sound. I switched out the light and slipped down beneath the covers. Had I dreamed the knocking? Not more than five minutes passed before the rapping came again, reverberating through the tower. I jumped from bed, still half asleep, and stumbled to the tower entrance. There was a swift, shadowy movement above me—

"Who's there?" I called. *"What do you want?"*

Hunter's Green

Phyllis A. Whitney

A FAWCETT CREST BOOK

Fawcett Publications, Inc., Greenwich, Conn.

I

I have no past, I have no future. I have only the immediate present.

Today I looked out among the sculptured yew shapes of an English garden and saw my husband for the first time in two years. Today I stood before the gates of Athmore, lost among other gaping visitors. I climbed the long walk to the high front terrace of the house where I had once lived—and found myself anonymous.

Ahead of me the stones of Athmore glowed like warm honey in the spring sunshine, instead of frowning cold gray upon an American intruder as they had once done. I meant nothing to the house. I had been put aside once and for all. I had loved Athmore and I'd hated it—but I had not come here to see the house.

It seemed necessary to make my approach quietly, to get well within the grounds and establish my presence before I could be caught and sent peremptorily packing. Fortunately, I had found it simple enough to get down from London and make my secret assault upon the gates. As soon as the airport bus brought me into the city I had hurried to an agency office and learned that a tour would leave shortly on an overnight trip, stopping at another house or two along the way and winding up at Athmore in the afternoon. I had booked my place and taken my suitcase aboard the tour bus, meaning to stay at the village until . . . until whatever I had come for was completed.

I cared nothing about seeing the other houses just then and I had found myself waiting in strange gardens, sitting idly in the sun, or aboard the bus until we could be off again. In between I rode the miles away in my window seat, lost in the turnings of my own mind.

All those contradictory turnings! Somehow I must free myself of old ties, as I had not been able to do back home in New York. The only thing to do with dead love is to bury it. The letter from Maggie Graham had reached me a week ago, and I'd spent the hours since reading it over and over, assuring myself that Justin North meant nothing to me anymore, and that my marriage to him was an impossible mistake. But emotion cannot be buried by words, though it can be aroused by them. Only seeing him again would set me free.

There was no more need to hate him furiously, as I had when I ran away from Athmore. Surely I had grown up enough in these three years to know that hating was never the way out of anything. But surely if I saw him again, if I felt that cold look of his upon me, I would understand how thoroughly love could die. I would be released from—from what? From hope, perhaps? From whatever it was, released I must be so that I could get on with my own life without any thought of Justin and Athmore to tug at my memory and weaken me at the wrong moment. I was young and it should be easy. It must be done.

I had shut out the warnings which stormed my mind, taken leave from my travel agency job and come headlong across the Atlantic by the first plane that would have me. I had sent no word to Justin's cousin Maggie Graham, who still kept Athmore for him, or to anyone else. Three years ago, at nineteen, I had married Justin. Two years ago I had run away from Athmore. Had I grown up at all since then? Sometimes I wondered.

By the time the long trip was over, taking longer than its usual four hours by car, and our bus pulled up before handsome wrought-iron gates that I remembered all too well, the others on the tour were friends, chatting among themselves. I pleaded a headache, took sympathetically proffered aspirin, and kept to myself. If I told them my name was Eve North, what a stir it would cause!

It seemed strange to find Athmore gates closed and barred, so that it was necessary to summon the gatekeeper to open them. In the old days the gates stood hospitably ajar most of the time, and the old man who occupied the gatehouse had little to do. Certainly he wore no uniform like that of the husky young fellow who came to let us in. The locked gates were my first hint that all was not well within, and I felt the first stirring of a new uneasiness.

While we waited for the ceremonial unbarring, I fumbled with the camera strung over my shoulder and stared at the

fancifully wrought crest of a wolfhound formed in the iron-
work. This was the Athmore crest, and at sight of it pain
stabbed through me. From earliest days, long before this
house was built, the crest of an Irish wolfhound had belonged
to earlier Athmores, and the motif was repeated at intervals
throughout house and grounds, even appearing on the notepaper. It had been an Athmore tradition to keep live wolfhounds as well, though the need to fend off evil intruders no
longer existed, as it had in another day.

The very first puppy born after Justin brought me home
from our honeymoon had become, without any formal giving,
my own dog. "Deirdre" we had named her in honor of her
Irish ancestors. But Justin had always called her "Deirdre
McIntosh" with that flash of humor that sometimes surprised
me in him, and often he shortened it to "Mac." There had
been crossbreeding in the strain for many years, he said, and
there were Scottish deerhounds on the pup's family tree, so
we must bow in all directions.

Deirdre had been *mine*. The only thing that was wholly
mine at Athmore. Even now when I remembered her I ached
with sadness. The thought of Justin left me dry-eyed and staring, but I could weep for Deirdre. Where was she now? I
wondered. Would she know me if we met? Probably not,
since a year-old dog would have a short memory.

"You feel everything too intensely at the very same time
that you don't trust your own feelings," Maggie used to tell
me. "It's one thing to be joyful, but quite another to agonize."

During the last two years I had tried not to agonize in the
old, self-pitying way. But there had been no joy in me either.

The bar was off the gate, the latch raised, and our tour
streamed through. I let the others carry me along. We went
on foot, crossing the curve of driveway to follow the brief
walk interspersed by steps that cut through several levels of
lawn. That impossibly green and velvet lawn I remembered
so well! There had been rain in the morning, but now only
puffs of white cloud sailed a pale blue sky. The sun gave us
Athmore at its impressive best. I made myself look at the
house as we walked toward it. I even tried to recapture my
first feeling of seeing it when I was nineteen and had wandered through the open gates unbidden and unannounced.
My grandmother had lived in the nearby village as a child,
before she had grown up to marry an American, and she had
told me marvelous tales of the house and those who had lived

in it. So I had come to it with open-hearted eagerness, and I wished I could experience the same feeling again. But all that young emotion seemed lost to me forever.

The sun-tinted stones rose ahead of us in their familiar H form, and I stopped like any tourist to take a picture of the house. Strange to think I had none. This time I wanted something graphic to recall its details when I was far away. Even as I snapped the shutter, however, I smiled wryly at my own action. Here was another of those contrary, diverging pathways. I wanted to forget Athmore—so I came with a camera in order to recreate its memory when I left it for the last time.

I put the contradictions from my mind and gave my attention fully to the house. All this stone had come from the quarry—now long unused—on Athmore land. A three-storied wing on either side held the main rooms of the house, while the long bar across the H housed the entrance and those great halls and galleries that had awed and sometimes depressed me. Athmore was not one of the larger "stately" homes of England. Indeed, it had a satisfying compactness and neatness about it that I preferred to such echoing, castle-like structures as I had visited on other estates. Still, it was larger than any house I had ever set foot in at home and there was a certain splendid arrogance about stones that had stood for nearly two hundred years. The original Athmore Hall had been built in Elizabethan times by one John Edmond Athmore, and it had burned down twice, so that the present Athmore was young as such houses go, having been built in the first decade of the nineteenth century. Still, nearly two hundred years can give anything an air of supreme confidence.

My own years were now twenty-two and my confidence was uncertain. "Believe in yourself," Justin used to say to me impatiently, but I could find little in myself to justify such faith. My father had been a well-known illustrator, and my mother had devoted herself to him contentedly. She had been devoted to me as well and I had been surrounded by love for the first seven years of my life. After my mother's death I had my father to myself for three more years before I lost him for good to the woman who became my stepmother. That was when the loneliness and the uncertainty began, the loss of confidence, when nothing went right. My grandmother was too ill to take me herself, though her love and interest never failed. Eventually I was sent away to a series of schools, where I could grow up without making a nuisance of myself, as I always seemed able to do at home. Somehow I went right on feeling uncertain and unsure of myself until Justin fell so unexpectedly in love with me and I thought everything had changed.

It had not worked out that way. I knew now that I'd never had anything real to offer him. What he had seen in me had never actually existed. Perhaps what I believed I had found in him had never existed either. And here I was back at Athmore to make very sure of this.

Our tour went up the sloping walk, with wide lawns spreading out toward circling driveways on either side, and beyond to drowsing clumps of beech and oak, obviously painted by Turner. The terrace was just above us, its stone balustrade running on either hand, to divide in the center where broad steps led upward. A big red setter crossed the terrace as we approached, giving us a casual look of indifference out of great sad eyes.

My heart had begun to thump unbearably and my mouth was dry. How could I tell who might be looking out from spacious windows in either wing? Those second-floor front rooms on the left had been Justin's—and mine. But surely Justin would be in London, busy at the work that so absorbed him, and against which I had always rebelled. Cars—the designing and improvement of cars for a man like Justin! I could imagine him a diplomat, or occupying a seat in Parliament, or even as a writer of note. He had the intellect for any of these careers. Yet he concerned himself with the turn of a fender—"bumper" the English called it—the purr of an engine, and I remembered him at the wheel of a car racing with grim speed about the parklands of Athmore. That had frightened me more than once, because there was a strange contradiction in him—he disliked driving. When he drove like that it was to release springs of tension, and it made me afraid.

But even if Justin was not here, others might look out and see me. I pulled up the collar of my hunter's green trench coat so that it hid brown hair that reached my shoulders, and ducked my chin into the bright yellow scarf at my throat.

If Maggie saw me first it might not matter, since she had written me to come, and if she looked out and recognized me she would have the good sense to move quietly and raise no alarm. She had, however, wanted me to stay in London until she could see me there—so she might not be pleased to find I had come on alone.

It was really Maggie I wanted to see, I insisted to myself —though unannounced and not in London. If Marc saw me it might be different. The very thought of Justin's younger brother made me wince. I wanted to avoid seeing Marc ever again! He had always preferred city to country living, and Maggie had mentioned in an earlier letter that he had a job of sorts in a London art gallery, so he might well be away.

Her letter, which had brought me here, dealt only with Justin and me. Quite naturally, she still found most of the fault mine for what had happened. I was not sure why she had written me at all, after more than a year's silence, and only occasional letters before that. Why had she felt called upon to let me know that Justin meant at last to instigate proceedings for a divorce, and that he intended to marry again? Why had she begged me so urgently to come to England? She mentioned no names, but one in particular leaped immediately to my mind. If it was Alicia Daven he meant to marry—! Suddenly my fingernails were pressing crescents into my palms. Was I here mainly because of Alicia and because old jealousy would not die? How was I ever to be sure of my real motivation?

Ahead of us on the terrace, waiting as we climbed the steps, was a young woman, blond and poised and very English. Maggie's latest secretary, I supposed. Maggie had a good many interests and civic duties. Athmore fortunes being at low ebb, her charities were not great, but she needed the part-time help of a young woman from town who came in for a few hours two or three days a week, and she had always assigned these girls to the task of showing visitors about and introducing them to Athmore. I was glad this one was a stranger.

We climbed the wide steps and stood in a self-conscious circle, while she told us that her name was Miss Davis, and welcomed us to Athmore. I huddled, still anonymous, among the others, but my eyes strayed from where she pointed and followed the line of the two square towers that crowned the front corner of each wing. At the back of the house were two more such towers, invisible from where I stood, with flat rooftops dotted with tall chimneys stretching between. The bar of the H connected the four towers by means of the roofs, with parapet walls all about, where one could stand

and look out over much of the estate. From towers and roof-tops my eyes moved downward to where afternoon sun fired the windows of the great library, and, a floor below, to the columned doorway—that neoclassic touch that gave this Georgian house a special grace without being ostentatious. The term "Georgian" could cover all sorts of imaginative architecture, I knew, but the remarkable woman who had built this later Athmore had restrained her taste to a creditable degree.

Recessed in stone to the right of the front door was a niche that held a bas-relief statue of the Athmore wolfhound. Here the dog stood in the traditional pose, its long, strong neck turned so that it looked over one shoulder. I thought of Deirdre, who had loved me for whatever I was, and mourned her loss again.

"Before we go into the house itself, ladies and gentlemen," Miss Davis was saying, "you must see the old ruins of Athmore Hall. Some of the walls of the original building are still intact, you know, including the famous arch of the chapel window. If you will come this way, please."

Like an airplane stewardess guiding her charges, Miss Davis followed the terrace briskly to the right of the house, and started along a winding path that led across lawns toward the road. Her nose pointed straight ahead, and so confident was she of being followed that she cast no glance behind as she led the way. Everyone streamed after her—except myself. The last place I wanted to visit in chattering company was this ruin deep in Athmore woods. There I had experienced my first joy over finding the house, and there I had suffered the pain of saying goodby to it. I wanted to see the place again, but I must be alone when I did. Perhaps if I could get there first—!

Obeying sudden impulse, I ran through Maggie's garden toward the shortcut, while the tour plodded off by the main road. The way through the woods was quicker, and I could take my snapshots and be back at the house before Miss Davis was through with her lecturing.

Beneath the trees it was quiet, save for the crackle of twigs under my feet, and the scolding of birds I disturbed in my hurry. I ran until broken stone walls lay across my path, outlining the boundaries of what had once been Athmore Hall. The great arch of the chapel window still rose against the sky, and it was a sight to break my heart all over again if I gave in to sentimental lingering. But the nearness of the tour prevented that. I pointed my camera haphazardly in one direction and then another, snapping pictures almost at random. Later I would have these to remind me, and I could be as sentimental as I pleased in the privacy of my own room. No matter what I told myself, I had come here to remember, not to forget!

I took several quick views of the arch from different angles, caught the broken stone doorway to what had once been the house, and had time left for a few other shots as well. As I finished the roll in my camera I heard distant sounds of the approaching tour, though they would not be here for another few minutes at least.

Unexpectedly, a voice spoke from beyond a crumbling wall, calling my name: "Miss Eve, Miss Eve!"

I whirled to see Old Daniel, Athmore's longtime gardener and guardian dragon, watching me from the chapel corner, a light of such welcome on his wrinkled, ancient face that I was startled. During my year with Justin, the old man had never liked me. He considered me an intruder, an upstart, and certainly no proper mistress for Athmore. He had been far more friendly toward Alicia Daven, whom he considered a proper English gentlewoman, no matter what reckless escapades she might sometimes indulge in. I had learned from him how much could be forgiven one born to the purple, and how little was forgiven the outsider like myself. Yet here he was hobbling toward me with an air of anxious greeting, as though there was no one he would rather see.

In dismay over being discovered, I waited while he came to speak to me. He reached for my hand at once and held it in bony, earth-stained fingers, almost as if in pleading. His faded eyes looked out from the creases of age with an air of conveying some gravely important message.

Yet all he muttered under his breath was, "You're back, Miss Eve, you're back!"

I withdrew my hand from his dry clasp, more than a little uneasy. He disliked me, yet he welcomed me in almost maudlin fashion, as though he might not be in full possession of his wits. I was suddenly aware of the loneliness of the green-shadowed ruins about me.

"I'm only here to see Miss Maggie," I told him. "I won't be staying at Athmore."

He seemed not to care whether I came or went from Athmore, if only I would stay and talk to him here.

"You remember the chess game?" he pressed me, his man-

ner as secretive as though he conveyed some matter of state.
"You remember the fine chess game in the top'ry garden,
Miss?"

I could only nod my bewilderment. The topiary garden,
with giant chess figures carved in ancient yew, was one of
Athmore's curiosities, and Old Daniel was the preserver of its
tradition, carving the yew year after year to keep the traditional forms intact.

"Of course I remember," I said.

His pale eyes stared at me without blinking and his lips
moved tremulously as he tried to speak. It struck me suddenly that something had terrified him.

"It's the rook's play next," he said in the tone of a conspir-
ator who spoke of evil. "The rook's play! Don't you forget
that, Miss Eve. Don't forget as how Old Daniel tol' you it's
the rook's play and the king had better watch out."

I tried to calm him with my promise. "If you say so, I'll
remember," I said, wanting to escape his wild look and the
way he reached for my hand.

Miss Davis's high voice came to us clearly as the tour
neared the ruins. I would not stay to watch strangers tramp-
ing over a place that had once belonged to me. At least I had
my pictures, and I told the man a hurried goodby and ran
back through the woods by the way I'd come. Miss Davis
would deal with him now, find out what was troubling him.
She would know how to manage, if indeed he had become
senile in the last two years.

The day was cool and in spite of my hurried return to the
house, I was glad of the trench coat I had brought along
against England's cold and rain. Once more I hunched into
its collar, as all the disguise I could manage, and walked idly
around the side terrace. Because of Old Daniel's odd urgency
I wanted to see the topiary garden again. I passed the tall
French windows of the red drawing room without daring to
give them more than a glance, and stepped out upon the narrow strip of sloping lawn behind the house.

At the foot of the grassy slope began the Victorian garden
of trimmed yew that Old Daniel had cared for nearly all his
life. Each geometrical figure was hewn to the exact form he
had preserved out of the past. It was a curious work of art,
yet somehow I had never cared for the garden. Maggie was
ridiculously proud of it, but to Justin it was an oddity, like a
Victorian whatnot. Though he objected to the expenditure of
working time required to maintain it, he nevertheless suffered

the garden as a showpiece of Athmore, and he knew it would
break Old Daniel's heart to give it up. So it had continued
year after year repeating itself in all the fantastic growth that
was forced upon the yew. For me, even now, there seemed
something repellent about these dark, still figures, poised in
their unending game.

The topiary chessboard spread away from me across the
rear of the house, wide and deep, with those pieces which remained in play meticulously represented, from king and
queen down to a number of pawns, all engaged in a game
and already in play.

I stood at the edge of the garden and was glad that the sun
was shining. Once I had played a moonlit game of hide-and-
seek with Justin in this place and I had lost him—a tall, black
figure among other black, tall figures of yew—and I had lost
myself too in the midst of alien, inhuman shapes. It had been
oddly frightening until he found me and pulled me into his
arms, held me close so that I turned from shivering child to
woman and forgot the chessmen.

But I must not think of that now.

Since no one hailed me, I stepped out among the chessmen
and wandered through the maze they quickly formed around
me, their heads hiding me from the view of overlooking windows. All the yew figures were of great size. Even the pawns
came to my shoulder, with kings and queens towering high,
and rooks and bishops looking down upon me. I stood in the
shadow of the prickly greenish-black mass of a mitered
bishop and felt safe from being sighted at the house. My
knees had a tendency to weaken and I let them buckle under
me and dropped to the velvet grass.

It was easy to lose myself in the grotesque shadow of the
yew, and I bent my head forward so that my long hair swept
across my face, veiling me further. Sitting there I gave myself
up to nothingness. I wanted neither joy nor agony. I wanted
only to live a full, busy life at home and forget about happiness that was only an illusion, about a love forever lost. I did
not need Justin anymore. Here in the topiary garden at Athmore I told myself this and let my mind and my emotions go
blank.

Only my outward senses were still alive. I could feel the
prickle of yew at my cheek, the springy turf beneath my
knees. I could respond to a butterfly flitting past, yellow as
the sunlight, and breathe the marvelously clean, green-gold
air of country England. My hearing was alert enough too,

and I caught the sound of a voice not far away—and stiffened.

It was a man's voice and I would never forget the deep timbre of those tones, or the faintly grating quality of harshness that could underlie it when Justin was angry. The harshness was there now.

"Every bit of glass in the place was smashed," he said. "But very quietly. The guard heard nothing and the dogs barked too late to do any good."

"Is the damage serious?" a woman's voice asked. "Or is it the further delay that matters most?"

This voice was Maggie Graham's. I'd have recognized her low, softly clipped tones anywhere. I whipped back the dark curtain of my hair and looked around the yew bishop. The two were coming toward me and I was helpless to move. Maggie looked tall and sturdy and fit as always—a handsome woman in her slightly old-fashioned brown tweeds. She would be forty now—five years older than Justin, and still a vital, striking woman. But it was not upon Maggie that my attention focused so helplessly.

"Both," Justin said in answer to Maggie's question. "Both serious and delaying. Nearly all of one phase was destroyed. This is more ugly mischief. The worst yet. I'll put a guard on duty tonight."

Their words meant little to me, though perhaps this was the reason for the barred entrance gates. Now, however, I wanted to look rather than listen. To look at Justin's face until I was satisfied—as I had longed to look during all those empty nights when I conjured it up before me from more than three thousand miles away.

He seemed older and a bit thinner than I remembered. The crease down his left cheek had deepened and his mouth had a straight, grim look about it. The white streak running back from his forehead through light-brown hair—that streak I had once thought romantic—had widened. His aristocratic nose seemed more than ever like the beak of some bird of prey—a hawk perhaps. Its slightly flared nostrils could widen in moments of stress, and it was the moments of stress I remembered best because there had been so many of them. None of the Norths were known for keeping their tempers.

I could not move. I could neither jump to my feet and confront them on their own level, nor crawl miserably away to hide among the chessmen. They continued toward me, and it was Maggie who saw me first. As a rule she was equal to anything, poised and unruffled, no matter what the crisis, as she had needed to be, playing more mother than cousin to Justin and Marc ever since her own mother had died years ago. But now she blinked and gave me a brief stare before she looked away. The look was enough to make Justin turn. His expression did not change except for the deepening of the crease in his cheek, the tightening of his mouth. He stared at me for a long, dreadful moment and then came directly toward me.

I had not thought it would be like this. I had imagined myself facing him coolly, wondering what I had ever seen in such a man. I'd never expected to shiver, I'd never expected that I would warm to fire, then freeze into ice. I dared look only at his long feet in their scuffed country brogues. I dared not raise my eyes higher than his shoes and gray trousers.

"Get up!" he ordered me. "What are you doing hiding in the bushes? Was it you last night in my workshop smashing about out of pure devilment?"

He had not changed. He had always been capable of saying outrageous, arrogant things when he was angry. Though why he should fly into a rage at the sight of me, I didn't know.

"Don't be ridiculous, Justin," Maggie said. I think for once she was not as calm as she pretended, though she went on to lie with quiet assurance. "Eve is here because I invited her to Athmore. Though I can't think why she's come into the garden without announcing herself."

Her words were a reprieve I had not expected. At least I was not to be thrown out ignominiously, even though I had not waited for Maggie in London. When she bent and held out her hand to me, I saw the sparkle of a star sapphire on her engagement finger, where before she had worn only her widow's wedding ring. I noted, but did not think about it till later. I gave her my hand and let her pull me to my feet with her strong grasp. Once standing, I braced myself, with hands thrust deep in my coat pockets, and my feet well apart. My eyes were on a level with Justin's chin, and again I looked no higher. What an impossible, unlovable man he was, I assured myself.

"Of course she can't stay here," Justin told Maggie. "I won't have her at Athmore." And then to me, roughly, "How did you get in?"

"Through the gate," I said. "I came with the tour."

"Then we owe you a tea, at least," Maggie put in cheerfully, paying no attention to Justin. "Did you know we have Thursday Tea Tours nowadays, Eve? With one of us presiding. It's a way of getting visitors to come all that way from London. And it's much better for business."

Justin looked as if he might explode. His lean face had darkened and his eyes were the color of Athmore stones on a winter day. But he could not strike us, shake us, or crack our heads together, as he might very well have liked. So he turned on his heel with such force that he ground a hole into Daniel's turf and strode away toward the house. Maggie watched him go and shook her head sadly.

"He had a good deal to upset him just now. And you'll be one more worry. But perhaps that's how it must be."

"I—I won't stay," I faltered, growing a little angry, now that I need not look into Justin's cold eyes. Angry not only with him, but with myself—a mixture that was hurtfully familiar.

Maggie studied me. She had dropped my hand once I was on my feet and she offered no warm, welcoming move in my direction. There was no reason why she should. All her loyalties were given to Justin—and even more to Marc, who had always been her favorite, as I knew only too well. I must come very low in the scale of her consideration. Yet she had kept me here by the lie she had told Justin.

"Why did you come here by yourself?" she asked quietly. "I would have brought you."

"I—I'm not sure. I suppose I haven't felt anything at all for a long time. Until your letter came. Then everything began to hurt dreadfully—the way something hurts after you've been frozen to a state of numbness and the blood starts to flow again. So I didn't want to wait. I couldn't live with a feeling like that. I'd rather be angry. I'd rather feel misused—and I knew I could count on Justin to give me that. When was he ever fair or kind? Now he's given me exactly what I need. And he gave it to me right away. I'm over caring. I'll go home at once!"

Maggie reached out and took my left hand in hers, turning it curiously about. She touched the finger that wore no wedding ring, looked at the palm as though she might do her amusing little palm-reading act.

"You're shivering," she said. "And no one can go on being angry forever. Americans give in to their emotions too easily,

I always think. I suppose that's why they get on so well with
the Italians and the Irish. You were always one to talk about
loving and hating in one breath and at high pitch."

The old twinge of irritation went through me. How the English loved to generalize about Americans—even Maggie,
who had an enthusiasm for us most of the time.

From a distance we could hear the sounds of the tour returning. Miss Davis's tones were cultured, but carrying, as
she pointed out the charms of Athmore on the way back to
the house.

Maggie dropped my hand. "Go with the others. Come in
with them when Caryl brings them to the drawing room for
tea. In the meantime I'll get a room ready for you. You have
a bag?"

"But—but Justin—?" I began.

I remembered her generous smile that could nevertheless
be a touch shrewd and knowing. "Hurry and join your
group," she said.

I did not hurry. I trailed after them slowly, knowing the
way well enough and still trying to get myself in hand, feeling betrayed by the intensity of my own reactions. I threaded
my way through tall yew shapes and returned to the terrace
in time to follow the last member of the tour between white
columns and under the wide fanlight of the door.

"This is the famous Hall of Armor," Miss Davis was telling her charges, sounding a little more by rote than she had
in the beginning.

I stood just within the door of the long echoing room that
connected the two wings of the house. The ceiling was remotely high, and ornate with plaster whimsies. Across the
room's great width the marvelous staircase, recessed in its
own bay, wound upward with stately grace. I stood with the
toes of my shoes resting upon a red marble diamond set
among the white. Spreading away from me, the great expanse
of red and white marble gleamed in sunlight cast through tall
windows that rose on either hand. Along the walls, between
the windows and at the far ends of the hall, stood the pieces
of Spanish armor John Edmond Athmore and his sons had
taken pride in collecting—some of them perhaps at first hand
from the bodies of Spaniards. Many of these pieces had been
saved from the fires that had attacked the original Athmore
Hall, just as a few of the precious paintings had been saved.

In its place of honor opposite the door hung the famous
portrait of John Edmond in the prime of his life, shortly be-

fore his tragic death. Sometimes I had thought Justin looked
a little like him, and for that reason I would no more than
glance at the picture as Miss Davis mentioned it.

Her low heels tapped the marble, and we followed her to
the door of the red drawing room in the south wing. I closed
my eyes for an instant before I stepped across the sill, long-
ing foolishly to recapture my first sight of the room as it had
seemed when I'd first entered it so eagerly and timidly when I
was nineteen.

The red and gold damask of the walls had been brought
from Italy, Justin had told me, and I heard the echo of his
very speech in Miss Davis's pronouncements. I let my attention wander in further recognition, paying little attention to
her words.

The great rugs were richly faded Persian, the chairs and
sofa upholstered in a muted Chinese red. And there were
touches of chinoiserie everywhere—a cabinet of red lacquer
here, a small inlaid table there. On the shelf above a black
marble fireplace stood the lovely Ming horse I remembered.
In fact, I remembered everything—from the tall French windows that opened upon the side terrace and were framed in
dusky red draperies threaded with gold, to the burnished
brass scrollwork of andirons on the white marble base of the
hearth. The draperies were not as old as the red damask
walls, but they were old enough to carry the smell of ancient
dust. I need not put my face to them to feel the tickle of remembered sneezes in my nose. I did not need to go close to
see that they were worn and mended, as much of Athmore
was worn threadbare.

We all stood close together at one end of the big room,
herded there by Miss Davis, and I looked about at the individual members of this group I had joined, realizing what a
mixed lot we were. There was a red-faced man whom I had
put down as a butcher, though for all I knew he might be a
judge. There was a wizened little Englishwoman in her seven-
ties, who seemed to be absorbing her surroundings as though
they were indeed sustaining meat and drink to her. There was
a middle-class mother-and-father, son-and-daughter group,
well-to-do and bent on putting their best foot forward. In
fact, Sonny was nudged now and then by his mother to make
certain of this.

Behind me someone came into the room, and I forgot my
itemizing and turned uneasily. Justin would not come to tea,
I knew. Not with me present—if he ever came. But the per-

son whose name flashed into my mind was Marc. Marc
would regard such tours as cause for high amusement,
though he would play the role of gracious host to the hilt, so
that hardly anyone would suspect him of mockery. But it was
Maggie who had reappeared, and I breathed again. The man
who came in with her I did not immediately recognize.

They had tactfully appeared before anyone was sitting
down, so there need be no awkward jumping up again, and I
watched as Maggie went gracefully from visitor to visitor,
learning names with real interest, saying a few words to each,
asking questions, inviting everyone to find a chair—turning
the whole affair from a paid-for tour to a social occasion,
with herself the more than gracious hostess, and ourselves her
most welcome guests. It was make-believe, of course, but
done with kindness and genuine interest.

I hadn't expected her to come to me, but she was suddenly
at my side, holding out her hand, her brown eyes challenging
me.

"And your name, young lady? I don't believe you've told
me."

I mumbled something a bit wildly, and she accepted the
mumble with a kind nod and saw that I was seated next to the
elderly Englishwoman who was so enjoying this experience. I
could feel comfortable there, and I let her tell me how many
of the great houses of England she had visited, and how, as
an American, I must value an experience that was surely not
possible in my own country. When she paused for breath I
asked a question.

"When you visited the chapel ruins did you happen to see
an old man there?"

Her attention focused on me shrewdly. "Why, yes, we did.
Odd that you should mention it. He was quite old—a bit dod-
dering, I should say. Miss Davis told us he was the gardener.
She had to stop him from interrupting the tour. Somehow I
had the impression that he was upset about something, even
frightened. But when we left he stayed behind. How did you
know?"

"I saw him too," I said vaguely, and did not explain. Fortunately, she lost interest and turned to speak to the man on
her right.

I sipped strong English tea and thought about Old Daniel.
If he had been frightened—what was the cause? And why
had he hung about those ruins? But there was no one I could
easily ask, so I gave myself to nibbling at wafer-thin biscuits,

tiny sandwiches, and little frosted cakes brought in on an old-fashioned tiered silver tea tray. I remembered the tray, as I remembered the honey flavor of the cakes, undoubtedly made by the same cook who had ruled the kitchen when I had lived at Athmore. For the moment I forgot about Old Daniel.

There was only one near giveaway for me. That was when the maid, Nellie, who was passing cakes, the picture of perfection in her black uniform and white patch of organdy apron, looked straight into my face and nearly dropped the plate in my lap. I thanked her hastily, managing to shake my head slightly at the same time. She recovered with a gulp or two and went on about the room. Once Nellie had been my friend in an alien place.

The man who had come in with Maggie took no part in the ceremony of the Tea Tour. He bowed courteously enough to everyone in general, but he did not accompany Maggie about the room. He stood, teacup in hand, looking out upon a sun-dappled terrace through the farthest French window. I caught the shine of jewels in his cuff links—and suddenly knew who he was.

Nigel Barrow had come to Athmore on a visit from his home in the Bahamas when I had met him here that other time. His complexion had been far more tan from the islands' sun than it was now, and he had not worn a mustache then. His graying hairline had receded a bit more too, though he was only a year or so older than Justin. The ostentatious cuff links identified him for me. They had always puzzled me, being worn by so quiet and unassuming a man. His business, as I recalled, had something to do with building and real estate in the Bahamas, and I gathered that he had made enough money to sport jeweled cuff links if he chose. He was unmarried, and Justin and Marc and Maggie had long considered him one of the family because Justin had taken him up when they were boys together in the same school. Justin had come to the school by right of birth, while Nigel Barrow had attained it the hard way—by winning himself a difficult scholarship. Justin had brought him home one holiday, and the family had more or less adopted him. I remembered him especially because of a rather embarrassing conversation I had once had with him.

He saw me looking in his direction and smiled faintly, raising his cup in discreet greeting. Maggie must have warned him of my presence. He was a quiet, well-mannered man, rather slight in build, but wiry and active. I recalled that he

could outride the gentry at hounds, and he had taken up the
sport, riding whenever it was possible. I remembered this fact
very well, because all I could do with a horse was tumble off
it. Once, when Justin had ridden past me in a fury, Nigel Barrow had come to pick me up and dust me off. Justin had
never been able to understand why everyone could not learn
to stay in a saddle. He thought I was stubborn and fell off to
annoy him. After all, as he so often pointed out, wasn't my
chief mission in life trying to torment and annoy him? Justin
had never understood anything about me—never! And I
mustn't start shaking again.

Maggie moved from guests to tea table and back, and once
she stepped to the window to speak to Nigel. I saw her put her
left hand lightly on his arm, caught again the shine of the star
sapphire on her engagement finger. The jewels in Nigel's cuff
links were star sapphires! My heart sank a little. How could
he be right for Maggie Graham? He was an outsider. For all
that Athmore had once been almost like a home to him, he
wasn't born to it, or born to what it stood for.

I choked on a crumb of biscuit, catching myself up. Was I
really such a snob? I, who was never more of an outsider than Nigel
could ever be! I who had never lived comfortably at Athmore
and never could—not if I were here a hundred years. Not
only Justin, but the house itself had rejected me. So what was
I doing here in the red drawing room drinking English tea and
thinking critically of a man who was essentially kind, if not to
the manor born?

The tea hour ended at last, and Miss Davis made little
shooing gestures that brought us to our feet. I meant to leave
with the others. I meant to plant myself solidly in their midst,
but Maggie went smoothly into action and cut me out from
the rest. They flowed through the Hall of Armor without me,
and Maggie led me toward the stairs.

"Your room is ready," she said. "I've had your bag brought
in from the bus and it was explained to the driver that you're
staying over with us. Run upstairs and get settled. Ring for
Nellie when you're ready and let me know when we can have
a talk. Nellie is yours again while you're here, in between her
other duties."

There was no resisting her. I was like that nineteen-year-old
I had once been—ready clay for anyone to mold, and eager to
be molded. I had been trying desperately to find out who I
was in those days, and only too eager to be what anyone I
liked thought me. The difficulty was that I had never set prop-

erly in any one pattern. I could never stay fired in the Athmore kiln. Afterward I always crumbled back into my own uncertain American shape, and Athmore had been decidedly upset by me.

Nellie waited for me at the foot of the stairs, prepared for me now. In the old days an upstairs maid would never have been expected to double in the parlor, but such times were gone forever. Nellie worked where she was needed, anywhere in the house.

Except for my dubious encounter with Old Daniel, hers was my first real welcome to Athmore. "It's fine you're back, Miss Eve," she said, and I hadn't the heart to tell her that I was far from "back."

How well I remembered the white staircase, its iron grillwork painted white to match and rising gracefully on either side of the steps. A red velvet carpet flowed smoothly around their elliptical curve, and the shining banister carried the eye upward and upward, from floor to floor. That staircase had always seemed to me one of the masterpieces of the house. The vast expanse of wall above, unbroken by windows, was covered with handsome family portraits, the prominent position above the lower flight being given to a full-length painting of that Mrs. Langley who had built this house and graced it with her own inventive imagination. She had ended by living in it as a widow with five marriageable daughters. How they must have made the place ring with their merry parties before the eldest found a husband and brought him home to carry on the Athmore tradition by adding a new name to the roster. The name of Dunscombe, which continued to haunt Athmore in its own particular way, though there had been no descendants of that name. The portrait of the unfortunate Mr. Dunscombe had been relegated to an upper floor. In a way, the present family was proud of him, though he was something of an embarrassment as well. Mrs. Langley had probably never approved of her son-in-law's marriage to her darling Cynthia, but the lovely face of her eldest daughter, visible in its own portrait told its story of willful determination and perversity.

Nellie paid no attention to the paintings as she climbed. Her curious sidelong glances were all for me. She had been my favorite of the Athmore staff when I'd come here three years ago, and while I had never been able to resign myself to the ministrations of a lady's maid, Nellie and I had got along very well. I knew about her deaf grandfather and her rheumatic mother. I knew about the young man from the village who was courting her, and I noticed now the wedding band on her hand.

She told me readily as we climbed the stairs. She had married her Jamie, but recently he had taken a fall from a roof he was helping a neighbor to shingle. His back had been that bad he could not work as helper to the village chemist for a time. So Nellie had returned to Athmore, which was always understaffed, and glad enough she was to be helping out with her man. He was better now, but she would stay on awhile.

"Miss Maggie has put you in the blue lady's room, Miss Eve," she said. "Up on the second floor, rear. Where you can see the top'ry garden and the lawns."

"Second floor" meant the third floor to me, and I always called it so. English houses started at ground floor, with the first floor above, and I was constantly confused.

"Oh, it's right that you're back, Miss Eve!" she ran on. "We've been proper fearful for Mr. Justin, I can tell you. It will be a pity if he marries that—"

"Hush!" I said. "I haven't come to stay, Nellie. It's just that there are some—some things that need doing before—"

I floundered and she did not help me. She simply looked at me with sad reproach on her plump-cheeked face, and said nothing more as we mounted the stairs together. Mrs. Langley's five daughters watched us climb, and probably mocked me from their separate portraits, knowing very well that this time I would not last even as long as I had the first.

Nellie took me through the long gallery on the top floor and into a corridor in the north wing that led to the blue lady's room. When she had left me I stood in the center of the room and looked about at blue canopied bed, blue carpet and draperies, blue upholstery—all very rich and faded and worn. The old nonsense ran through my mind. Was this the *blue* lady's room? Or was it the room of a blue lady? Oh, the latter, surely. I thought a little wildly. Of course it was the room of a very blue lady!

There were tears on my cheeks without warning. It was a lovely room, but it was not *my* room. The room I had shared so joyfully—and sometimes miserably—with Justin was far larger than this, and adjoining it had been a lovely small dressing room which Justin had let me decorate especially for myself.

Nellie had already unpacked my things, and a dressing gown lay across the bed, with slippers on the floor beside it. I kicked the slippers away and flung myself down across the blue coverlet. Two years ago, when I left, I hadn't been able to cry except when I'd said goodbye to Deirdre. But I wept now, and pounded my fists upon the pillow. Tingling blood throbbed again through frozen veins, and the pain was almost more than I could bear.

Almost. Not quite. One endured what had to be endured, I was learning. Or did something about it. That was why I was here—to do something. To make the amputation complete. A missing part could throb endlessly, no matter how lost, unless both mind and body accepted the severance, admitted it, said "gone is gone," and learned to get along without.

Tears were a waste of time. Therapeutic, perhaps, but I had too much to do. I must see Maggie, settle matters once and for all, and be out of this place tomorrow. I would leave word that I would not oppose Justin's action. I would behave with dignity and firm decision. My meeting with him had made everything quite clear, so that now I could act.

I got up resolutely and washed my face, combed my hair free of tangles and fastened a band around it to hold it back. It was a style Justin had always liked—young and free and without artifice, he said. Like Alice in Wonderland, I thought looking in the mirror. And who else could I possibly be? That was the trouble, and I felt every bit as confused as Alice, no matter what I told myself about acting with firm decision and dignity. There was no certainty in me, no confidence which lasted. That was the trouble. Yet now, somehow, I must acquire these qualities. I could not go on playing Alice all my life.

I found the bell and rang for Nellie, who came so quickly she must have lingered down the hall. I asked her to see if Mrs. Graham would speak with me now. Then I went to stand at one of the two windows of my corner room. The window was open, of course. Windows were always open in English homes, it seemed to me. I reached to pull it shut against the late afternoon chill and heard the sound of singing coming from another room on my own floor. I knew that voice from American radio and television, where the singer was currently popular.

Who in the world at Athmore could be playing a recording of Petula Clark? I wondered and leaned into the window opening to listen.

II

The singer's voice came to me clearly and the words of the song:

> *For all we know*
> *We may never meet again . . .*
> *Tomorrow may never come . . .*

The plaintive song of some years before was brought to fresh life with the modern beat of Petula Clark. I didn't want to hear it. I did not want those words, that tune to start humming through my mind.

I started to close the window when movement on the ground arrested me. This was the side of the house which overlooked the garage and stables. The buildings were set back at a fair distance from the house and partly screened by a splendid row of young beech trees. The driveway wound between these buildings and the house, and two men were crossing into view—Justin and his brother Marc.

Hidden by the blue draperies at my window, I studied Marc warily. His fair hair shone in the later afternoon sun, and I knew his eyes would be as heartbreakingly blue as ever. Not that they had ever broken my heart. Marc was too ultra good-looking to appeal to me. I liked a man to be more virile and rugged. There was a delicacy about Marc's features which gave them that slightly inbred look one sometimes finds in young Englishmen of good family.

My flesh crept a little as I watched him approach the house with Justin. Even though the fault for what had happened two years ago had been as much mine as it had been Marc's, and I had tried to use him for my own angry purpose, he had managed to use me far more cleverly. I had never quite fathomed his motives—they were too devious and obscure for any sim-

ple understanding. Certainly he had done nothing to help me
once the chips were down. I knew more than ever that I
wanted to be away from Athmore before I met him again.

The brothers seemed to be arguing heatedly as they approached the house, and Justin looked more glowering than
ever. Once Marc glanced up toward the window from which
Petula Clark's tones were throbbing and I drew hastily back,
lest his eyes pick me out at my window. Had he been told that
I was here? I wondered. And I wondered too—as I had so often—how he had reconciled his position with his brother after
I had fled from Athmore.

Since I could not bear to watch these two, I turned to the
rear window which overlooked the topiary garden, thinking
once more about my strange meeting with Old Daniel in the
woods. His curious eagerness to see me—whom he had always
regarded as a foreigner, with no right to stay at Athmore—
had been altogether out of key. What was it he had tried to
tell me about the chess game? "It's the rook's play," he had
said. I was to remember that. But of course it was the rook's
play! That, at least, I understood. Out on the grassy spaces of
the vast chessboard one move of the black rook would place
the white king in check. So it was forever up to White to save
the game and save the white king by counterstrategy. Everyone knew this who lived at Athmore. So why had Old Daniel
urged the fact upon me and warned me that the white king
had better "watch out"?

Nellie's knock on my door rescued me from unanswered
questions and I hurried to open it. The news that Maggie
would see me in her sitting room right away was welcome.
Now I could finish what I had to do and leave for London tomorrow. There must be no wavering, no more indecision. I
told myself there was just one thing I wanted to make sure of
first—that the pictures I had taken had turned out well. I removed the film from the camera, talking to Nellie as I did so.

"Your Jamie used to make a hobby of photography, didn't
he? Do you suppose he could develop this roll for me and
print a set of pictures? I'd like very much to make sure they
came out before I leave tomorrow."

She took the roll and slipped it into her pocket. "Of course
he'll be glad to do them for you, Miss. I'll bring them for sure
when I come in tomorrow morning. He's sold off his enlargement camera, but he can still do developing and printing."

We went into the corridor together, and Nellie cocked an

ear in the direction of the music that came faintly from behind a closed door toward the front of the house.

"She's at it day and night that one," she said, with no great
respect for the presence of a guest, and free with me as she
would never have been with other members of the family.

"Who is she?" I asked.

Nellie rolled her eyes. "That's Miss Dacia—Mr. Marc's latest." Her shrug indicated disapproval. I had no interest in
Marc's women and I asked no more questions.

"You needn't come with me, Nellie," I said. "I haven't forgotten the way."

A little uncertainly she left me and went off toward the
back stairs, perhaps remembering how I had managed to get
lost in the house when I had first lived here.

I hurried through the long gallery that connected north and
south wings, with a fleeting glance at the remote wall to which
Mr. Dunscombe's portrait had been relegated. There had been
a time when I had felt a certain comradely sympathy for that
unhappy son-in-law, but I had no time to pay my respects
now. On the floor below, the stairway opened into the great
library, and I went through the doorway with a familiar sense
of recognition.

The word "great" aptly described the room. The library occupied the area directly above the Hall of Armor. The wide
boards of its darkly polished floor were bare except for occasional small rugs, and bookcases reached from floor to high
ceiling along every available wall. Three chandeliers marched
the length of the ceiling, and there was comfortable room at
either end for two fireplaces. Chairs and sofas grouped themselves down the room, but there were oases for the solitary
reader as well, with a lamp suitably placed, or a tall window
which could light the room brightly when the sun was shining.
I had always liked the library, for all that it could turn to
gloom and shadow by night, or on a gray winter's day.

At the far end a doorway let me into the second-floor corridor of the south wing, and I followed it toward Maggie's
rooms at the rear. Marc's apartment had occupied the front
end of the house off this corridor, I remembered, and was
probably still there, since Athmore was not a house given to
change.

Maggie's bedroom was a spacious affair, with a smaller sitting room opening off it and overlooking the rear corner of
the floor. It was at the open door of this room that I paused.

Inside, a fire burned cozily—in my honor, undoubtedly, since Americans were always cold in English houses.

Maggie was waiting for me. "Come in," she called, "and do close the door after you. We'll need to have an uninterrupted chat, won't we?"

Her tone lacked warmth and I knew that we had moved a long way from our old affectionate relationship. In the beginning Maggie had not accepted me with enthusiasm as Justin's impulsively acquired bride, but lame ducks had always been her specialty, and when she decided that I was one she had given me her ready friendship—even guardianship—providing I took a willing third place to Marc and Justin. Of course in the end she had discovered that instead of being a satisfactory lame duck, I was only a square peg—and a bit defiantly so— unable to fit into the well-grooved round holes of Athmore. But I had loved Maggie Graham, and I hated to lose her as my friend.

At least I was glad to see her alone in this small private sitting room which had been carved off from the larger bedroom. Here Athmore grandeur had been very nearly banished. The rug had long ago faded to pale yellow-green and the walls had only a hint of sunlight painted into them. Most of the furniture was shabby, though of good vintage, and the upholstered things were slipcovered in plain materials. Maggie would have no Athmore ancestors looking down from her walls. Instead, there were outdoor scenes—watercolors of woods and hill-surrounded lakes, and one of a fox running, with the red-coated hunt coming after. I had once looked doubtfully at that very picture, and Maggie had said, "Don't worry—the fox will get away. You can tell by the clumsy seat of those riders. It's a ridiculous picture, but I like its colors. They cheer me when things are going badly, and its absurdity makes me smile."

Things had often gone badly for Maggie. She had come to Athmore as a young girl when her mother took charge after the death of Justin's and Marc's parents in a tragic, flaming auto crash. After her mother died, Maggie, though only a few years older than Justin, had stepped into the breech so that Athmore continued to be their home. She had eventually married, only to lose her young husband at El Alamein during the war. She had not married again. Maggie never lacked courage and the ability to act, so that I found her a comforting and sustaining presence during my year at Athmore. Her optimistic belief that she could make things turn out for the best was reassuring, if not always practical. Now it was disconcerting to find this coolness in her despite the lie she had told for me.

I sat in a chair drawn invitingly near the fire, while she took the soft-cushioned sofa opposite me. Staring at a picture above the mantel—one Maggie herself had painted of an Athmore mare with a crescent of white on its black forehead, and sensitive velvet nostrils—I found an opening to break what seemed a too watchful silence.

"What about the stables—the horses?" I asked. "There was talk before I left of getting rid of them."

"That's been done," she told me brusquely. "Cars are a necessity these days. There are three or four of those around the place now. The horses were a luxury and they had to go. Marc never cared for riding, and Justin no longer has time for it."

So of course Maggie, who loved horses and riding, had made the necessary sacrifice in order to economize. I hoped that Nigel Barrow—if she married him—would give her a stableful and a place to ride them.

"I noticed your ring," I said.

She glanced at the star sapphire on her left hand. The choice was a good one for her strong, capable hand. The delicacy of other jewels would have seemed a contradiction of her nature.

"Nigel chose it," she said.

That was one up for old Nigel, I thought. I'd not have expected him to be so perceptive.

"It was Nigel who persuaded me to write and bring you here," she added.

"Nigel?" I could not have been more surprised. "But why? Why did he think I should come?"

Maggie Graham was as honest a person as I had ever known—except where Justin and Marc were concerned. For them she would lie, or cheat, or do whatever was necessary to protect the charge she had taken so willingly upon her own shoulders when she was young. I had seen her do it. Now, however, she attempted to be frank, even though she watched me uneasily as she spoke, so that I wondered what it was she held back.

"It's this possible marriage of Justin's that appalls me. Nigel knows how worried I am. And since Justin has been like a brother to him, Nigel is worried too. Neither of us believes it can turn out well under the present circumstances."

I'd had enough of evasion. "Is it Alicia Daven Justin means to marry?" I asked bluntly.

Maggie's answer was indirect. "You're the only one who might stop it, Eve. There were reasons for not sending for you, as you very well know. But Nigel thinks they no longer matter. What matters now is how you feel about Justin. That's what I meant to talk to you about in London. Because there was no use in your coming here if you no longer care for him."

This was something I could not answer—not even to myself. What Justin did was up to Justin and I could not interfere, no matter now much I hated to think that Alicia might someday be his wife. When he and I had married he had not told me about his past affair with her. In what I considered his arrogance, he had not felt it necessary for me to know, and consequently I had blundered unprepared into learning about her.

The facts had been simple enough. When Justin would not discuss Alicia with me, Maggie had told me about her. Alicia was Justin's age and she had grown up at Grovesend, her parents' house, not far from Athmore. Justin had known her all his life. After her mother died her father had lost heavily through unwise investments, so when she was old enough Alicia had taken a job in London on a fashion magazine. For several years she did not see much of Justin. Then a wealthy uncle had left her a tidy sum in his will, so she had chucked her job and returned to take over at Grovesend. Upon her father's death she stayed on alone, and that was when she set her cap seriously for Justin.

"I could have liked her," Maggie had told me. "She has beauty and a great deal of poise, and she was born to Justin's world. But she always had a reckless, irresponsible streak that led her into escapades. I suppose their affair was a bit sultry, though things don't last forever on that level alone. You came along and spoiled everything for her. She wasn't able to hold him."

This was the thing I had never understood. The why of Justin's turning to me.

I looked up from the flaming coals of the fire and met Maggie's gaze directly.

"Why?" I said. "Why did he marry me instead of Alicia, when he must have been in love with her all the time?"

Maggie snorted. "Athmore blood never seems to prompt its owners to reasonable behavior. Justin manages to keep his driving impulses under control most of the time. Perhaps that's why they break out of bounds when he lets go."

"But if he loved Alicia—"

"Oh, he did. For a time. But he didn't trust her, and that always held him back. I've an idea the affair was thinning out a bit when you turned up. Somehow he trusted you at once. Don't think he didn't sing your praises to me! You know how he sets integrity above everything else, and you had all that straightforward American honesty on display. Besides, you had a special young appeal of your own, and you knew a great deal about Athmore. So he made the mistake of marrying you."

I stared at the fire again. I knew what was coming now.

Maggie jumped restlessly to her feet, a tall figure in brown tweeds as she paced the faded yellow-green rug. "You could hardly have behaved more outrageously, Eve. Carrying on with Marc practically under Justin's nose. Not that it fooled me—or Marc, either. You had to make Justin jealous because of Alicia, didn't you? You had to destroy his belief in you. You had to behave like an absolute idiot!"

"Which I was," I admitted.

I reached my hands toward the fire because the chill of Athmore had seeped into my bones. What Maggie accused me of was true, yet what had happened had not been exactly as she claimed. There had been circumstances that I might have explained at the time—if anyone had been willing to listen and believe me. I had been stupid, but I had not been faithless.

"What I found hardest to take was the way you deliberately involved Marc," Maggie went on. "I've never forgiven you for that."

So this was what Marc had told her, leaving no loophole for anything I might say. And of course this was what Justin believed.

Maggie was still pacing. "I had a dreadful time persuading Justin not to send Marc away from Athmore for good. I've never thanked you for what I went through for Marc at the time."

"Apparently you succeeded," I said wryly.

She came to a halt in front of me. "I've never understood it—never! Oh, I knew you were trying to slap out at Justin, but this seemed a cheap thing to do. I'd have expected more of you. I thought you loved Justin."

"I did," I said.

"And don't you now?"

I would not look at her. I wanted to answer furiously that I hated him. Yet I could not.

"I—I don't know," I said truthfully. My emotions were a tumult of confusion. How could I know how I felt while I was being tugged in so many directions?

Maggie turned from me and went to a window where the trumpet flowers of an azalea plant bloomed deeply pink in a green pot. Beyond lay the lawns and woods of Athmore that she had loved and served so well.

"What sort of an answer is that—you don't know?" she asked after a moment.

"It's no answer," I admitted and gathered my courage for the hard thing I must say. "There's nothing I can do. Justin has made his choice. Tomorrow I'll be gone and I won't have to see him again. I only came here to—to get myself back."

She swung about so suddenly that I was startled. Without warning she swooped across the room, to put her strong, square hands upon my shoulders, pulling me up to face her. Like all the Norths, Maggie was tall, and I had to tilt my head to look up at her.

"Shaking me isn't going to help," I said.

She dropped her hands from my shoulders as if I'd slapped her and ran the fingers of one hand through her short graying hair, so that it looked the way it did when I'd seen her come in wind-rumpled from a ride on her favorite mare.

"I'm sorry, Eve," she said. "Along with other traits I seem to have inherited the Athmore spleen. You're the last one I should be angry with. When I saw you suddenly in the topiary garden this afternoon, I began to hope that Nigel was right and that just as you rescued Justin from Alicia before, you might save him again. You're my last chance, I suppose, but I mustn't blame you and scold you. Let's sit down quietly, my dear, and talk this over."

I dropped into my chair by the fire and braced myself to resist this softening, to resist any pressure she might put upon me.

"Justin can't possibly marry that dreadful woman," she told me flatly.

"Why not?" I challenged her. "If Justin wants her, what can you do?"

"Listen to me," she said more quietly. She sat opposite me, her hands clasped about her knees. "I never wrote you about how it was here after you left. Justin was like a wild man. He was sickened by your behavior and he was through with you, but I think he loved you and he didn't take kindly to suffering over you. Goodness knows, Alicia would have offered him solace, but he was in no mood for her then. She was clever enough to wait. She went out of the country, took a jaunt around the world, and stayed away for a year. In the meantime her investments went well and she came home a richer woman than before and flung herself into a new venture. She bought a small casino in London—the Club Casella. She retained its original owner—a man named Leo Casella —as general manager. It was the sort of thing to satisfy her taste for gambling—though she doesn't play the tables. She likes to appear as hostess—quite elegantly, you know—several nights a week, and she has made the club very smart and popular. Very jet set and swinging, and open only to the right people. Gambling's quite the thing in London now, and Alicia fits in well."

I wanted to hear none of this. None of it mattered except the fact that Alicia and Justin were together again. But Maggie showed me no mercy, and I had to listen.

"The odd thing about Alicia is that she seems to have come home a different woman. Outwardly. If anything, she's more fascinating than before. But she seems to have learned a new serenity as well. I think she's developed a lovely act, so that she seems to be offering comfort and peace to a lonely man. What used to exist between them seems to have deepened and matured."

I swallowed hard. "Then why am I here?"

Maggie leaned toward me. "Because Nigel and I both believe that Justin is being thoroughly fooled. What Alicia has learned in her year away is how to play the role that will most please Justin."

"He isn't stupid!" I cried. "And he can't like this gambling club. That's not his sort of thing."

"He doesn't like it at all," Maggie agreed. "But Alicia has convinced him that it's a toy with which she amuses herself —though Nigel suspects that it's a major source of her income. Anyway, she's promised to give it up when she and Justin marry. She'll come to him as a rich wife who will take the curse of poverty from Athmore."

"That's not why he'd marry her," I put in indignantly.

"Of course not. But her money wouldn't hurt, would it? Besides—if you love him so much that you must spring to his defense, why are you running away? Why don't you stay and fight for what you want? Aren't you woman enough by this time?"

I stared at her, appalled. After what she had told me, how could she possibly expect me to stay?

"I don't love him," I said as calmly as I could. "I don't even hate him. I don't feel anything at all about him except the need to go home and forget him. I can do that now. I'm glad you brought me here because you've made that possible."

"If you must lie," Maggie said, "learn to do it with more confidence. If you blunder into statements like that, with your fists flailing, no one will ever believe you."

There was nowhere to hide my hot face. "Do you think I want to stay and be abused by Justin, insulted by him—treated the way he treated me today in the garden?"

"He treated you as he did because you upset him so badly," Maggie said. "That's the thing that gives me hope. He couldn't take the sight of you calmly. He couldn't shrug you off as he wanted to, so he had to fly into a rage and take his anger with himself out on you. How can two people be such total idiots about each other? Why don't you wake up and face the truth about yourselves?"

I heard her out bleakly and said nothing more. I had done enough damage by trying to argue with Maggie Graham. She had always believed what she wanted to believe, and I must not let her words sway me into some impossible course that would hurt me more in the long run than if I turned tail and fled. The difficulty between Justin and me was no mere matter of a misunderstanding that could be cleared up with a little discussion. Quite aside from Alicia, there was too real a basis for our incompatibility and no chance at all that either could change enough to live with the other. A physical attraction there had certainly been—and so strong a one that it had clouded even Justin's better judgment, while I had been too young to have any sort of judgment about my own emotions. Once the edge was off a little, we saw each other as the strangers we really were, and the trouble began. It wasn't in me to play a role, as Alicia had apparently learned to do. If he couldn't love me as I was, then I didn't want his love anyway.

Maggie continued to watch me, and her look made me increasingly uneasy. Like Justin, she was never one to give up on a direction she had settled upon.

"Don't you know what brought you here?" she asked

abruptly. "You're a grown woman and it's time you faced up
to a few things. At nineteen we couldn't expect much of you.
Now the least you can do is think this through sensibly. Face
it and figure it out with your perfectly good brain, instead of
using all that uncontrolled American emotion. Come downstairs tonight and join us for dinner. Get into the order of
things again. Justin won't be here. He's going to Grovesend
—you've frightened him that badly."

So he had run from me straight to Alicia!

"Please—I don't want to come down to dinner," I said.
"It's not only because of Justin. I don't want to see Marc either. The things he told you and Justin weren't wholly true.
Marc wanted me to leave. I never realized it until the end,
but he wanted our marriage to break up."

"And you helped him along," Maggie said.

Marc was her darling, but there were times when I suspected that she had few illusions about him. She gave evidence of that now.

"Of course he was against your marriage. Marc would like
to stay next in line as heir. Children could spoil that for
good. His approach to such matters is fairly simple—he is always in need of money. In fact—that's his main difficulty
now. I might as well tell you that one of the reasons I feel
about Alicia as I do is because she's encouraged Marc to run
up huge debts at her club. She's using him—perhaps as a
weapon to hold over Justin's head. Though she'd be skillful
in using it, and she hasn't let Justin know about this as yet."

"Marc's troubles are nothing to me," I said. "And Justin
can take care of his own head. I've told you—I never want to
see Marc again."

Maggie drew a long, deep breath and I knew she was
angry with me. "You needn't have any concern about Marc
now. He has found a little girl who seems able to lead him
about by the nose."

"The girl who plays Petula Clark recordings?" I asked.

"Endlessly. Dacia Keane. She's been rather a shock for
Athmore to absorb. Far more than you ever were, since she's
the new England. She considers us terribly square Establish-
ment, but she tolerates us kindly and forgives us our shabby
luxury. She knows all about turning the world into something
more swinging, and doesn't mind telling us how we muff our
chances. But you can come downstairs quite safely, Eve,
since Justin won't be there."

"I'm not hungry," I said.

Maggie sighed, but she gave in to my stubbornness more gracefully than usual. "Very well—stay here by the fire, and I'll send you an early supper tray. After that flight across the Atlantic, you'll be ready for a long night's rest. Tomorrow we'll have another chat. I've a number of things to see to now, so you can have this room to yourself for the evening, if you like. I'll send up an old friend to see you in a little while. Perhaps someone more persuasive than I've been able to be."

"Not Justin!" I cried in alarm.

"When were you two ever friends?" she said dryly, and was gone before I could offer further objection.

I sat beside the fire and watched the coals flame and redden, turning gradually to dead gray. I lacked the energy to get up and put on more coal before the fire went out altogether. The afternoon had darkened into evening, and as the light outside diminished, the room lost itself in shadow. Even to get up and turn on a lamp would take too much effort. All I wanted was to sit here and think carefully and clearly about what Maggie had said. The things I'd said to her had rushed out easily, defensively—and she had not believed them. So what did I believe? What did I feel? Was it possible to face what I felt about Justin? When was I going to accept the truth about him and give him up?

"Maggie?" said a voice from the doorway.

I had no need to look around to know that Marc stood on the threshold of the dusky room. He was the last person I wanted to see. If I stayed very still perhaps he would go away without noticing me. It was a futile hope, since my shadowy figure must have shown up against the last red coals in the grate.

"So it's you, Eve," he said easily, and came into the room. "I'd heard you were here, but I could hardly believe you'd come back."

I said nothing as he turned on a lamp and went to poke up the fire and put on more coal. I blinked in the sudden light and forced myself to look at him when he turned from the fireplace. I had been wrong to think when I saw him from my window earlier that two years had not changed him. Firelight touched his pale hair to gold in the old way, but he seemed thinner than I remembered and there was a tension about him that was new. The mockery in his intensely blue eyes was the same, however, and the faintly teasing quality I had mistakenly thought good-natured.

"What a time for you to come back, Eve old dear!" he said, and draped himself gracefully upon the sofa opposite me. "What on earth do you expect to gain by it?"

"I've nothing to say to you," I told him stiffly.

He stretched his long legs upon Maggie's fawn-colored slipcovers and leaned one elbow on a cushion, the better to observe me.

"You look rather different," he said. "Less wide-eyed and trusting. Older, I suppose. It's becoming, I must say. But you're too late, you know. I suppose Maggie has told you that Justin has cast the die with Alicia, and all that sort of thing. Justin's in a rage about your coming, of course. He's not after offending Alicia at this late date. We all rather need her in the family now, you know. Or don't you know?"

"It's none of my affair what you need," I said. "Just go away and leave me alone."

He did not move, but his rather delicate features lighted in an angelic way I remembered. How many hearts had he broken by the deceptive sweetness of his smile? I wondered. Mine had been safe enough from him, though my wounded ego had not been. But everything was changed now. I mustn't be afraid of him.

He continued to watch me, obviously speculating. He had always been enormously curious and ready to probe callously for answers to anything that puzzled him. My attempt to ignore him only amused and intrigued him.

"What can you hope to gain by coming here?" he repeated. "With Alicia's money to help out, Justin can afford to make you a much handsomer settlement than before. If you don't rock the boat—"

I sprang up to face him, my temper as easily lost as ever. "I don't want any settlement! You would never understand why I came. Not in a thousand years. And I'm leaving early tomorrow anyway. So there's nothing for us to discuss—nothing at all!"

He listened to my outburst without getting to his feet, and his sweetly wicked smile did not waver. "They've put you in the blue lady's room, haven't they? Dacia's at the other end of that hall. You must meet her before you go. I've told her all about you, you know."

There was something about Marc that had always made me not only angry, but uneasy as well. Even during that reckless time when all I'd cared about was punishing Justin, I had been a little afraid of Marc. And my fears had been jus-

tified. But in this tenser, older man, there seemed to lie some
deeper threat. I started toward the door and he let me go, but
before I could reach the corridor my way was blocked by the
appearance of Nellie with my supper tray, and Maggie's secretary, who followed beyond. Miss Davis smiled at me, and
Marc got to his feet and drew up a table before the fire so
Nellie could set down her tray.

"I wanted to make certain you have everything you need,
Mrs. North," Caryl Davis ran on, her voice at conversational
pitch, now that she was not lecturing. "Fancy not knowing
who you were when you joined our tour this afternoon!
When Mrs. Graham told me, I was quite upset about not giving you a proper welcome."

Marc winked at me. "I hope we've made up for that by
now. I'll run, and let you dine in peace. There's all that glass
mess in Justin's shop still to be seen to, and a guard to be
arranged for tonight. Cheerie-bye, my dear." Marc loved to
affect any vulgarism.

Nellie had her antenna out, as always, and she had seen
my face. She bent toward me. "The soup's hot and strengthen-
ing, Miss Eve. See you eat every scrap of it, now. And I'll go
fetch a hot-water bottle for your bed, the way I used to do.
Not that this is the season for it, what with its being so warm
outdoors. But I remember how you liked your hot-water bottle, and you shall have one now. Do eat up."

She looked at me so kindly that I felt weak tears in my
eyes and I had to blink to keep them back.

"I'll try," I told her. And to Miss Davis, "Thank you. I'll
be fine now. You needn't trouble about me."

Nellie hurried off, but Miss Davis lingered. I pulled my
chair closer to the table and took a spoonful of thick soup
with beef chunks floating in it, hoping she would go quickly
away. Instead, she moved about the room, turning the pot of
azaleas, straightening the hunting picture a trifle, tugging the
corner of a slipcover—all empty gestures to give her an excuse to stay. I could hardly bear to swallow, but I kept on
with the soup in order not to watch her.

"I suppose you've heard about what happened to Mr. Justin's workshop?" she said, perhaps experimenting with this
topic because she was curious about me. "It's quite dreadful,
really. All those glass bottles and vials broken and his work
spoiled. It's the third time in as many weeks that someone
has broken into his shop. They say he's really onto something

this time, and we're afraid someone is trying to stop him, or even steal what he's trying to do."

This, at least, interested me. "What is he trying to do?"

She glanced at me a little coyly. "Ah, that's what we mustn't talk about, Mrs. North. Not that we know anything. Not really. But with the way he drives about testing that new experimental car of his, we know it's something big coming up. You can tell by the look of the car it's not regular. Though of course this is nothing any of us can work out, is it? Mrs. Graham is terribly concerned about him now, and a new, added worry—" She broke off apologetically, but the tenor of her remarks was evident. I was the new worry.

"You needn't concern yourself—I'm leaving tomorrow," I told her abruptly.

She had the grace to flush. "Please enjoy your supper. And I do apologize for not recognizing you on the tour this afternoon. Though how we could know—"

She left me at last and I put down my spoon and stared without interest at the food on the tray. All I wanted was the thin bread and butter, and I'd have liked a cup of strong American coffee. But I sat with my hands in my lap, all energy drained from me. How I was to face the long walk upstairs to the opposite wing of the house, I didn't know. The numbness was coming back again—and perhaps it was better to be numb than to feel, than to face the fact, as I must inevitably, that Justin was lost to me forever. His coming marriage to Alicia was irrevocably set, and only Maggie, prompted by Nigel, who could not really know, was ready to pin some faint hope on my coming here. Maggie was a born optimist, who always believed she could wrench a change of mind from fate, even when everything was at its worst. At least she need not stay at Athmore and share it with Alicia when Justin married her. Nigel Barrow would take her away to the home of her own she so richly deserved.

I must rouse myself, I thought. I must finish what I could eat and return to my faraway room. But as I sat listless, something cold and damp thrust its way beneath my hand and came to rest on my knee. A long muzzle and lean head, shaggy-haired, lay beneath my hand. Round brown eyes looked up at me, questioning.

"Deirdre!" I cried, and the dog wriggled, coming as close as she could with her great, rough, brindle-gray body. Her long tail, curved upward at the tip, thumped on the carpet as she snuffled at me hopefully, and her small neat ears pricked erect at the sound of my voice.

"You're only hungry," I said. "You don't really remember me!"

I put my arms about her and let her sniff my neck, lick my cheek. This was the way it had been when I had said goodbye to her that other time. Legend had it that Irish wolfhounds were gifted with second sight, and certainly Deirdre had been remarkably sensitive, even as a puppy. When I'd said goodbye to her she had whimpered and whined, and her tail had drooped sadly. But now she was full of joy. When I encouraged her, she put her paws upon my knee and raised herself to a height greater than mine in my chair. It wasn't only the food she was interested in, after all. Whether she truly knew me or not, I couldn't tell, but she recognized someone she felt at home with, and certainly she must feel my response.

When we had greeted each other thoroughly, I persuaded her to sit at my feet, and I shared bits of ham with her as I ate. I had a friend at Athmore, after all. Dear Maggie had known and had sent her to me.

Suddenly I felt hungry and considerably stronger than I had a while ago. I put all hard thoughts of the future away from me and finished every bite of my supper, while Deirdre watched me with love, her proud neck arched, her tail occasionally thumping out her approval. Somewhere in me courage stirred. All the cards seemed stacked against me, but I wasn't beaten yet.

III

The library was empty as before. Deirdre and I met no one on the stairs on in the upper corridor of the north wing. No music issued from Dacia Keane's room, and I gave the girl no more than a passing thought as we followed the long bare hallway toward my room. Except for a console table, an occasional stiff chair, and one or two paintings on the walls, the corridor was unfurnished and lighted only by three sconces along the way. The sight of it reminded me of how dismal Athmore could seem in the darkness of winter.

Nellie had been in to turn down my bed, and I knew the promised hot-water bottle would be waiting for me. She had left the window closed, but the room was as chill as the corridor and I would be glad to go quickly to bed.

Deirdre came in with me at my invitation, but once she was in the room her manner became strangely hesitant. She stood uncertainly in the center of the worn blue rug, sniffing the air and looking about her, as if for something alien that she did not like.

"What is it?" I asked, and she gave me an uneasy look and growled low in her throat. "I always thought it was the green-velvet room that was haunted," I added, and put my hand on the dog's bristling coat to quiet her. She went sniffing across the room, found her way behind a huge Victorian dresser and made a whining noise to summon me.

Behind the dresser was a corner door that I had forgotten about, though I knew where it led. I opened it quickly upon the wedged stone steps that circled upward to the tower—one of Mrs. Langley's whimsies in building this house. A draft swept down upon me and I could look up at the rise of stone wedges to a rectangular sentry window open to the sky. No wonder my room was cold. The tower had the damp, musty odor of old stones, and as Deirdre sniffed she growled again,

43

and I felt the bristles of her coat rise eerily beneath my hand.

"Hello?" I called. "Anyone up there?"

There was no sound, no answer. I knew that the tower door opened upon the connecting roofs and that all four towers had access to those roofs. From the four corners of the house anyone could go up to the roof and retreat with a choice of exits. I spelled them out in my mind. There was this room, and at the front of this north corridor the room Marc's girl occupied. In the opposite wing the front guest room had access to a tower, though I did not know whether it was occupied or not. The room that opened on the rear tower was the one known as the green-velvet room—a room I had reason to know all too well. However, identifying the tower rooms told me nothing, gave me no answer to Deirdre's suspicious manner.

I backed from the opening and closed the door. "There's nothing up there," I told her. "No one runs around the roof at night."

Nevertheless, I examined the door for a bolt and found none, found there was no key to the massive lock. Deirdre would not stay with me in the blue lady's room. No matter how I coaxed, I had to let her go. Wolfhounds of all species were known for their courage. They had once been fighting dogs and their loyalty to the death is proverbial. If there had been an enemy for Deirdre to face, she would have been up on the roof like a flash. As it was, she was merely disturbed and uneasy, anxious to be away from the place.

Her distress touched off uneasiness in me, and I felt bereft without her comforting presence. My room was far removed from the rest of the house, yet all I could do was shove the great bureau before the tower door and get ready for bed.

Once I had put on my blue-sprigged granny gown, brought especially for the chilly nights of an English spring, I opened the side window and leaned upon the sill. Lights burned in the garage and stable areas, and between the trees I could see a man moving slowly up and down. The guard, I presumed, since Justin had said he would put someone at this post tonight.

What was happening here at Athmore to destroy its former peace and seclusion? Maggie was worried, Marc cold and a bit secretive—and everything appeared to be moving in Alicia's direction. Yet there seemed, as well, some threat, some enemy within the gates. A malicious hand had been at work to play havoc with Justin's experiments. Even Old Daniel, when I met him in the woods, had been touched by the secret threat—perhaps frightened by it? My encounter with Maggie had made me forget about the old man. Now I wished I had mentioned that meeting among the ruins to her, and told her the odd warning he had given me about the rook's play. Tomorrow I must seek out the old man and ask him to tell me plainly what he meant.

I almost smiled at the thought. In spite of my stated intention to leave, I was already making plans for tomorrow!

A cool breeze blew in at the window and I went to bed, to warm my feet on Nellie's towel-wrapped hot-water bottle. In my old life at Athmore I had seldom been as cold as I was now. In those days Justin had slept beside me, close and warm and always ready to open his arms and shelter his freezing little American.

Now I lay on my back in the huge bed, looking up into distant blue-canopied depths, perversely as wide-awake as I had been sleepy before.

How had this all come about? How had my grandmother's words led me so inevitably to this bitter outcome? If only she had never told me her tales of Athmore; if only she had not built romantic pictures in my mind and urged me back to the village where she was born! But no—she wasn't to blame. Every step along the way there had always been choices for me to make. I had no one to thank for such steps I had taken but myself. My grandmother was long dead by the time I came to England as a student just before my third year in college. Dad had staked me to the trip I wanted so much to make—only a few months before his death. I had not seen him again. He had not lived to know about the fiasco of my marriage, and since I avoided my stepmother, I did not have to listen to what she might say.

How innocently I had stood before the open gates of Athmore that other time, that first afternoon when I'd taken the bus down from London. I had not expected that it would be so easy to walk in. Though, having come so far, I might have entered, even if there had been a sign up ordering me to stay out.

On that afternoon I wandered up the same straight walk I had followed today, spellbound by the sight of Athmore glowing warmly beneath a summertime sun. The lawns were greener than any I had ever seen, the flowerbeds more glowing and lush. No one stopped or questioned me, and I did not go so far as to walk up to the front door and ring the bell.

My grandmother had been the daughter of the village vicar, but that hardly gave her granddaughter an introduction to Athmore.

There was no one on the terrace. I wandered around to the rose garden at the side and found Maggie Graham cutting a basketful of long-stemmed beauties. She saw me and smiled a ready welcome. I stammered my name, told her about Gran, and how I had grown up on stories of these gardens and parklands.

"The walls of the old hall are still standing, aren't they?" I asked. "And the chapel window? Do you suppose it would be possible . . . I mean, the bus I must take back to London doesn't leave for another hour and——"

"Of course you may look," she told me readily. "Come along and I'll show you the way."

She sensed that I was hesitant, aware of my own intrusion and thus ill at ease. She knew I would enjoy my exploration better alone, so she indicated the walk through the woods and sent me on my way.

"Mind you don't miss your bus," she called after me. "There's not another through here until tomorrow morning."

I smiled and nodded vaguely. My feet were set upon a way that I had followed often in my imagination as a romantically inclined girl. I fancied that I knew the very trees I walked beneath, and indeed there was a great old beech that Gran had mentioned, with the initials of forgotten lovers cut into the bark, the carving now grown high and far from the ground.

The tree made me feel very small and unimportant. It gave me an awareness of the need to hurry if I was to do any living at all. Life went by so fast. Where were those lovers now? Where were the first Athmores who had opened the forest and built in its depth an Elizabethan mansion whose ruins still lay hidden by these woods?

A final curve of the path led me almost unwittingly into the clearing. The place had been allowed to return in part to forest growth, and a green carpeting covered the old stones, covered fallen mounds of brick, almost hiding them from sight. Only where the scorched and broken chapel walls remained had brush been cut away and grass planted to a smooth green floor. There between broken walls, rising serenely against the sky, stood the great arch of the window.

It was so beautiful I could hardly bear it. I went out upon

the green carpet and sat cross-legged on the grass, where I could stare up at the marvelous arch that had been raised here hundreds of years before by those who understood beauty.

Every stone was intact, forming the great Gothic point at the apex, pointing into the sky, and falling away in eye-pleasing curves on either side. Beyond the window the forest had been cleared for some distance, and I could sit there on the grassy floor and look through to the expanse of blue English sky. I sat so quietly that the birds came close, to hop upon the walls and sing in the trees about me. Because I wanted to hear a nightingale, I was sure that one penetrating birdsong must really be that of a nightingale.

As I watched and listened, a jet plane moved across the sky in a great arc, leaving its vapor trail behind, so that through the window the sky was streaked with the signature of my own time. It was not incongruous. Indeed, there seemed a continuity to life at that moment that the white trail in the sky intensified. Others had been here before me and left their heritage. Others would follow me, and if there was any force to my own small life, they might profit because I too had lived.

I had never felt this before, even though, unlike many of my contemporaries, who seemed to scorn the past and lived only for the present, I had grown up with a sense of history. Now for the first time I sensed a continuity to being alive. Even my small flash in time was part of some pattern that would go on, no matter what new forms it took in the future. In those brief moments while I sat upon the grass in a place that had long ago burned down, I had an exultant feeling of life welling up in me, a feeling that for the first time I held its clear meaning in my hands.

Of course so intense a vision had to fade, but as I sat there the threads of history began to weave themselves through my mind in colorful warp and woof. Here in this place, before this arched chapel window, John Edmond Athmore had fought for what he had built and believed in, and for the safety of his wife and children. Fought with a sword in his hands and been wounded to the death while the flames that devoured Athmore Hall leaped greedily about him.

So vividly was I immersed in another time, with the very roar of those flames, the clash of ringing steel, the shouting which echoed through the woods sounding in my ears, that when a man in modern dress walked into my line of vision I felt no self-consciousness. I simply accepted him as part of the scene and spoke to him eagerly of what I saw.

"That was where he fought his last battle—that first Athmore," I said, rising on my knees to point toward the arch. "John Edmond slew Glanbury on that very spot, and then he picked Margaret up in his arms, and although he was mortally wounded, he vaulted through the window, where the glass had already been broken out by vandals' swords. I know he carried her away into the woods to safety, but I wonder where he died, exactly? I wonder if they still keep his sword at Athmore?"

The man who had walked in upon my vision answered me gravely. "I can show you where he died. I can even show you his sword."

"Oh, I'd love to see that!" I cried, aglow with excitement over this reliving of history. "But there's one thing I've never understood. That stone window ledge is fairly high, and I suppose it was the same in Athmore's day. So how did he manage—wounded as he was—to pick Margaret up and go vaulting through that opening as they say he did?"

The tall man looked down at me and under his blue, intense stare I remembered that I was a stranger here and that I'd been informing someone who actually lived at Athmore of Athmore history. Still—his expression was not ominous, and his blue eyes appeared to be dancing. Before I could scramble to my feet, he swooped down upon me, scooped me up in arms that held me lightly as he swung me toward the window, lifted me through the opening and set me on my feet upon the grass beyond. Then he vaulted the sill and stood beside me.

"I fancy that's how it was done," he said. "History may have embroidered a bit. I used to play the game here when I was a boy and I had it all figured out. Desperately wounded men have been known to perform heroic deeds, and he would have been bent on getting Margaret to safety. But she was whole of limb and unhurt, so I doubt that he'd have gone carrying her through the woods. More likely, she supported him a good part of the way. Fortunately the children had already been sent far off and they were spared the whole murderous affair. Come along and I'll show you where John and Margaret went that day."

It seemed natural that I should go with him, that we should take each other for granted. The path beneath arching branches of beech and oak was still there, still kept clear in these times. It was some little distance that he led me through the woods to the edge of a small clearing.

"There was a woodsman's hut just here," he said. "It was empty that day and Margaret brought her John into it. He died there in her arms. Glanbury's men had run away at the death of their leader, and it was Athmore's tardily arriving forces who found them there—Margaret rocking him in her arms, white-faced but very brave, with his blood upon her dress, and John Edmond dead of his terrible wound. There's a picture of her at the house, painted when she was old—a grand lady with fire still burning in her eyes and the stamp of pain and courage about her mouth. That gown of hers has been preserved as well. She would not have it destroyed, and it is under glass, torn and stained with faded brown."

Somehow I managed to shake myself back to life, back to the present. "You know so much about all this—you must be the present Athmore," I said. "Though of course I know that's not your name."

"My name is North," he said. "Justin North. Now tell me yours and tell me how you know so much about Athmore history."

"I'm Eve Milburn," I said. "My grandmother's name was Appleby and she was born in the village. She was Vicar Appleby's daughter."

He smiled at me and held out his hand. "Welcome home, Eve Milburn," he said.

His clasp was warm as he held my hand, studying my face, as though something about me puzzled him. Perhaps he would have tried to put his puzzlement into words, except that we heard someone calling his name from the chapel ruins.

"Oh, good Lord!" he cried in consternation. "That will be Maggie—my cousin, Mrs. Graham. She sent me to remind you that your bus would be leaving before long, and I forgot the bus completely. So now it's gone and I am to blame."

I forgave him without question. "I forgot it too. And I'd much rather have had this happen to me, no matter where I stay tonight."

"Come," he said, and took my hand. "We'll go and break the news to Maggie and see what can be managed."

We went together through Athmore woods—or rather, he went ahead, his legs much longer than mine, pulling me behind as we ran.

Maggie Graham was gracious and kind about having an uninvited guest thrust upon her. The fact that my grandmother was an Appleby and local weighed in my favor, but I'm sure Maggie would have taken me in no matter what.

It was planned that I should stay overnight—but somehow my visit extended into the week. Justin was home on holiday and there was so much he had to show me. I had given him back his boyhood memories, he told me, so that when he showed me Athmore's sword hanging in its honored place in the Hall of Armor, he could recapture his own young feeling about it. When he showed me Margaret's blood-stained dress —glass-protected in the great library—he even opened the case so that I could touch that brown stain wonderingly, reverently. The cloth felt dry and old, but once a warm, loving woman had worn this gown, and warm, brave blood had spilled upon it. I took my hand away and there were tears in my eyes. Because of old suffering, and old loss, because life lasted for only a little while—and because I was young and had no one to love, or to be brave for.

That was when Justin kissed me for the first time. The kiss was only meant to comfort me, I knew, but I had the first inkling of what might happen to me—with this dangerous mingling in me of love for Athmore history and more than liking for the man who was the Athmore of the present.

We went on and he showed me drawings of how Athmore Hall had been rebuilt after its first fire. The second fire had been more prosaic and had done far more damage, so that afterward it was decided to build a completely new house— the present Athmore. But that marvelous chapel window in the woods would always be preserved. Some of the remaining walls had been shored up and were kept in repair. Such restoration could be authentic because the quarry was there from which the original stones were brought.

Nevertheless, before the week was up I was ready to leave —ready to fly, to run, to escape. By that time I knew what was happening—for me, at least. There was an unreality about the entire experience that made me not myself. Perhaps I was a figment of both Justin's imagination and my own at that time. For the moment I had no life outside of Athmore, and everything I saw and learned about the house and its history enchanted me—literally laid a spell of enchantment upon me. Only now and then did I surface and realize that I was falling foolishly, hopelessly in love with Justin North. It could not have happened any other way, granted my youth

and particular susceptibility. He was "Athmore," the hero of
Gran's stories, and of course I fancied myself as Margaret.
Only now and then did I remember that I knew nothing
about this modern man who escorted me on forays through
history. My head was filled with romantic nonsense and the
heady realization that he seemed to be paying attention to me
as no other man ever had. Only toward the end of the week,
when I began to feel more pain than pleasure, did I tell myself that I must leave. There was still such a thing as reality,
and for all that this was an enchanting interlude, Justin
North of Athmore was not going to marry a foolish American girl who was years younger than himself.

I told Maggie I was leaving, and she approved, though
gently and with understanding. I did not tell Justin. It was
better to be gone first, and not disgrace myself by letting him
know how I felt. It was my undoing that I must say goodby
to the ruins of Athmore Hall, if not to its present master.

Justin came home unexpectedly, saw my bag sitting in the
Hall of Armor near the front door, queried Maggie, and was
furious. Like his forebears he had a formidable temper and
an impetuous, unruly nature that he usually kept well in
check. He did not now. How dared I leave without letting
him know? he demanded of Maggie. How dared she connive
with me in this? She tried to talk to him sensibly, appalled by
the direction he was taking, but he could be arrogance itself
when the occasion called for it, and he came storming arro-
gantly out to the chapel where I was saying my sentimental
farewells, with tears streaming down my cheeks.

He was rough with me as I had never seen him. Indeed he
frightened me half out of my wits. He shouted that even if I
thought so little of him that I had to go sneaking away behind his back, he could at least drive me up to London, and
see me aboard my plane for home! There was to be no arguing about that. He put me in his car with my bag and
drove off furiously. Expert in cars that he was, Justin could
never forget that a speeding car had killed his parents horri-
bly, and he disliked driving. Yet he was a skilled, superbly
controlled driver, and for all his smoldering rage, he managed to get us to London alive and unarrested. He deposited
me alone in a hotel, and when he returned he had obtained a
special license for our marriage. So it was in London, without
my having very much to say about it, that we were rather
angrily married three days later. The ceremony took place in
a small church after Justin and I had indulged in so furious a

quarrel that we should have been warned. I'm sure the vicar
who married us must have shaken his head gravely, wondering at our ill-temper and apparent distaste for each other. I
hadn't even a ring, except for the signet Justin took off his
own hand to put on my finger—telling me it served me right.
If I hadn't behaved in so idiotic a fashion I'd have worn the
traditional Athmore ring, and I'd have had a wedding dress.
Now I must wait for my ring, and there'd be no formal wedding for this Athmore bride. I marveled that so brilliant a
man could be so thoroughly bereft of reason and calm judgment, but I was not exactly calm and reasonable myself. More
than anything else, I think I was frightened. Yet there was no
power in me to swim against the current that swept me along,
even if I'd wanted to struggle against it.

After that violent marriage, we walked out into rainy London and were quickly wet through. Yet, quite inconceivably
and unreasonably, we walked together hand in hand down
Piccadilly in the pouring rain and were beatifically happy—
Justin's rage gone, as though it had never been.

Maggie must have been shocked by the news, but she sent
what Justin needed from Athmore and he bought me new
clothes in London's best shops, and put the heavy, emerald-
studded Athmore ring that Maggie sent upon my finger. That
ring which I left behind me when I fled our marriage.

I had never known such joy, such happiness. This euphoria
lasted through our honeymoon in Greece until Grecian ruins
reminded us too often of Athmore and Justin began to long
for home. What was home to him was not home to me, as I
quickly discovered.

Having behaved recklessly by following our emotions without benefit of any reasonable doubt, the piper now waited to
be paid. We began to look at each other more critically and
found to our mutual dismay that Justin was not Athmore, and
I was not the brave and loyal Margaret. We were simply two
people who had let their passions run away with them and
who did not know each other very well. What was worse, we
did not very much like what we began to find out.

The house itself—that magnificent Athmore which had
seemed to accept me graciously as an American visitor—now
would have none of me. Its history-ridden halls and echoing
rooms were like those of a museum—and who could live in a
museum? I was cold and lost and lonely. I could not live and
breathe history—I wanted a life of my own. The man who
had given me his all-absorbing attention at Olympia and

Nauplia and Delphi, was now absorbed elsewhere—with cars, with machinery, with his work for the manufacturers who employed him in their plant this side of London. Often he was gone during the week, returning home only for the weekend—and I had no husband. When winter came and the days were coldly gray, I shivered through the daylight hours and was warm at night only when Justin's arms were about me and love warmed us as we could not be warmed by day.

Even then, perhaps I would eventually have grown up a little. Perhaps. Simply because I loved him utterly and blindly and without due process of reasoning. Perhaps I had begun at the wrong end, with love instead of understanding, but love was there. It existed for me. Far more for me than for Justin, as I quickly knew.

But before there was time for growth and adjustment, I learned about Alicia. It was Marc who told me, Marc who pretended sympathy and pity and offered comfort for my wounded pride and empty loving.

Now in my wide bed in the blue lady's room, I turned and twisted and tried to turn off the memories that streamed through my mind. Not until the thought of Alicia, and the betrayal of my trust by Marc, rose in my mind, did I manage to put up a barrier that I was not yet ready to pass. There was a painful comfort for me in other memories. But in remembering Alicia and what Marc had done, there was no comfort at all. So I blocked out the problem of those two. To think of them was to destroy my ability to live from day to day in the present—which was all I had.

Wind whispered eerily down the tower that occupied a corner of my room, and at length the sound furnished the soporific I needed. I fell at last into a sleep of physical and emotional exhaustion. Yet even then my dreams would not let me rest. At some time during the middle of the night I dreamed that Athmore Hall was burning—as it had burned out there in the woods some two hundred years ago. I could hear the crackle of flames, the shouting voices—and I waited for swords to clash, for someone to come and lift me through the window.

Instead, the sounds grew louder and wakened me. I opened my eyes and stared into a room that was no longer dark. The flare of moving light was reflected upon the blue canopy of my bed, the shadow and flicker of flames moved in replica across my ceiling.

I rolled out into the cold room and ran to the window.

The stable and garage areas were alive with the red of flames, and the shouting voices were real. It looked as though Justin's workshop was on fire and men were there fighting to save it. Between the screen of beech trees I could see darting figures black against the flaring light, their shadows long upon the ground. The night air was cold and I slammed the window shut and belted on my blue woolly robe. I thrust my feet into furry slippers, pinned my hair back hurriedly with a comb, and went into the corridor. I knew only that where Justin was I had to be. If everything that had meaning for him was being threatened, I could not stay helplessly in my room. I had to go downstairs and learn whether there was something useful I could do.

After the flickering in my room, the hall seemed dark, its lighted sconces dim as candles. But there was movement at the far end and I went quickly in that direction. As I neared the doors to the long gallery, where they opened midway, I saw that a child stood shivering in the chill of the far corridor.

She was a flat-chested little thing, inappropriately dressed in a pink shorty gown, tied in bows over each shoulder, with romper panties showing below the hem. Her long legs and her arms and feet were bare and she stood with one foot atop the other, her arms close to her body as she hugged herself in the cold. Her fair hair was cut like a boy's—indeed it looked so thatched that she must have taken shears to it herself— and she had the largest dark-brown eyes I had ever seen.

She turned these upon me as I approached, and spoke between chattering teeth. "Th-th-there's a fire! Something's b-b-burning down out there! Do you suppose it will catch the house?"

She seemed more excited than frightened, but I tried to reassure and calm her.

"I should think the house is safe enough. The fire seems to be in the old stable area. But shouldn't you go and put on something warmer? Is your mother about?"

She continued to stare at me out of those enormous eyes, while her face broke into a gamine smile that showed her rather uneven teeth and wrinkled her small, pert nose.

"My mum wouldn't be chasing after me, even if she was here. I'm not all that young. But you're right about me needing something warm. If you'll wait half a mo' I'll go down with you."

She flew toward the open door of the front room, and then turned back to me with a broad smile.

"I know who you are! You're the long-lost Eve—that's who! You're my Marc's old girl friend. Mind you wait for me!"

She vanished into her bedroom, leaving me to stare after her in astonishment.

The "child" was Dacia Keane, the girl who Maggie reported was leading Marc North around by the nose. Apparently he'd had the effrontery to tell her that *I* had once been his "girl friend."

I was of a mind not to wait, and I went into the long gallery of this upper floor, seeking the doors to the stair bay that opened off its center.

The girl was quick, however, and she came after me promptly, thrusting her arms into the sleeves of a bright orange coat that stood out about her like a tent, striding toward me in brown leather boots that rose almost to her knees.

When she saw me, she came chummily to tuck her hand through the crook of my arm as though we were already friends. As though some inevitable weaving of fate had brought us together. I'm not sure whether or not I actually felt this, but there was something between us at once—some curiously guarded approach that neither tried to deny as we started down the elliptical stairway together, hurrying toward the scene of Athmore's latest disaster.

IV

Before we reached the library floor, Nigel Barrow appeared. He had put on brown corduroys and he was still pulling on a sweater as he ran down the stairs from the opposite wing above.

"What's up?" he called as he came after us. "I heard shouting, but from my window I can't see a thing."

"There's a fire in the stable area," I told him.

He hurried past us down the stairs and was out the front door before we reached the lower hall. Below us the great chandelier burned brilliantly, lighting the red and white marble diamonds of the floor to a shining gloss. All the suits of Spanish armor stood along the walls, watching through the slits of their crested helmets. The portrait of John Edmond seemed to watch as well, as though he might step down from his picture at any moment to join us in defense of Athmore. Members of the household staff rushed about in various stages of disarray and confusion, lacking direction.

As we reached the hall, Maggie came in through the outside door, muffled in a heavy gray sweater and warm wool trousers, her gray-blond hair rumpled, her expression one of shocked concern.

"Daniel's been hurt, Morton," she called to one of the men. "Do get me first-aid things quickly, and ask someone to ring up Dr. Highsmith."

At mention of the old man's name my heart leaped in sudden dread, and I watched anxiously as Justin and Nigel came in from outdoors carrying Old Daniel between them. Justin heard Maggie's words.

"The phone's out," he said grimly. "Someone's cut the outside wire, I've already sent for help."

"I'll manage Daniel," Nigel said. "Take care of yourself, Justin."

Justin paid no attention, though he looked dreadful. Apparently he had dashed outdoors in his shirtsleeves, and his shirt was torn, his face streaked by sooty smudges, his eyes burning a furious blue in his thin face. But Old Daniel looked worse. Gray and still, with a terrible wound in his skull—a wound that no longer bled. They laid him upon a couch and stood back.

"We found him too late," Justin said grimly. "There's nothing we can do now."

Maggie cried out in alarm. "Oh, no! Justin—where was he? What happened?"

Justin answered in short, clipped phrases, obviously fighting his own grief. "When I discovered the fire, I sent one of the boys through the woods to get help from the village. He took the shortcut by way of the ruins and found the old man where a wall had fallen over and crushed him. He's been dead a long while, I'm afraid."

I gasped. "But I saw him there this afternoon. I saw him and he was perfectly all right!"

Justin looked at me and then away. "The wall must have fallen in on him afterward."

Maggie had dropped to her knees beside the couch where Old Daniel lay. She was trying vainly to bathe his wound, to coax him back to life.

"Look out for yourself, Justin," Nigel repeated more sharply. "That's a nasty burn."

At his words Maggie would have risen to see to Justin, but he waved her back. "Never mind. I'm all right."

He was not all right. His left sleeve hung in scorched shreds, and beneath it the flesh of his forearm burned an angry red.

"I'll help with that," I said firmly, giving him no chance to refuse. Morton had brought the first-aid tray and he pulled up a high-backed chair of Spanish leather for Justin. I found shears in the tray and began to slit the sleeve Justin was attempting to rip from his arm. I felt shocked and confused—horrified by what had happened to Old Daniel since I had seen him this afternoon, yet questioning as well. If I had stayed longer, I might have been there to help him when the wall collapsed. Or he might have been talking to me and nowhere near the wall when it fell.

"He knew those walls," Justin said, paying no attention to what I was doing to his arm. "He should have had better sense than to get near the one we were going to shore up."

Maggie relinquished her place to Morton and got to her feet. "What about the fire? Do you know how it started? Are they putting it out?"

"It's not too bad," Nigel said quietly. "Just one corner of the workshop seems to be damaged. But why didn't the dogs bark? What happened to the man on guard?"

Justin answered savagely. "He's all right now, but he was knocked out by someone who came up from behind. And the outside dogs were drugged. They're still sound asleep. Only Deirdre raised a rumpus here in the house. That's what wakened me, so I looked out my window and saw the flames."

He was giving me a hard time with his arm. "Don't pull away," I said. "You can't hit anyone right now."

After that he held still, though his head was turned from me, as if in distaste for my nearness. Scorched skin showed that flame had already cleansed the area and there was only need for a loose bandage until the doctor came and treated it properly. I worked as gently as I could, and he did not permit himself to wince.

Once I looked around for Dacia Keane, but she had apparently gone outdoors, and I suspected that she would be in the thick of the excitement.

I dared not think about Old Daniel now. I tried to be as impersonal as Justin, and attend solely to what I was doing, forgetting the man whose arm I bandaged. Instead, I found myself consumed by an unwanted tenderness. All too well I remembered the shape of the long-fingered hand I touched. I remembered the way that hand had once smoothed my hair, my shoulder, and how roughly it had shaken me. I knew the very line of his jaw as he looked away from me, knew the way his brown hair grew at each side of his head, with that light streak cutting through above. All these were part of me, part of my knowledge of him, whether I liked it or not. His pain was my pain and I could not work this close to him unmoved. Fire and death must be dealt with in good time, but for the instant I was aware only of my husband and the fact that he had been hurt.

Not until I was through did he finally look at me, and then with a curious expression, as if I were some species he could not comprehend, someone whose very existence he questioned.

"Thank you," he said in a surprisingly subdued tone. "I'll go back to the stable now and see what's happening. I heard the town fire equipment arrive a little while ago."

I watched him cross the hall, but before he reached the door, Marc came in from outside, pushing the orange-clad Dacia ahead of him. He was as soot-streaked as Justin, and he looked thoroughly keyed up—yet as though what had happened did not altogether distress him. That he was annoyed with Dacia was evident at once.

"What a bloody little fool you are!" he said, shoving the girl through the doorway. "Pulling a trick like that! If I hadn't fished you out you might be dead of smoke poisoning by now."

"But I wanted to see!" Dacia wailed. "There were still flames and I'd never been that close to a real fire before."

"Getting close to a real fire can be dangerous," Maggie said tartly.

Dacia swung about, her great brown eyes alive with excitement. "But that's what I like, Mrs. Graham—the danger! How can anyone be really alive except when there's danger?" Her gaze fell suddenly upon the body of Old Daniel on the couch, where Morton was drawing a sheet over him. Her color blanched. "Ow! Who's that?" she cried.

Apparently Marc did not know about Daniel. He crossed the room and jerked back the sheet. "What's happened here?" he demanded.

Maggie told him and he heard her out, his expression stony. I remembered that Marc and Old Daniel had never been friends. As a boy Marc had constantly teased the old man about the topiary garden and Daniel had never forgiven him. Now, at least, Marc might have shown some compassion, some feeling, but he only turned and spoke again to Dacia.

"Do go back to bed, will you, darling? You're not needed down here."

Maggie put her hands to her face. "What can be happening to us? We've never had so much trouble at Athmore!"

"Not for a few hundred years, anyway," Justin snapped. "Old Daniel's death is a miserable accident. I blame myself for that wall. But the fire was *set*. And I don't know why. There's apparently been no attempt at theft. All these things have been nuisance interruptions, though why anyone should have it in for us—"

"My brother's a trusting bloke," Marc interrupted mockingly. "It never occurs to him that it might be to the interest of others to interfere with what he's doing."

"Don't talk rot." Justin was impatient. "I'm not that important. Not yet."

Dacia had paid no attention to Marc's efforts to send her upstairs. She was staring at them all, wide-eyed and still over-exhilarated. "It's just like in the films! I saw a flick in London last week—with spies trying to get hold of the secret formula, and—"

"Do shut up, darling," Marc said, regarding the girl with amused tolerance.

Maggie spoke to her across the room. "Do as Marc says and go back to bed, Dacia. You too, Eve. I'll stay with Daniel and wait for the doctor."

"And I'll keep vigil with you," Nigel said, and drew up a chair for himself.

Justin spoke to his brother. "Come with me, will you? I want another look before the police come."

At once Dacia was at Marc's elbow. "Do let me come too!" she pleaded, but Marc shook his head and gave her a quick, light hug before he pushed her in the direction of the stairs. Over the top of her head he cocked a whimsical eyebrow at me and I turned away. Justin was watching, and I did not want to exchange so much as a look with his brother.

When the two of them went outside, I said goodnight to Maggie and Nigel and started upstairs. At once Dacia came clattering after me.

"Fancy you coming here at this very time!" she said, her boots clacking up the steps beside me. "Whatever brought you back, anyway? Nothing's going to switch Justin in his tracks now, you know. In fact, it'd better not. Not with all that money of Alicia Daven's coming in so handy."

I had no wish to discuss my life with this avidly curious girl and I hurried up the stairs. She kept pace with me, her chrysanthemum-shaggy head close to my shoulder.

"You've given Marc a dreadful fright, you know," she confided brightly. "Though you mustn't let him guess I tipped you off. Of course he's got good reason to panic, what with owing money up to his ears. It would be a nice mess if Justin decided he had to stay married to you, after all, wouldn't it? Imagine me marrying old Marc and taking on all those debts! Maybe that's what he's got in mind. I wouldn't put it past him. Not that I blame him. After all, it's everybody for himself first, don't you think?"

I climbed the stairs in silence, glad enough to have her chattering about herself instead of me.

"Of course I know I won't be sitting on top forever," she ran on. "Not as a model, anyway. Though there're some people who say I've got something that's especially me, so I can be somebody on my own account, once the Twiggy craze dies out. Right now I'm her type and they're playing that up. But I do want to be *me*—not an imitation of somebody else."

This revelation accounted for quite a bit, I thought. Her hair, which looked as though she had taken the kitchen shears to it, might very well be the creation of someone like Vidal Sassoon in London. She was certainly the type for the current craze, with her slight, straight body and blank little face on which nothing much had as yet been written. Even her huge expressive eyes only expressed her youth and eagerness to be alive. As for Marc's debts, they were nothing unusual. Justin had long ago despaired of keeping a tight rein on him, and Maggie had been foolishly indulgent.

We reached the top landing of the stairs, and I walked briskly toward the double doors into the long gallery. Dacia bounced beside me, rather like a puppy whose blunders were persistent but good-natured. I wondered how old she was. Seventeen, perhaps?

For all her open curiosity about me, she seemed willing enough to overlook my lack of response to her hints and questions. She shrugged it off and ran to a wall of the darkened room to touch a switch.

Two lighting fixtures on either side of the central doors came to life, while the rest of the long hall remained shadowy and dim.

"Ooh, what a hideous place!" she cried, wrinkling her nose in disrespect.

I had to agree. This was a room I had never liked. Down its entire length the walls were ornately paneled in carved wood that had darkened over the years until it was almost black, and everywhere there were gloomy hints of the Gothic touch. There was Gothic in the arches above the doors, at the highest point of the window frames, even in the panel carving. The ceiling was a vast, ornate pattern of linked plaster rings, and there were two enormous stone fireplaces at either end. Tall chairs from some doge's palace marched stiffly along the walls, with console tables, or low upholstered benches set at intervals between. Here and there down its length hung portraits of lesser members of the family, with the pale and sad-eyed Mr. Dunscombe facing the stairway doors. I nodded in secret greeting to this unhappy first son-in-law of Mrs. Langley's. Dacia wasn't looking.

"What's a room like this good for?" she demanded, flinging her thin arms wide to encompass its great space, while her orange coat stood out stiffly about her. "With everybody here claiming to be so poor—and all this to keep up! Not that they seem poor to me. They manage to have somebody work on the grounds, and there are servants for indoors. It looks pretty posh, I'd say. Maybe I make more in a year right now than Justin does, but I don't live like this. Wouldn't know how. What's the point, anyway? It's all out of touch, that's what it is!"

I had felt something of the same thing when I had lived here. Dacia was right and it was out of touch—if you reckoned that the modern world was what counted most. But perhaps I had a bit more perspective and knew more of Athmore history than Dacia did. I could not remember without being moved some of the things Justin had told me, so there was an ambivalence in me toward the house.

Dacia took a few steps into the huge room. "Imagine! All this space and nothing to do with it. It's a bit spooky, don't you think—with horrible, dark woodwork, a miles-away ceiling, and that ghostly Mr. Dunscombe staring from the wall! Why don't they hang him in the green-velvet room where he belongs?" Dacia looked suddenly aghast at her own words and then giggled. "Oops!—no pun intended. I suppose that's where he really hanged himself, isn't it, so that wouldn't do. But just think—you could be up here screaming your head off and nobody'd hear you. It must've given you the shivers when you first came. How did you get used to it, anyway?"

"I never did," I said shortly and started toward the door to our corridor in the north wing.

She came after me, doing a saucy dance step in her high boots. "That's what I'm afraid of. What if I marry Marc and he brings me here? I'd perish of the dark and the way every ancestor in the lot would look down their noses at me. As they must have done with you. Is that why you ran away?"

The question was rhetorical. By now she expected no answers. She simply rushed on, letting her voice go ringing a bit shrilly down the room—challenging the ancient echoes with her here-and-now approach. I felt a twinge of unexpected pity for her. She was right, as I very well knew. The house would no more welcome her than it had me. It would have as little taste for Bow Bells as it had for America.

Dacia swung about as we reached the corridor door and flung both arms wide again, as if she dared the room to snub her. "Never mind! If I come here, I'll give the old digs a surprise or two. What a place this would be to hold a fashion show! Marc could bring some of my friends from Carnaby Street and we could get into our mod clothes and give the house the shock of its life. What do you think?"

I had to smile at her eagerness, and at the impertinent tilt of her boyish head. Three years ago I had given the house a few shocks myself—but Dacia's shocks would be shriller and more colorful, though perhaps no more shattering. Mine had been on the quietly stubborn side, but they had smashed things up in the course of a year anyway. Mainly they had smashed up what had existed so tenuously between Justin and me. I had only wanted his love, but he could not accept me as I really was and keep on loving me.

We left the lights burning behind as we went into the corridor leading down our wing. The room seemed safer lighted than dark.

Dacia was considering me again. "I suppose I should worry about you coming here more than I have," she said, suddenly sly. "You could tip over Marc's applecart entirely if you got Justin back. Because then where would the money come from to pay his debts? Alicia would stop holding him up and the whole jig would be over. Of course Maggie knows this, all right. She's a smart one. I think that's why she's considering marriage with old stick-in-the-mud Nigel Barrow. All that Bahamas money of his would help now, wouldn't it? And she'd do anything to keep Marc and Justin out of trouble."

I could not bear to listen any longer. "There's an old man lying dead downstairs," I reminded her, "and I don't think—"

"So what?" Dacia had recovered from her first shock at seeing Old Daniel on the couch downstairs. "People are alive and then they're dead. It happens all the time. Besides, he was a mean old codger. He used to watch me every time I stepped out on his silly grass chessboard—as though I might hurt it someway."

I hardly listened because of my own disturbing thoughts. "I keep remembering that I saw him in the chapel ruins this afternoon and that he seemed glad to see me, even though he never liked me. I think he was trying to tell me something. If only I could have understood!"

Dacia paused at the door of her room and swung about.

"What do you mean—tell you something?" I could almost see her vivid imagination taking a leap into space. "You mean there's something more to how he died? More than a wall falling over accidentally?" she demanded.

"I don't mean anything," I said. "Don't be absurd."

I hurried toward my room, while she spoke to my retreating back, her attention once more upon her own affairs.

"Oh, well, if I lose out here, I can always keep on with my job. I'll not give it up till there's solid ground under my feet. So I might as well wish you luck."

I heard her door creak open and then close before I reached my room. For all my impatience with her, I found that I liked Dacia Keane. I might feel a real sympathy for her if Marc North married her and brought her home to Athmore. Though that seemed unlikely. Marc had never stayed with one girl for very long. His penchant was for playing the field, and I had never seen him with anyone like Dacia before. At least she had her eyes open. If she married Marc, she would know what she was doing—which was more than I could say for myself when it came to marriage.

I reached my room and went in to switch on the bed-table lamp. Then I stood in the eerie blue glow the room generated, sniffing doubtfully. Had someone been smoking in here? I had stopped smoking long ago to please Justin and I had never started again. So why should there be a faint aroma of tobacco in the room?—if that was what it was.

I went to fling a window open and stood huddled in my wool robe, looking out toward workshop and garage. There were no more flames to be seen, but the stench of smoke was thick on the air and I closed the window against it. Undoubtedly this was what accounted for the odor in my room. My hands were cold on the windowsill and I thrust them into the pockets of my robe, remembering again the urgent clasp of Old Daniel's fingers. Why had there been such urgency in him? What had he meant about the rook's play and his warning that the king had better watch out? Why should he have mentioned these obvious facts about the topiary game?

I wished I did not feel so uneasy. I wished that my own mind would not go leaping through space just as Dacia's had done. At tea this afternoon I had asked the woman next to me if she had seen an old man when the tour visited the ruins, and she had told me readily that she had and that he'd seemed frightened. Could there be any possible connection between tonight's fire and Old Daniel's death?

But of course that wasn't possible, since the wall must have fallen upon him hours earlier.

Before I got into bed, I went again to the unbarred tower door, drawn to it uneasily, wondering again at Deirdre's reaction to room and tower. I slipped behind the bureau and pulled the door open upon darkness and the chill mustiness of damp stone. Above I could see the narrow oblong of a sentry window that had never been intended for use. The circling stone steps between were black and I could see nothing close at hand, yet it seemed to me that some trace of smoke lingered here too, and that it was different from the outdoor smell of the fire. Still—with the fire stench so strong —it was impossible to balance a fainter smoke scent against it and be sure of any distinction.

I stood utterly still, listening, while an odd tremor ran through me, and my blood began to beat in my ears until it seemed to me that I really heard sounds up there in the dark tower. A creaking that was not the wind, a suppressed sigh that was like a human breath. I thought of the guard struck down at his post and backed hastily from the tower. Before I closed the door, I listened once more, trying to quiet my trep- idation—and heard no sound except from far away. That was Justin's voice calling, and Nigel Barrow answering out in the yard. But nothing closer. Nothing at all. My imagination had always been nervously stimulated by this house, and I must not heed it now. It would be absurd to go running downstairs with a wild alarm that would cause laughter. Besides, if any- one was up there, escape from the roof was too easily possi- ble. From either corridor the back stairs were quickly accessi- ble at this deserted hour of the night. I closed the door and shoved the bureau hard against it. At least the door could not be opened while I slept without a good deal of noise.

I returned to my bed and found that Nellie's hot-water bot- tle had lost its comforting warmth. This time I left the bed- table lamp burning, and the blue aura of my surroundings seemed to add to the chill as I lay shivering beneath the cov- ers.

Shivering—and thinking . . .

Thinking that I had no past, since it was lost to me. That the future was wholly doubtful. That there was only the pres- ent. And what was I to do with these few hours that already slipped through my fingers?

From far down the hall came strains of music. That would

be Dacia again, turning up her record player. She too had a tower bedroom. Had she smelled cigarette smoke in its dark reaches? Had she turned the music up loudly for comfort and company because the house was intimidating her in spite of her gay defiance?

I did not want to hear the beat of Petula Clark's singing. Those were words I wanted to forget:

For all we know . . .

But I could not forget. The memory of Justin that I had been trying to hold off returned to engulf me. When I bandaged his burn I had been close enough to him to slip into the curve of his arm, had he offered it. The memory warmed me, and it answered as well the question of what I must do about the present.

Tomorrow may never come . . .

I put my hands over my ears to shut out the words. I must be honest with myself. Honest about why I was here. There was no time left for subterfuge, for fooling myself because of hurt pride, worn by now to such shabby shreds that I could no longer hold it about me. It was absurd to tell myself that I had come here to make certain that I was no longer in love with Justin North. I was here because I had never stopped loving him, and probably never would. Yet how I had lost him, how we had failed, seemed clear enough—so how could I expect another chance?

During my marriage, before I knew what Justin meant to Alicia, and she to him, I had met her a number of times. Grovesend was part of our social community and could not be ignored. Once I knew, I tried to avoid her—which was not always possible. Remembrance of those encounters with Alicia still made me squirm in humiliation. Only later had I realized how cleverly she baited me and exposed me to ridicule, while always remaining well-mannered herself. More than once she had stung me to sharp response in front of Justin, her attitude one of quiet amusement that anyone so gauche and clumsy as I should play at being mistress of Athmore.

I turned miserably in bed, unhappy all over again because of what Alicia had done to me. At least I would know her baiting for what it was if I had to meet her now. Surely I would be able to smile and keep my temper, retain my poise as well as she.

I lay scowling in the dark, my temper anything but restrained, and once more tried to think honestly about Justin.

He had been furious at the sight of me this afternoon. He had not willingly submitted to my help in bandaging his arm, and he had looked at me strangely afterward—as if I were someone he did not know, someone different from the young girl he had fallen in love with. Was I too different—or not enough different—to win him back? Was all this questioning simply the straw clutched at by a woman when love has already slipped out of her grasp?

Still—Justin had waited. That was the thing which had brought me back. He had not called me, but neither had he divorced me for desertion. And I had at least one advantage over Alicia Daven. One enormous advantage.

I was Justin's wife.

Having faced the beginnings of truth, I turned over and fell asleep in the wide bed. If anyone crept up and down the tower steps or smoked a cigarette on the roof, I did not know it. I slept soundly until morning came.

V

Nellie came into my room, red-cheeked and smiling, to look at me as if I were a lazybones. She set her tray on the bedside table with a determined, cheery "Good morning" and went to start the fire.

"It will be a warm, fair day," she said. "But I remember you feeling cold in the mornings. We'll get you strengthened up again soon, but for now you shall have your fire."

I propped myself onto one elbow and sipped my tea strong, with no hot water or milk added. I could remember how I had hated to be thus awakened in the old days. "I don't want any tea!" I used to wail to Justin. "Why can't they just let me sleep?" But of course Justin wanted his tea early when he was driving off to London. I'd had only Athmore ahead of me, and nothing at all that I really wanted to do. Oh, I could learn to garden and to help run a house that did not need me to run it. I could accompany Maggie on her round of good deeds. I could visit other country families. But where was the world I had hoped for in all this? Worst of all, where was Justin? I had ached with my lonesome loving—while he had gone off to his machines and his formulas, his experiments, forgetting me for a good part of the time.

Would it be different now? What had I to offer except the fact that I was three years older than when I'd married him, and, hopefully, three years more mature?

"Drink up now, or your tea will be cold," Nellie said, and I returned to face the present.

"Is there any word about the fire last night?" I asked.

The girl looked around at me from the hearth, her determined air of good cheer falling away. "I didn't know a thing till I came this morning, Miss Eve. But everyone's running on about how some madman has it in for Mr. Justin. It's cruel,

69

that's what it is. And him working so hard and trying to do something for England."

"Oh?" I said. "Is that what he's trying to do? I thought he was working on a new car."

Nellie moved back from the fire as the kindling took hold, and brushed up the hearth, talking to me the while.

"It's that in part, Miss Eve. I mean he'll need a new sort of engine for the car, won't he—if it's a new fuel he's to come up with?"

A new fuel? So this was the hush-hush secret Miss Davis was being so mysterious about. Apparently it was common knowledge below floors.

"What sort of new fuel?" I prompted.

She moved about the room, pulling back draperies, opening a window to freshen the room, in spite of the hearth fire. "Oh—we'd not be knowing about that. Something that won't poison the air or burn up a car if there's an accident—that's what they say. A car that will be a lot safer all around. That would be fine, wouldn't it—for all of England?"

If Nellie was right, and Justin was really developing such a car, then this was very big news indeed. I had heard him discuss ideas along this line in the past, but in his experimental work for the company he had always been put at other things. Now, apparently, he had taken leave of absence to do something on his own. And someone was trying to stop him, or at least delay him.

"You've heard about Old Daniel's death, haven't you?" I asked. "Has there been any more news about that? Do they know whether it was really the wall that crushed him?"

She nodded sadly. "It was the wall, all right. It toppled over on him fair and square. Morton says the police came last night and again early this morning to have a good look at the place. The old man should have had better sense than to go near that wall. He knew it was dangerous. Oh—that reminds me, Miss. I've brought your pictures. My Jamie did them up for you last night—prints and all. We made free to look at them, and you've got some snaps of the very place where the wall fell down. And one snap of Old Daniel standing there."

This was a surprise, and I sat up in bed and took the packet of pictures she handed me. In my hurry to catch scenes I wanted to remember, I had not realized that Old Daniel was about, or that I'd turned my camera on him before the roll was finished. I sorted quickly through the snapshots and found the one with the old man standing in the shadow of a large bush. So lost was he in leafy shade that it was no wonder I had not noticed him. This last glimpse of him alive was saddening, and I wished again that I had understood what troubled him.

Once the fire blazed properly, Nellie came to my bedside to regard me with approval. "It's good to have you back at Athmore, Miss Eve. You never used to stand by and take the old ways just because they've been old ways for a hundred years. You stirred things up a bit when you were here."

I smiled at her. "I'm afraid a lot of my sentences in those days began, 'In America we . . . ,' and everyone tired of that quickly. What a bore I must have been."

"Oh no, Miss Eve!" Nellie denied. "I like Americans. I'd like to go over there someday for a visit. And I don't see why you might not do some things in a way better than us."

I had noticed before in England—and in other places too —that often the working classes seemed more warmly friendly and less inhibited in their behavior toward the stranger than the more reserved upper classes. Fortunately for me, the working classes were very much "with it," as Dacia would say, in today's England.

"You're a darling," I told her. "But I'd like to learn more about Athmore as it is, instead of trying to turn everything upside down the way I used to."

"Anyway, we've got someone new doing that," Nellie said wryly. She rolled her eyes as she had done yesterday and nodded toward the hall. "Her nibs down there. Wait till you see her—skirts up to here, and sometimes red tights over those long legs. Colors enough to put your eye out! My man'd not let me in the door if I came home dressed like that."

"This is the country," I reminded her. "In London that's what you see on the streets every day, and only the tourists give it a second look. All this is supposed to be waking England up."

"I'd sooner stay asleep," said Nellie. She picked up my tray to carry it to the door.

"Wait a moment," I said. "Nellie—tell me something. Would anyone be likely to come into this room smoking a cigarette while I was downstairs during the excitement last night?"

Her rosy face sobered and she stared at me with frightened eyes. "Oh, no—not already! I thought maybe he'd stay away, what with you being an American and all. What would he want with you?"

"He?" I echoed. "Whoever do you mean?"

"That one from the green-velvet room," Nellie said. "He's taken to smoking cigarettes, he has—though how he manages that, I can't know."

I sat up in bed. "Nellie! You're not talking about poor Mr. Dunscombe who's supposed to haunt that room, are you?"

She cast a nervous look around, as though some shadowy figure might appear at her elbow, and put a finger to her lips. "Hush, Miss, do! These days he gets about. I'd swear he'd been in here yesterday before I came to make up the room for you. I smelled the smoke just as plain. And it's logical he'd come here, isn't it? After all, his wife moved into this very room while Mr. Dunscombe was still alive. They say her lovers could come to her easily across the roofs and down that tower there. Though of course the green-velvet room that Mr. D. moved to is a tower room too, and they say he came across the roof and caught her one night. Sometimes there's a knocking here—just like he's still trying to get in."

None of this ancient legend troubled me. But a ghost who smoked cigarettes was something else.

"Have you told Miss Maggie about the smoke?" I asked.

Nellie nodded vigorously. "I have indeed. But she says I've always been afraid of dark corners at Athmore, and it's time I grew up. I don't think she took me serious. But when I—" She broke off abruptly, as though she had said too much, and went to the door with her tray.

"Wait," I said. "Don't stop. What were you going to tell me?"

She seemed to turn something over in her mind. "It's just that—that Mr. Marc was there, and I think he believed me. He didn't speak a word, but he looked like he was thinking hard about what I'd said and didn't much care for it. In fact, he went off in a hurry before Miss Maggie was finished with me."

I wondered what Marc had done to follow through, and whether Justin knew about this. Since a secret enemy was abroad at Athmore, this should be looked into.

Nellie transferred the tray to one hand and opened the door before I could ask more questions.

"I'll start your bath for you, Miss Eve. Nice and hot the way you like it. Her nibs—Miss Dacia, that is—sleeps for ages every morning. We're supposed to be a rest cure for her right now, you know. Ran her to a frazzle, they did in London—poor skinny little thing. So Mr. Marc brought her here for fresh air and some feeding up. He's home on holiday too, from that art gallery place where he works. But what rest she's getting. I can't see—the way she stays up half the night. Anyway, you can take as long as you like with the bath. Mr. Nigel's on the other side of the long gallery, in the front room, so you and Miss Dacia are here by yourselves."

I let her go and moved about collecting the things I'd need for a bath—my "sponge bag," now that I was back in England. Then I went down the hall to where steaming hot water roared from huge faucets into such a tub as one never saw in America. I poured in pink bath salts from an apothecary jar on a table, and got into the tub for a wonderful soaking. Athmore water might not be this hot again until evening, so I had to take advantage of it now.

The room filled with steam and the mirrors misted over with sweetly scented fog. It wasn't exactly bracing, but I luxuriated, trying to put off the moment when I must go downstairs and face all the insoluble problems that awaited me. A mind fresh awake in the morning will seldom let one be, however. Strangely enough, considering all the other difficulties which awaited me, it was the recurring thought of Old Daniel that nagged at my mind. There was some meaning hidden in my chance meeting with him, and I must find it. The accidental snapshot I had caught of him might well have some bearing on the puzzle.

I got dripping from the tub to wrap myself in a bath towel as big and thick as a rug, and thoroughly warmed from a hot-water-pipe rack. Then I snatched up my robe and scooted back to my room.

There I spread out the snapshots on my bed for a more careful look, studying them while I toweled myself dry. Only the last few I'd taken were important—the shots of the chapel ruin—and only one of these had a particular significance for me. I picked it up and studied it more closely than I had before.

The figure of Old Daniel was blurred, indistinct, lost in shadow. He stood beside a bush near a high portion of crumbling wall. I could just make out his dark jacket and the peaked cap pulled low over his face. He must have stood there watching while I took my pictures, not approaching me at once.

I put the packet of prints and film away in my suitcase,

holding out only the one I'd caught of Old Daniel. Whether it would have any significance in explaining the accident, I did not know, but I slipped it into my handbag and left it in a bureau drawer. I would mention the picture to Maggie or Justin later on.

In twenty minutes I was dressed and I hurried downstairs for breakfast. I needed to ask no one the customs of the house. There would be chafing dishes to keep the food hot on the dining-room sideboard, ready for irregular breakfasters. There would be cold toast waiting in open racks, because no one in England seemed to mind cold toast, and there would be wonderful marmalade, hot water for tea, hot milk, and abominable coffee. I was home again at Athmore.

Nowadays the large dining room was used only for dinner parties, and the small Wedgwood room for family meals. It was a room I had always liked, and I stood in the doorway for a moment while nostalgia swept through me. All heavy, gloomy colors had been banished here. In the morning light it was a cheerful blue-and-white room with blue Wedgwood insets around the white marble fireplace, blue walls that were less intense than the walls of my present room upstairs, and a white Wedgwood frieze where walls met ceiling. The table not nearly so large as that in the adjoining gold dining room, was Hepplewhite, as were the blue-upholstered chairs set invitingly around it. In the beginning of our marriage Justin and I often breakfasted together in this room—and sometimes we'd held hands under the table.

There was no one here now. I went to the sideboard to help myself, and Morton looked in, faintly superior as I remembered him, to see if there was anything I needed. Morton belonged to the vanishing school of butlers who stayed with one family forever and partook of their fortunes, good and bad, presenting a dignified and correct demeanor, behind which his own opinions and notions carried on a vigorously secret life which the gentry pretended did not exist. Justin had told me once that a good butler, a good waiter, should be gracefully invisible—but I always forgot this and wondered about Morton as a person. His opinion of me was undoubtedly low, but I greeted him warmly, ignoring his lack of welcome.

Of kippers and grilled kidneys I would have none, but I managed scrambled eggs, toast and marmalade. And when I had finished I went outdoors.

At least I knew how to dress for spring at Athmore and I

had put on a gray woolen skirt and yellow pullover sweater, a
fresh yellow band to hold back my hair, and low-heeled
walking shoes. The morning was brightly cool, but the air
still bore a taint of wet ashes as I walked down the slope toward the workshop and garage area.

The screen of beeches on the embankment shielded me
from view, and I took care to stay behind the trees. One of
the yard men was working with Justin, carrying out charred
wet wreckage and dumping it on one side of the driveway.
An upper corner of the building that had once stabled Maggie's beloved horses was smoke-blackened, and repairs would
be necessary—but the rest of the stable workshop appeared
unharmed.

Next to it was the big garage which Justin had built a few
years before I had come here. Horse-poor they might be at
Athmore, but cars, as Maggie said, were a necessity in the
country. I recognized the black Morris Oxford that was Maggie's. I had sometimes driven that very car in the old days,
since Justin's car was always busy taking him to and from
London. The other two cars I did not recognize. The newer
English model—a blue car—was probably Justin's everyday
car, since his taste did not run to the spectacular. The red
Mercedes-Benz was undoubtedly Marc's, since he usually
managed to get what he wanted, in spite of always being
short of cash. There was no car to account for Nigel's trans-
portation, and I supposed he must use Maggie's when he
needed one. Once more I wondered about his being here, and
about his engagement to Maggie Graham. Did he still have
connections in the Bahamas, and would she go there if she
married him? Somehow I could not imagine Maggie living
away from Athmore, but I did not want to recall the thought
Dacia had dropped into my mind last night—the suspicion
that Maggie would marry Nigel only to save Athmore and
her precious Marc. I would hate to believe that, but I knew
very well how far Maggie would go for Marc's sake. She had
proved that to me long ago.

Next to the big garage with its open doors was a small,
neat, new building I had not noticed until now. It, too,
looked to be a garage. Its doors were closed, but through a
front window I could glimpse a long gray car. This, I supposed, must be Justin's new, experimental car. Fortunately,
the fire had not touched it.

A sound from the direction of Athmore's front gates
reached me and I stepped close to a tree trunk, reluctant to

I

reveal myself. The car that came toward the garage was a
cream-white Jaguar, and I knew at once who it belonged to.
Alicia Daven had always driven a white car and she was at
the wheel now. I leaned closer to my shielding tree trunk.
There was no way to return to the house without being seen,
and I wanted to avoid her.

The Jaguar drew up on the concrete apron before the garages, where I could look down on it from my embankment.
Alicia seemed as golden and beautiful as I remembered. Her
masses of fair hair were drawn into a French twist at the
back of her head, as she wore it much of the time. It became
her in its elegant simplicity, as everything she wore became
her, from the white cashmere of her sweater to the heather
tones of her tapered trousers. She was Justin's age, but she
looked younger, with her fair English skin and delicate features. I remembered her heavy-lidded eyes and that perfect,
straight nose, with the nostrils that could lift with the unconscious disdain of the aristocrat. All at once I was nineteen
again and wildly jealous, hating the woman who meant to
have my man. That he had been hers first was an indigestible
fact which I had never been able to swallow.

Perhaps she felt my gaze upon her, for her deeply blue
eyes turned my way and she saw me there, peering out from
behind my tree trunk. Saw and recognized me, and said nothing at all, though she did not look away. The next move was
left to me, and there was no easy choice. I could not go on
cowering like a child behind a tree. Nor could I turn and run
toward the house as I might have liked. That would be retreat, and I would not give in to the impulse. What about
that sturdy resolve of mine to meet poise with poise? I must
go down there and speak to her, whether I wanted to or not.

She held to her silence as I descended the embankment toward her, watching me with that air of confidence which was
hers by birth. The calm of a born assurance had never been
mine, and as I neared her I became less and less confident of
my ability to deal with her on any level. This was regression
and I hated it. Yet I could not stem the slipping away of my
self-possession.

"Hello, Eve," she said, and smiled at me in her remotely
kind, rather pitying way.

I knew very well how treacherous any seeming kindness
from Alicia was likely to be, yet her manner disabled me.
Open warfare I could meet. But her manner of being a bit
sorry for me sent my blood pressure soaring in the old, hate-

ful way. I could not even return her greeting casually. I simply stood beside the white Jaguar and stared at her with the baleful air of the child I had once been.

"Maggie tells me you've been doing very well in New York," she went on lightly, ignoring my lack of response. "Your work there sounds fascinating."

There was nothing sensible I could find to say. I would not be a hypocrite and simper about my job at the travel agency.

She knew very well that I was furious, and she knew why. At least she now chose to put aside her pretense at conversation and took a direct thrust at me. "You shouldn't have come here, Eve. You've only made it hard for yourself and more difficult for Justin. He hates to hurt anyone."

Even her choice of the word "anyone" was a cut. "Justin can take care of himself," I told her, and knew I sounded sharp and angry.

By contrast her tone grew more velvety. "Not altogether," she said, her implication plain. She meant that she would take care of Justin far better than I ever had.

"You aren't married to him yet!" I cried, and heard the outraged Victorian ring of my own words. What should have sounded triumphant bore a petulant sound. This was what she had done to me in the past, and she was succeeding again. I knew it and knew the fault was mine for responding as she wished—yet I could not help myself.

"You've always insisted on injuring yourself," she said, speaking an irrefutable truth with all the honeyed gentleness she could put into her voice.

The honey—absent till now—warned me. I stepped back from floundering in utter quagmire and smiled at her stiffly. It was a smile that promised her battle, and she knew it very well. But her tone had put me on guard, and I looked around to see Justin coming toward us from his workshop. How much he had heard I couldn't tell. There was thunder in the look he gave me, though it was to Alicia he addressed himself.

"Hello, darling," he said and came to the side of her car. She raised her face sweetly and he kissed her with an elaborate tenderness. At least I took some satisfaction in knowing that his kiss, at this particular moment, was more a slap for me than a kiss for her, and I hoped she sensed that too.

She slipped gracefully from under the steering wheel and slid along the seat. "Do drive, will you, Justin darling? I'm feeling lazy this morning."

"I like you that way," he said and set the car into motion, turned it around on the apron a bit too sharply for as good a driver as he, and went off toward the front gate.

I looked after them, shaken by wild, futile anger. Now he would go with Alicia and she would offer him this new, deceptive serenity with which she could surround herself. Like Maggie, I was unconvinced that it was the true serenity that comes from being at peace with oneself, but it must serve well enough to give Justin the surcease he needed from the strains of his own troubled spirit. When had I ever done anything but trouble him more? Yet I could not be another Alicia—and I did not want to be!

At least I was trying to be honest about myself, trying to face up to all that was wrong. I doubted that Alicia had ever bothered to do that herself, or ever regarded herself as less than perfect.

As the car disappeared, something dug into my ribs so sharply that I jumped. Dacia Keane had come quietly to stand beside me. The sharp instrument that had stabbed me was her small, pointed elbow.

"That puts your nose out of joint, doesn't it?" she said, nodding in the direction of the departing white car.

I turned my back on the car resolutely and gave Dacia my startled attention. This morning she was dressed like a boy, yet she looked not at all boyish. Her orange coat hung open, and beneath it she wore a shirt of Italian blue, unbuttoned at her skinny little throat. Boys' shorts of the same color stayed up mysteriously, though belted low on her narrow hips, and below them long blue tights covered surprisingly well-shaped legs. On her feet were square-heeled, silver-buckled black shoes. She had slicked her wispy yellow hair down with water, and her face was devoid of make-up except for the meticulously careful job she had done on those enormous eyes with false lashes and pencil, even at this hour in the morning. More than anything else, however, it was her mouth that kept her from looking boyish. Her uncolored lips were full and slightly pouting in repose, though she could flash a dazzling smile when she chose. Young as she was, this was the mouth of a temptress.

"Do you still think you can get him back?" she asked, moving her elbow as though to prod me again.

I stepped out of range. "Aren't you ever afraid of dangerous ground? Doesn't your mother ever spank you?"

She grinned at me impudently. "Not so you'd notice it. Do

you know about my mum? They always print it about her when they write me up. That she was a char, I mean. She scrubbed out offices after Pa ran off—and before too, since he liked the inside of pubs better than the inside of any place where he ever worked."

She waited for some exclamation on my part, cocking her brassy young head at me.

"Are you bragging?" I asked.

Velvet brown eyes stared at me for a long while before she wrinkled her nose, deciding.

"I suppose I am bragging. Why shouldn't I? There was a time in England when a charwoman's daughter couldn't amount to nothing. 'Anything,' that is. You notice, I'm trying hard to speak in a proper way. Marc made me go to a teacher to learn how to speak, he did. Anyway, now that everything's swinging in London, it's all the more special if you're a char's daughter. Sort of anti-Establishment, if you know what I mean. People get proud of themselves for taking you up and being so terribly democratic. But you don't feel that way, I can tell. I suppose it's because you're American. You're used to all those self-made men—and women. It's not so new for you as it is for us."

Once more she slipped her hand companionably through the crook of my arm and drew me toward the garage.

"I thought you slept late," I said. "Nellie told me you were up at night and in bed late in the morning."

Dacia shrugged orange shoulders. "Maybe I'm getting caught up. Besides, with you here there's more happening. More people having a fit. So I came down to be in on it. Breakfast I don't care for much, so I've skipped it. Come take a ride with me in Marc's car, will you? He's taught me to drive, and I like to practice."

Marc was as reckless a driver as I'd ever seen. He loved cars passionately, loved to drive, as Justin, strangely, did not —and he drove as though the world had to give way and nothing could ever harm him.

"Ooh! I don't drive like he does!" Dacia cried. "I want to live awhile, I do. Come along, Evie. We'll do the parklands course, and I'll show you a place I like. I'll even tell you how to get your Justin back, if you really want him."

"Thanks," I said dryly.

She never minded a snub. "It might be good for Marc if you did get Justin back, at that. I don't know if it makes much difference to me. Marc and I understand each other

pretty well, though whether I'll marry him or not is to be
seen. We fight a lot, you know. Though he doesn't try to
make me over—except the way I talk—and I don't try that
with him either. But just the same I scare him sometimes—
like last night at the fire. Is that what went wrong with you
and Justin? Did you try to make each other over?"

I laughed at her endless chatter. What "making over" there
was had been on Justin's side. Not that he had tried very
hard. He told me once that he wouldn't play Pygmalion—or
Henry Higgins. He simply took it for granted that I would
stop being the fairly independent American girl he had married, and turn myself into a suitable English wife. I'd tried to
do that, but it hadn't worked.

Dacia got into the bright red Mercedes and backed it out
of the garage, while the yard man who had been helping Justin watched her doubtfully. I joined her in the black leather
seat and she turned onto a road that led past the garages. As
we set off she explained the new testing course to me. To
some extent it followed the line of earlier carriage drives
through Athmore's parklands, and was shaped in the form of
a closed "m." The ovals on either side were of uneven size,
and the roads followed the outline of the "m" with a connecting bar making the middle stroke of the letter. The righthand enclosure was the largest, harboring Athmore itself at
its front, but leaving the ruins of Athmore Hall outside the
righthand loop of the course.

As I expected, Dacia drove too fast. The red car went
roaring down the connecting bar and took the well-banked
curve to the right with a speed that made the tires squeal.
Dacia flashed me a look of delight and did not lessen her
pressure on the accelerator. She drove like Marc, though with
less control.

Woods and a pond swept by us in a flash, and all we had
was speed and the wind whistling past our ears in the open
car. I could feel my hair whip back from my head as we
went, and put my hands up to the band that held it. She did
not slow until we turned down the outer rim of the righthand
course. Then she flung me a look of triumph.

"Wasn't that wonderful! Only danger is real! Only danger
makes me come to life."

"Danger could also be the death of you at this rate," I
said. "You're not a good enough driver for such speed."

"The car can do it and Justin built the course for speed,"
she said. "All I need to do is guide the wheel a bit. Besides,

dying young wouldn't be so bad, do you think? Who wants to
get old and dried up and see everything slipping through your
hands? Like Alicia Daven!"

"Alicia?" I smiled wryly. "There's nothing wrong with Alicia, by the look of her."

"Don't be a goop. She must be terribly old. As old as Justin. This is her last chance and she knows it. She'll be livid
because you've come home. After all, Justin was hers first,
until you came along and stole him from under her nose.
Maybe you hadn't any right to him. Do you ever think about
that?"

This stung me to a response. "No human being has a
'right' to any other. And in this case I didn't know she existed
until I'd been married for months."

"Oh, poor you!" said Dacia without much feeling. "Anyway, I suppose she should have been clever enough to hold
onto him in the first place."

"Perhaps Justin wanted a change himself," I said sourly.

Dacia grinned as she brought the car to a halt on the
shoulder of the road and stuck her long blue-clad legs out the
door.

"Come on, Evie. I want to show you a place I found a
couple of days ago. Maybe you already know it, but come on
anyway."

I followed her along a path through the woods, and knew
at once where we were going. This was the way to the old
ruins of Athmore Hall, where I had gone yesterday afternoon.

When we reached the area of broken walls and grassy carpet, kept neat and well-clipped before the great arch of the
chapel window, Dacia ran across the grass without a glance
for the sky and arching stone that framed it. I held back,
wanting to linger. Yesterday I'd had to hurry because of the
approaching tour. Now I could look about more carefully.

"Wait," I said. "I haven't seen this for years. I want to
stop."

She cast a look around without comprehension. "Grotty
old stones! Do come—there's something nicer to see."

I stayed where I was. The thought of Old Daniel intruded,
but I would not think of him now. A pointed Gothic arch
pierced the blue springtime sky. The stones were old and
moss-grown, but here and there gray markings gave evidence
of long-ago blackening by fire. Where the stones of the window ledge rose above the grass, tiny newborn flowers clus-

tered, yellow and pale pink—buttercups and primrose. As I stood watching just as I had done before, the vapor trail of a jet streaked across the sky.

Emotion could repeat itself, I found. In this place the sense of everything going on and on that I had felt before came again: a fleeting awareness that human pain mattered for less than a moment's breath in time—that others had suffered long before me, and would suffer long after. In a moment my universe would center around me again, as every man's must, but for this little while I was detached—part of a larger picture. There was something freeing about the experience.

"What do you see?" Dacia's tone was one of puzzlement as she watched me.

I gestured. "You can see it too. That jet streaking through the arch. The old England and the new. Everything moving on in spite of whatever dreadful things may have happened or may happen, and yet the old still standing, to remind us of what went before."

"Is that what you believe?" Dacia said. "That things really move on? I don't. I think it's all going to end—poof! So I'd better grab for the rosebud while I may."

The word "believe" brought back another memory. On that day when Justin had taken me about Athmore for the first time, showing me John Edmond's sword, Margaret's dress, and all the rest, he had used that word after he had kissed me. I'd not remembered for a long while.

"You're a believer," he had said, and when I asked him what he meant he would not answer directly. "Believing doesn't need to be talked about and explained. It simply is," he told me.

"I wish I could believe in something," Dacia said, sounding unexpectedly wistful. "In something good, that is."

A young softness had touched her face that was very appealing.

"Don't you believe in anything?" I asked her.

At once she was her cocky self again, facing me in her defiantly orange coat and blue tights, with her buckled shoes set wide apart in a boyish stance, and on her mouth a woman's smile.

"Of course I believe in something. I believe in money. And pain. Pain I'm afraid of. That's what makes danger exciting. But money is both for now, and for if I live to be old. When I'm old as Alicia, old as Maggie Graham—then I want to be terribly rich. I don't want to be the way my mum was when she got too old to scrub floors because of her rheumatism, and I wasn't making enough to help her. Now you should see her—the fine lady she is. Though she doesn't want a lot. Not nearly what I could give her."

The girl could be outrageous, and she could be hard, impudent, heedless of others' feelings—yet there was something touchingly winning about her in spite of all this. Something young and outgoing and generous that she often tried to suppress. Perhaps she believed in more than she knew.

"I'll come and see what you wanted to show me," I said gently, and she bounded off down a grassy path, her long legs flashing beneath the short orange coat. I knew the path we followed. It opened into the road to the old quarry where Athmore's stones had come from long ago. I had walked to the quarry often with Justin, and stood looking down into its steeply rounded pit where green growth had taken precarious hold along the precipitous walls, giving the whole a far less bald appearance than it must have had in the days when it was active. Perhaps before I left I would walk there again and take more pictures.

Now, however, we did not go as far as the quarry. We rounded a turn and came out upon the old road, and into the open. Dacia stopped at the edge of a field and flung her arms wide. I had forgotten the wild bluebells. I had forgotten how breathtaking this sight could be in springtime. In every direction the blossoms spread across the hollow of the clearing—a bright blue carpet, far bluer than the sky—their heads nodding delicately in a breeze that blew from the faraway sea. One could almost hear their springtime ringing. But after a moment or two of delighted staring, I looked at Dacia instead —at her lips that were parted because her breathing came quickly, at the wide delight in her huge brown eyes, at the wrinkling of a small nose that sniffed in all the scents of the outdoors.

"I never saw nothing like this in London!" She whispered the words, as though the scene might vanish if she broke the quiet. "Imagine flowers coming up every spring in a place like this. I'll close my eyes and think about it when I'm home again in London. Here's some of your keeping on and on, if you like. Stone walls and jet planes are only man things. This is different. If ever I could believe in much of anything, I suppose it would be this."

I kept very still, not wanting to break the spell of her mood, savoring with her the sight of that great sea of blue-

bells. But it was not in Dacia to be quiet for long. She bent
to pick a single flower and held it up in her fingers.

"I was never a brat who picked flowers in the parks," she
said. "It always seemed wicked to disturb them. I can't feel
happy when Mrs. Graham cuts flowers in her garden—not
even when they fill the house with their color and smell—and
that house needs them. But I think it's all right to take just
one, when there are so many, don't you?"

She thrust the blue flower into the top buttonhole of her
coat, where it held its own bravely and did not fight with orange dye.

The spell came to an end, and Dacia marched long-legged
ahead of me back through the woods. Where broken walls
commenced she stopped and pointed.

"See that pile of stones over there? That's where the wall
toppled over last night and killed Old Daniel. Marc says so."

I stared at the broken wall and something chill traced my
spine. A chill caused not only by realization of the old man's
death, but by a sudden feeling that something was very
wrong.

"I know," I said. "I met him here by chance yesterday. I
came to take some pictures, and he turned up in one of
them."

"How creepy!" Dacia cried, staring at me round-eyed.
"That's spooky—it really is! Where was he standing—right
there by the wall that fell over?"

I considered this, looking at the place with new eyes, now
that I could see exactly where the stones had fallen. Portions
of wall stood at intervals around the chapel, some of them
propped up by supporting buttresses. And the arrangement
was wrong.

"No," I said. "He wasn't anywhere near that wall in the
picture. He was in the opposite corner near that bush which
makes him blur out in the snapshot. I suppose he walked
over to the wall later." I was silent for a moment, still feeling
there was something wrong about all this, though I could not
think what it was. "He tried to tell me something when he
saw me," I went on. "Something that seemed important to
him about the chess game in the topiary garden. He said to
remember that it was the rook's play and the king had better
watch out."

This meant nothing to Dacia, who had not the slightest interest in chess.

"Too bad for Old Daniel," she said. "Marc says he should

have known enough to keep away from that wall. Anyway, we've seen the bluebells, so let's go back."

I did not want to leave right away. Besides, I had no wish to go racing back to the house with Dacia in Marc's red car.

"I'll stay for a while," I said. "Go along, if you like. And thank you for showing me the flowers."

She studied me thoughtfully. "If you want to get Justin back, I'll help you," she offered, as she had before. "I don't like Alicia Daven. I don't like what she's doing to Marc. I don't think her money will do Athmore all that lot of good."

"Please!" I begged her. "Let everything alone. I don't expect to be here more than a day or two, now that I know how things are."

She grinned at me, cheeky again. "All right then. But you may need me before you've done. And watch it, Evie, when you go back to the house. You have to follow the test course for a little way on foot, you know, and a car can come swinging around the curve just above here without much warning. Justin fixes it so everyone's warned away when he or Marc take out a car for real testing. But Marc gets careless sometimes. He almost ran Old Daniel down a few days ago. So mind your step."

She sauntered off through the woods by the way we had come, and I watched her orange coat swing out of sight among the trees.

Too much of history was repeating itself—yet not enough. There could be no going back to that other time when I had first come here. I was neither so young, nor so much of a believer as I had been then. I lay down upon my back on thick grass, with my hands clasped beneath my head, letting the morning sun warm me gently. I closed my eyes and tried to think of some sensible plan. Since I had seen Justin drive off with Alicia a little while ago my world had caved in upon itself. Until that moment I had not really believed that he was lost to me for good. But I had seen him kiss her, seen his face darken with anger at the sight of me. These were facts which I must accept. The end of love had come long ago for Justin, though not for me.

This was not the first time I had lain upon the grass in this spot. It had been my favorite place ever since I'd come to Athmore as Justin's wife. Yet I could no longer think about my times here with Justin. Alicia stood between, and there was another face besides. That of Old Daniel.

The puzzle concerning the old man seemed to be growing

ominously. How could it be that I had caught a picture of him as he stood near that other wall which still remained? Yet only moments later he had walked toward me from another direction. That was the thing that troubled me, the thing I had groped for. I had it now.

It would not have been possible, any more than it was likely that Old Daniel, who knew this place very well, would have endangered himself by going too close to a wall which needed repair. For the first time I began to wonder whether the man in my picture was really the gardener, after all. Now that I considered it, I was not even sure that the old man had worn a peaked cap when I had seen him.

I sat up on the grass cross-legged and stared at the blue sky beyond the great window, seeking comfort in a sight that had once given a repeated lift to my spirits. Behind me a dog came leaping suddenly out of the woods and nearly bowled me over in loving assault.

"Deirdre McIntosh!" I cried, and put my arms about the great beast, more than glad to see her.

She whimpered in joyful excitement, and then glanced behind her hopefully. Along the woods path her master came striding. The anger was gone from his face, but I liked anger better than the disdain with which he looked down at me.

"Dacia said you were here," he told me coldly.

That was Dacia—"helping," I thought, and did not thank her. I clung more tightly to Deirdre, my face against her rough, brindle-gray coat, so that I need not look up into Justin North's face. Whatever he had to say, while he looked like this—I did not want to hear it.

VI

"Deirdre likes me," I said by way of a delaying tactic when Justin did not speak. "Even if she doesn't remember me, she knows I'm someone she can like."

The dog responded with a loving lick at my cheek, but Justin still remained silent. After what seemed ages I stole a look at him and found that he had gone to sit upon the ledge of the chapel window, and that he was watching me in the same strange way that he had done last night after I had bandaged his arm.

"How does your arm feel this morning?" I asked him politely. All this was unreal and had no meaning.

He shrugged the question aside as though the subject of his injury had no interest for him. "I was rude to you yesterday, Eve. I want to apologize."

"That's rather unlike you," I said before I could bite my tongue. Why must I always be sharp with him? But I knew why. I wanted to hurt him before he hurt me. There had been too much of that before, yet here I was starting it all over again. Why couldn't I just let myself be hurt—and never mind slapping back?

For once he did not take me up with equal sharpness. "What are you doing here?" he asked. "Why have you come?"

I knew what he meant, but I chose to misunderstand. "Dacia brought me here to show me the bluebells. I'd forgotten how beautiful they can be at this time of the year."

I could sense exasperation rising in him, and I fed it, as I had always been able to do.

"If I'd known you were coming here, of course, I wouldn't have stayed in the place. But I saw you driving off with Alicia and I thought you'd be gone for the day."

He must be counting at least to fifty, I thought, and stole

87

another look at him. The exasperation was there, but he was smiling, however wryly. When he answered he sounded reasonable enough, reminding me of how angry his very reasonableness could make me.

"Alicia wants to give Maggie a mare for her birthday," he said. "I'm not sure Maggie will accept it, but Alicia wanted me to drive over to have a look at it. She brought me back right after, since there's plenty to do around my workshop picking up the pieces from last night."

I made a tremendous effort to do an about-face. I tried to let down that desperate guard of pride I held against him.

"I'm sorry about the delay to your work," I said. "From what Nellie tells me, it's something pretty important you're onto. Is it really a new type of fuel?"

"That's only part of it. Not that the fact of what I'm working on must be kept quiet. It's the method that's secret. The ingredients. Though whether they'll come to anything or not I can't tell. Especially not with all these beastly delays."

"How long has this mischief been going on?" I asked.

"Several weeks. But never mind about that. I hardly came here to cry on your shoulder. There's just one thing I want to know—when will you be leaving?"

I stroked Deirdre's proud neck and would not look at him. I was feeling stubborn again. "Maggie would like me to stay a little while."

"What use will that be? I'm sorry Maggie wrote to you first about my plans. I should have been the one to open the subject. She had no business to ask you to come to Athmore."

"She didn't ask me," I said. "I was supposed to see her in London. She lied for me yesterday."

"Then why did you come?" he demanded bluntly.

I fumbled for an answer. "Aren't there things we must discuss? The usual decisions to be made?"

"Such as whether you might get half of Athmore, I suppose?"

I pushed Deirdre away and stood up. I had to face him now. "I don't want anything from you, and you know that very well. I have a job and I'm not helpless. If you want to know why I came, I'll tell you. I wanted to know whether you really meant it."

He looked at me with an astonishment that was obviously real. "If I really meant it? But what else could you think after the way you behaved? How could you possibly believe I'd ever want to set eyes on you again?"

"I behaved badly enough," I agreed, "but not as badly as Marc made you think. Yet you seem to have forgiven him."

"One may have to accept a brother. But some things are unforgivable in a wife. I haven't much use for a woman who can't be trusted."

The old hopeless feeling of not being listened to, of not being understood, rose in me again. It was because of this futility that I had run away, hoping that somehow his feeling for me—if he missed me—might do what words could not.

"Yes," I said, "it was unforgivable. It wouldn't have happened if I had not let it. But I never thought you'd let me go. I went to London and waited. I thought you'd come after me."

"I don't play such games," he said. "You always could behave like an obstinate child, and I'd had all of that I could stand."

What could I say to him? That this was two years later and that I wanted to believe I might be more than two years older —that what I wanted more than anything else was another chance? Of course I could say none of this. I could not throw my pride away to that extent, or embarrass him by begging for a love he could not give.

I started toward the broken doorway and the path through the woods. "I'll leave very soon," I assured him. "Of course I shouldn't have come."

He did not speak until I reached the opening in the broken stone wall. Then his voice stopped me.

"I came here looking for you that day you left," he said quietly.

I stopped where I was, not turning.

"Maggie told me you were going," he went on. "She said you meant to walk about the grounds before you caught the bus, and I thought you might come here."

"I did," I said, and knew that the moment was somehow potent, that what was said now held my future on a balance scale.

Behind me Deirdre began to whimper, always sensitive to moods of the humans she loved. The tone of our voices worried her, and she began to run suddenly back and forth between us.

"Stop it," Justin ordered. "Sit down and be quiet, Mac old girl."

The dog obeyed him, sitting without question, but her

whimpering went on, sounding almost like words, pleading, beseeching.

"You had gone by the time I got here," Justin said.

Again I waited. If anything was to be offered, he must offer it. I had already said too much.

He left the window ledge and crossed the grassy area of the chapel. Up and down he strode, moving restlessly until he finally came to a halt before the tumbled stones of the wall beneath which Old Daniel had died.

"I blame myself for what happened here yesterday," he said. "The wall should have been repaired without further delay. I was busy and let it be put off."

I let my held breath go. His choice had been made. Nothing I might say mattered now. I might as well talk about Daniel.

"Do the police think it was really an accident?"

"Of course—what else?"

"I don't know," I said. "But I saw him yesterday just before he died and he tried to tell me something about the rook's play in the topiary garden. I haven't been able to think what he meant or why he should tell me so urgently."

"Old Daniel's been wandering in his mind lately," Justin said. "He's been hinting mysteriously and talking about old times in a maudlin way."

"Perhaps he knew something," I suggested. "Perhaps he knew something about what has been happening around Athmore lately, and—"

"Then he'd have told me." Justin was curt. "Don't let that wild imagination of yours get out of hand again, Eve."

I ignored the pricking of his words. "How was Daniel dressed when the wall fell on him? Can you tell me that?"

"Dressed? Didn't you see him when we brought him in last night? A jacket, corduroys."

"What about his head? What would he be likely to wear on his head?"

Justin was growing impatient. "What are you getting at? If he had anything on his head, I suppose it fell off when the wall crashed."

"We could search," I said. "If it's around here—"

Justin had endured enough of what he must regard as sheer whimsy. He looked down at me from his arrogant height. "Let's not run on about Old Daniel. I didn't come here to talk to you about him. I came to tell you that I don't want you to stay on at Athmore. You'd better understand

Hunter's Green

that Alicia is never going to be hurt by me again. Whatever happens, I shan't let her—or myself—down. She is everything I want, and under the circumstances you can offer no opposition to my plans. I hope this can be managed as speedily and quietly as possible. There is no point in waiting any longer."

He snapped his fingers at Deirdre, who bounded to his side, and then brushed past me through the broken doorway. The dog went with him, but only for a little way. Hard though the choice must have been, she left him after a few yards and came back to me. She pawed at my dress and barked, as though she scolded me—as though she believed that Justin and I belonged together and could not understand why we had spoken angrily and moved so far apart.

I went down on my knees beside her and held her tightly, past the time of tears, too frightened to cry. All the obstacles that had been set in my path were too large to be surmounted. Even the obstacle of my own sad-hurt-longing feelings were too much for me to overcome. There seemed no way to suppress or deal with them. If I had made a mistake about Alicia in that long-ago time, and if Justin had made a mistake about me, we ought to be able to say so. We ought to be able to admit our errors and go on from there. But "from there" was already gone in the past and it was too late.

Those were the words that hurt more than any others—"too late." They rang in my ears all the way back to the house. Everything had worsened and the way out seemed darker than ever, and more lost to me.

Dacia waited for me on the terrace. "Did he find you?" she asked.

"You shouldn't have sent him looking for me," I told her.

She studied me shrewdly. "Put your foot in your mouth again, did you? You Americans are good at that. You're always too touchy. When he asked me if I'd seen you, what could I tell him except where you were? I mentioned your yellow sweater, so if you moved about he could spot you through the woods. You know what he said? 'She always liked to wear yellow.' It wasn't just the words. It was the way he spoke them—as if he remembered something he had a bit of a liking for."

I could only shake my head as I went up the terrace and into the house. Remembering wasn't enough. It was only the present that counted—and the present was nothing. Nevertheless, I climbed the stairs to the top floor with Justin's words running through my mind: "She always liked to wear yellow." What a feeble straw for me to seize upon. But it was the only straw I had.

When I reached the long gallery I crossed its width to pause before the portrait of Mr. Dunscombe. He looked a gentle, sad young man—someone who had accepted his fate and taken himself out of the fight. In a way we had something in common, he and I. Both had married Athmores, and both had lost out in the end. His solution had been a desperate one. Mine was more dogged, more stubborn. I couldn't give up yet. There had to be a way to cancel out those hateful words "too late." Surely, as long as one drew breath it was never too late. Not even when Justin told me that Alicia was everything he wanted. Even when everything pointed to this truth, my stubborn heart refused to believe, refused to accept.

Perhaps it was time for me to go back and face what I had done to break up my marriage two years ago. Perhaps by reliving that dreadful time I could discover how to go on from here.

As I turned my back on the picture in the long gallery I had only to face right instead of left in order to reach the green-velvet room, where that last miserable scene with Justin had been enacted. I took the right turn. I walked through the entrance to the south wing and followed the corridor toward the tower room that was the opposite number from my own blue lady's room.

The door of the green-velvet room was closed, but it opened readily at my touch. From wide-flung windows a breeze came to meet me. Nellie must have been airing out ghostly cigarette smoke.

How well I remembered the central focus of the room—that great dramatic bed with its ornate coronet of a canopy, from which green cut-velvet curtains flowed to each of the four corners, and thence to the floor. Within the cave of the canopy and curtains a green-and-yellow tapestry of similar figure filled the wall behind the bed. On the other walls, covering them entirely, were green-and-gold tapestries depicting scenes from a stag hunt, which made this, I had always thought, anything but a restful room. A neutral gray carpet covered the floor, undoubtedly added in modern times, and across it were flung small East Indian rugs of rose and blue-green. Even the chairs were upholstered in green cut-velvet, grown shabby over the years. I remembered too the chest of drawers—of handsome English design with its mirror and serpentine front.

For a few moments I was still, recalling the emotions of that rainy evening when I had last stood here in green gloom, with candles lighted in brass candlesticks on a corner stand, and the shaded lamp on a center table shedding a pool of light. Marc had lit the candles before he brought me here. Marc, bent on mischief, playing on my jealousy, as I allowed him to do—his one purpose, as I later realized, to be rid of my presence at Athmore and break up my marriage.

But I had been blindly unsuspecting then. Dramatizing my loneliness, believing myself neglected by Justin, I had not found Marc's flattery altogether distasteful. If one brother did not value me enough, then it would serve him right if the other brother did—even though I cared for only one. I was too young to realize how foolish I was being, or how unlikely it was that so elementary a ploy would work with Justin. Or indeed where such a tactic could really lead.

The thing had begun, not here in this room, but when we were leaving the table after dinner to go to the drawing room for our evening coffee. Oh—it had been months before, really, with Marc hinting to me about Alicia, so that I had confronted Justin with my knowledge of her, and of the fact that he still saw her from time to time—in fact, that we all saw her.

"Why didn't you tell me?" I'd wailed to him. "How could you let me meet her so innocently, never dreaming what you two had been to each other?" I had been wildly dramatic in my accusations, and Justin had been cool, scornful.

"Do you think I've lived no life of my own before I met you? There's no reason why Alicia and I should cut one another when we live in the same community. I hope we may always remain friends. This has nothing to do with you."

Perhaps if I had not been so headlong and violent in my accusations, he would have been kinder, more reassuring. But having alienated him, I could not bear the results of my own actions. I could not accept reality. I did not want to share Justin with the past, I must own him wholly—as no man is willing to be owned. I began to watch him jealously, to question too much, to imagine constantly. What I wanted from him was a love as overwhelming and single-minded as my own—and Justin was not one to be overwhelmed, or to overwhelm anyone else.

That last night at dinner I was edgy and suspicious. I knew

Alicia had called him on the phone and that something was up. When we rose from the table and Justin announced curtly that he would not stay for coffee but was going out for an hour or two, Marc stepped behind me and put his hands openly upon my shoulders, looking past me at his brother.

"Don't worry," he said, laughing at Justin's glowering look. "I'll keep you entertained, Eve dear. Justin's business is important. So you must wait for him patiently."

Justin strode out of the room and Marc whispered in my ear, "Alicia's called for help again, and Justin has gone to Grovesend. Let me ring her up in a little while and ask for him there. Then you'll know for sure."

"Why do you hate him so?" I had asked, shrinking from this open betrayal, yet terribly, humanly, tempted.

Marc only smiled at me. He could be as enigmatic as Justin when he chose.

The tempting won, as it always had with girls named Eve. Marc rang up Alicia's house while I stood by, hoping somehow that he would be proved wrong, that I would be reassured as Justin would not stoop to reassure me. But when Justin came to the phone, Marc held the receiver out so I could hear his voice. Then he replaced it quietly.

"Of course Justin will guess it was you calling," he said, mocking me, now that I could not undo the act.

I ran away from him, hating myself as much as I hated Marc. I went to the library, where Maggie was talking quietly with Nigel Barrow. I took a book and sat far away from them, though I did not read. All my senses were keyed to listening for the sound of tires on the driveway that would mean Justin had come home. I did not know what I would do when I saw him. Would I fling myself into his arms and weep—an action he would detest. Or would I fling accusations at him instead and be equally detestable? Growing up did not occur to me. I did little of that until it was too late.

By ten o'clock that night it had begun to rain and the evening seemed doubly dreary. But I did not want to go to the room I shared with Justin. I could not bear to get into that big empty bed and torture myself by picturing my husband wth Alicia Daven. When Marc came into the library looking for me, I still sat staring at unread pages.

He was gentle now, as though he pitied me, and coaxed as if to distract me. "This is a perfect night for our Athmore ghost," he told me. "Wouldn't you like to meet him?"

"Ghosts walk at midnight," I said grumpily.

His face grew bright with mischief. "Not this one. He was husband to Cynthia, the most beautiful of Mrs. Langley's daughters, and he knew he was being cuckolded. He was not much of a man, I'm afraid, since his way out was to hang himself from beneath the high canopy of the bed in the green-velvet room. Now and then over the years someone will see him looking out the windows of that room on a rainy night. Or servants will swear they've come upon him sleeping in the bed, and that he faded away as they watched He's a harmless enough ghost, concerned with his own troubles, which he seems doomed to go on enduring forever. Rainy nights like the one on which he died are always best for him."

Marc took away my book and pulled me from my chair. Maggie watched us doubtfully as we left the library together, and Marc called to her to tell Justin, if he came, that we had gone to visit the Athmore ghost.

The room waited for us with rain whispering at the panes and the bed lost in canopied green darkness. A draft crept in from closed windows and the candle flames dipped, setting long shadows to bowing. Marc turned off the lamp, leaving only pale candlelight.

"Our ghost doesn't care for too much illumination," he said.

That night I had felt the mood of the room in my very flesh. I had sensed its aura of old despair, of futility, of black hopelessness, and these things became my own. Knowing what I must see, I stepped close to the bed and peered between flowing curtains. Was there a pale, lost face looking out at me? Did cavernous eyes burn from those greenish shadows? Suddenly I knew there was danger for me here. My happiness, my very life, was threatened and I must get away from all this somber green velvet as quickly as I could. If a misty face watched me, that was its message. Mr. Dunscombe would know that we were kin in despair.

But when I turned from the bed, Marc caught me in his arms and held me close as if to still my trembling. In the beginning I was scarcely aware of him, except as comforter to my distress. All my being was given to an inner listening, a sensing that was paramount. When I heard the sound of a distant door it was with an inner ear, as much as with an outer. When Marc began to make love to me, I fended him off almost absently. How could he think I would turn to him when it was Justin I so obviously loved? Not until his mouth forced itself upon my own, did I begin to struggle. I was to blame for this, but I wanted it not at all.

Then, quite suddenly, before I could break the grip of Marc's arms about me, he raised his head and I saw his gaze move toward the door. His look told me exactly what I would see if I turned my head. But when I would have stepped free of Marc's clasp, he whispered in my ear, his lips barely moving: "Here's your chance, sweet. Here's your chance to make Justin suffer too."

He put his lips upon mine, and I stood angrily still for his kiss, hating it, but filled with a savage desire to hurt Justin as much as he was hurting me. If he could go to Alicia—! I let my arms creep about Marc's neck.

Justin walked into the room—not raging, but utterly cold and arrogant. Not jealous, but disgusted. When Marc released me and I turned about with my mouth bruised, my eyes angry, Justin nodded toward the door.

"Get out," he said to me.

I think even Marc was a little frightened, but I dared not stay to see what might happen. I ran all the way—through the dark reaches of the long gallery, down the stairs, slipping in my haste, through the library, empty now, and finally to Justin's room. It had always been Justin's room—never mine. I ran through it to the small adjoining dressing room where there was a chaise longue that I sometimes used for napping. This place, at least, was my own, and I spent the night there, sleeping not at all.

Justin never came. Perhaps he went out of the house and back to Alicia, who was conveniently alone at Grovesend.

The next morning there seemed only one thing to do. I packed a suitcase and told Maggie I was leaving. It was sheer flight—a running away because I could not face Justin. No explanation could be given. How could I say, "I played up to your brother because I wanted to punish you for hurting me?"

Before I left I wandered about the grounds, dramatizing my tragedy before I had learned what pain could really be. I said a tearful farewell to Deirdre and Maggie and went to London, believing that Justin would come for me and somehow solve the problem I could not solve for myself.

Now, these years later, standing again in the green-velvet room, I faced all that had happened in its full appalling detail, and took upon my shoulders the blame I had never truly accepted before. By now I knew—through letters from Mag-

gie—that Justin's visit to Grovesend had been innocent
enough. Alicia claimed concern about some business matters
she had become involved in which were not turning out well,
and she wanted Justin's advice. He could hardly refuse her,
whatever her motive might have been. It was Justin's misfor-
tune to have a wife with so little faith in herself and her husband.

I shivered now with the chill of self-blame, and went to
close the windows upon bright daylight. Then I stepped before the serpentine bureau and looked wonderingly into its
mirror. My face did not look so very different from three
years ago when I had first come to Athmore. I still looked
ridiculously young with that pointed chin, wide brown eyes
and softly youthful hair. Yet there was a difference. About
my eyes, about the set of my mouth, there was a difference.
Gaiety was gone, and all the old eagerness that had won Justin to me. The eyes of the girl in the mirror seemed more
watchful—they doubted *me*. I did not like what I saw, but I
did not know how to change what was happening to me.

The glass of the mirror was slightly crazed and it seemed
to impose itself mistily between real face and reflected one.
How long had this glass reflected this room? I wondered.
Once it had mirrored me in Marc's arms and shown Justin
behind me. Beyond my own figure I studied the reflected
room. I could see the canopied bed and I knew the glass must
have beheld other, more dreadful acts which had occurred in
this room. Yet the mirror continued to give back only innocent pictures of the present, unmarked by all it had seen in
the past. The human face was not like that. It changed and
carried in itself the tarnish of all that was experienced.

Since I had closed the windows, an odor had begun to
make itself known in the room. I sniffed the air uneasily.
There was no mistaking the smell of cigarette smoke. Not
old, dead smoke that might cling to bed and window hang-
ings, but a fresh, distinct odor that floated gently about the
room, as if someone unseen stood near me smoking. For an
instant fear touched me, but I flung it off and looked about
for the source of the smell. The counterpart of my own tower
entrance in the blue room bulged into this room as well. Beyond, I would find stone steps circling to the roof. Could
someone be on the stairway smoking?

But the smell did not seem to come from that direction.
Across from me was another doorway which had no dupli-
cate in my own room in the opposite wing. I went to it

quickly and turned the knob. The cigarette odor grew strong and I saw that I had opened the door of a small dressing room. Draperies were drawn across the single window and the room was so dim that I stood blinking for a moment, trying to accustom my eyes to the gloom.

"So you finally found me?" Marc said, and reached out a hand to switch on a table lamp. "I heard you come in some minutes ago."

The room sprang to view, and I saw that he lay upon a chaise longue, lazily smoking and watching me.

"What are you doing, Eve—reliving history?" he asked.

My first impulse was to flight. I had a dreadful feeling that history might indeed repeat itself and that Justin could walk in upon us at any moment. But this was no time for repeated cowardice. Sooner or later Marc had to be confronted.

"So you are Nellie's ghost?" I said, and went to the window where I flung back the draperies and let in air and daylight. From the window I could look out upon the side lawns of Athmore, with woods rimming the far side. Maggie was down there, walking in her garden. "Perhaps I can ask you the same question you've asked me," I went on. "What are you doing here? Besides frightening Nellie, that is?"

Marc stood up and ground out his cigarette in an ashtray. Then he sauntered to the window and stood beside me, too close for comfort. I could never again be near Marc without uneasiness rising.

"Perhaps I'm watching for Nellie's ghost," he said. "Isn't that as good a reason as any? But I'm more interested in how it happens you haven't left early this morning, as you planned. Dacia reports that you're staying on, in spite of Justin telling you straight off that he doesn't want you here."

"There are things to be said and things to be done before I go," I told him, moving away from the window, away from him. "There's a lot I want to know. I never learned what happened in the room next door, for example—after I left that night. How did you save yourself? What lies did you tell Justin about me?"

Marc's smile was as sweet as I remembered, and as dangerous. "It took a little doing, I must say, but I managed. After all, is any man ever as much to blame as the woman who flings herself at his head?"

"You told him that?"

"Not then. Not in so many words. I just let Maggie know how it was so she could stand up to Justin for me. He wouldn't listen to me at first. I couldn't talk to him until later."

I had known about Maggie's efforts to keep Marc from being sent from Athmore peremptorily. She had written me about that, seeming to believe that I might worry about her poor darling Marc.

"Do you really think yourself so innocent?" Marc asked, very close to me again.

I drew sharply back before he touched me, and he laughed in the old, mocking way I remembered so well.

"That caught you on the quick, didn't it?"

"Stop being theatrical!" I cried. "Of course I blame myself. I was stupid not to see how you were feeding my jealousy in order to be rid of me. Though I never fully understood, until Maggie explained it to me yesterday, how you wanted Athmore one day for yourself, rather than have it wasted on Justin's heirs."

He laughed as though I delighted him. "Naturally that was part of my feeling toward you. Why wouldn't it be? Fortunately, Alicia Daven doesn't care for children. She'll never give him an heir. So if I marry Dacia, who is mad for children, everything will eventually come to my side of the family. That's probably the one reason she might marry me. Providing, of course, that Alicia first takes care of a few little debts that are hanging fire. You know, Eve, it's an odd thing, but Dacia seems to have taken to you. I believe she really likes you."

"I like her," I said. "She's much too good for you, but she's tougher than I was. She can look out for herself."

He nodded. "And for me, too, if she decides to make a go of it. But what's all this Dacia reports about a picture you took of Old Daniel yesterday? The police think he must have been dead since afternoon, so you could have snapped him shortly before that wall fell over."

I had not thought of the old man since I'd parted from Justin, but now I found myself wishing Dacia were less prone to gossiping about all she knew. I did not want to discuss anything with Marc, but at least I could ask him the question Justin had not answered.

"What would Daniel have been likely to wear on his head when he was there yesterday?"

Marc regarded me thoughtfully. "This morning when I went out early to look around, I found his cap. Why? What made you think of such a thing?"

I shrugged and let it go. There was something more important I must ask of Marc before I went away. Futile though it
might be, I had to try.

"Now that it no longer matters to you, won't you at least
tell Justin the truth about what happened here that night?"

Unexpectedly Marc reached out to touch a lock of my hair
where it fell against my cheek, and when I would have drawn
back, he caught it tightly and I held my head still against the
hurt of the pull.

"The truth, Eve? But did you ever know the truth? Did
you ever stop to think how I might have felt about you?"

I reached up to release the strand of hair from his fingers
and saw that his eyes were dancing in the old wicked way.

"What an innocent you were! Fresh from college and sure
you knew all there was to know. Such a pretty young thing
—a lamb, really, with all that eagerness to experience, and all
that trusting belief! And your notions about making over the
world. Of course here at Athmore the world was a bit out of
your reach, but you could work on us. And God knows you
tried. Justin couldn't take it, but if you had been my girl I'd
have given you something to sink your teeth into. I'd have
taken you away from this mausoleum and given you London
to work on—and me!"

I walked away from him into the other room. He meant to
start trouble all over again, and this time I had no intention
of listening.

He followed me at once. "I used to wonder what you'd be
like when you grew up. There's a touch of the lemon now
that was missing before. It's an improvement, I'd say. I like
a hint of sour with the sweet."

He crossed the room so that he stood between me and the
corridor door. The feeling that I'd had yesterday in Maggie's
sitting room came surging back—an almost frightening distrust of Marc North.

"Do you remember the way you kissed me, here in this
very room?" He was mocking me again.

"You'd better remember Dacia now," I snapped.

His laughter carried assurance. "Dacia knows well enough
what I'm like. While I may struggle to change her speech, I
don't try to change her. We leave each other free."

I had to pass him to make my escape through the door,
and I moved toward him slowly, ready for whatever he might
do. When he reached toward me, I stepped back quickly.

"Let me by," I said.

Instead he pinioned my arms to my sides, laughing down at me, his face close to mine. Behind us a door opened—and was held ajar, as if someone behind me stood in waiting silence. I broke Marc's clasp and sprang away from him. If it was Justin again—! But it was not. Nigel Barrow came through the tower door carrying an empty wine bottle, and a handful of twisted cigarette packets. We must have surprised him, but except for that moment of hesitation, he hardly blinked. He came into the room and held up the bottle for Marc to see.

"I had an idea there'd been somebody up on the roof. I've just had a look and collected these things. I suspect he's been hiding out in the blue room, until Mrs. North moved in. Or perhaps he's even been serving as the house ghost by smoking in this room. I think he's not been down my tower stairs, and Dacia has seen no evidence. I've checked with her. It's the empty rooms he'd pick, of course. But where is our intruder now? That is what we need to know."

Marc was quickly alert, watchful. "If this is the answer to what's been happening, then it ought to be easy to stop," he told Nigel. "All we need do is post someone on the roof for a few nights. But I must say he's a bold one. Give me that lot and I'll speak to Justin about it right away."

Nigel hesitated for a moment, almost as though he mistrusted Marc's word. Then he turned bottle and packets over and Marc went off, with only a sidelong glance of mockery for me. I read it well. "Let's see you get out of this!" his eyes were saying. I could not help my long sigh. Once more I was faced with the impossibility of explaining what could not be explained.

Nigel's mustache twitched into a faint smile, but his gray eyes seemed chill and a bit disapproving.

"Don't worry, Mrs. North," he assured me stiffly, "I'll not say anything about this."

I made a gesture of impatience. "There's nothing to be secretive about! I can only tell you that I detest Marc utterly."

He considered this as though it might be a new idea. I supposed that Maggie must have given him Marc's story of what had happened before I left Athmore that other time.

"At least that's an understandable reaction," he said. "I don't always like Marc myself, though I've known him since we were boys. Come now, you mustn't be upset and on the defensive. Let me take you downstairs to Maggie's sitting room where you can pull yourself together. All this haunted velvet can give one the tremors."

"I don't want to talk to Maggie," I said. "No one can talk to her about Marc."

"Do you think she doesn't know exactly what Marc is like?"

"Then how can she love him so much?"

He smiled ruefully. "Does love—whatever it may be—have very much to do with reason? Or haven't you discovered that yet?"

"I've discovered it," I said.

He held the door for me and I went through ahead of him. I would never be wholly comfortable with Nigel Barrow because I could never forget that time during my last month at Athmore when he had thoroughly embarrassed me. I thought of it uncomfortably as we walked along the corridor. He had come here from the Bahamas on an extended visit, though no one had seen him in England for years. He had gone to the islands as a young man and he'd made a sizable fortune there. But during his years away he had rather cut his ties with Athmore, as he had with England. Only Justin, returning from a trip to New York by way of Nassau had seen him a few times during that period, and then only at Maggie's urging, since Justin felt that Nigel wanted to be left to go his own way alone. Not until long after his success was assured did he return to England. Then he had written Maggie, asking if he might come on a visit. Maggie had welcomed him warmly and forgiven his long absence, perhaps understanding Nigel's innate pride and the need he had to make his own way without further dependence on Athmore and Justin.

"As a boy," Maggie once told me, "all Nigel could give us was gratitude, and he was too young to suffer that without offering anything in return. Now everything is changed and he is his own man. But a lonely man, I think. I want to make him welcome."

So Nigel had stayed for a visit, never seeming entirely content, yet yielding himself to Maggie's fond efforts to make him feel that he had come home. He must have visited England several times in the years since I had left. That Maggie had finally accomplished her purpose now seemed evident.

As we went through the long gallery and down the stairs, I thought of these things, prodding my memory, reaching for more generous understanding than I had ever given him before.

On the occasion when he had upset me, I had somehow stubbed my toe on one of Athmore's traditions, bringing down upon me Justin's disapproval. Nigel had found me weeping angrily in a corner of the library and he had been kind, when I did not want his kindness.

"We're alike in some ways," he told me that day. "We're both outsiders, aren't we? But we mustn't let that hurt us. You mustn't mind being an American, any more than I mind the roots I came from. We make up for these things by what we become. We live them down."

I had nearly exploded. "I like being an American!" I cried. "I don't want to live it down. Athmore traditions are ridiculously stuffy and I won't bow to notions that belong to the Middle Ages, or pretend that English ways are always better than American!"

He had been quite gentle and reasonable with me. "Give yourself time and you'll come to love the house and all its traditions, stuffy or no. I understand how you feel. I had no traditions of my own when I came here, and I suppose I resented having other people's thrust upon me. Perhaps that's why I had to make good on my own. I couldn't come back to Athmore until my perspective was better. Give yourself time, Eve, and you'll be all right."

I had not been willing to allow for time. I had been too young and rebellious, and I had not thanked him for counseling me. Now these several years later, I remembered and was uncomfortable all over again. It was Nigel, I realized, who had brought me back here this time, urging Maggie to write to me, even though I had not treated him very well in the past.

We found Maggie's sitting room empty, and Nigel went to a small cabinet for a decanter and glasses.

"Sherry?" he asked. "You need a bit of something to relax you. I hope you're not like Dacia, who feels the only thing to drink that's with it, as she says, is vodka and lime—at whatever hour."

I took the glass of sherry and sat in the same chair where I had faced Maggie yesterday.

There was no fire in the grate this morning, but the pot of pink azaleas still brightened the room, and Maggie's shabby possessions seemed comfortable and familiar, so that I began to relax in spite of myself.

Nigel stepped to a window, giving me time to recover. He never moved suddenly, or restlessly, as Justin might. I think he had learned long ago that it was safer not to take the center of the stage. Fewer mistakes were noticed, if one did not call attention to oneself. A sensible course that never occurred to me in time.

I seized on the subject of Dacia in order to make conversation and show that I no longer resented him.

"What do you think of Dacia Keane?" I asked him. "What do you think of this swinging set she's part of in London?"

He smiled. "I'll admit they leave me behind. But I admire them, I think. They're a bit uncertain about a number of things and they overdo the matter of being in, as they say. But most of these youngsters have jobs of one sort or another and they work harder than some of their elders do. Dacia and her sort are breaking down barriers faster than my generation ever did. She already knows pretty much where things fit in. On the other hand, I don't think she'll ever appreciate Athmore the way you and I can appreciate it."

"Now you're erasing barriers too," I said.

He took no offense. "Yes. It's an odd do, isn't it? Me marrying Maggie Graham after all these years."

This seemed treacherous ground, lest I say the wrong thing, and I was silent.

He read me well, as sensitive as ever, and when he spoke again his manner returned to the stiffly formal.

"I hope you'll stay for a while, now that you're here, Mrs. North," he said.

I tried to smile at him. "You used to call me Eve. But aren't you echoing Maggie now?"

He turned from the window to look at me with that quiet authority which always surprised me when it appeared. Though he never seemed like a man who might take command, I supposed he must have done so in the business field away from Athmore.

"I never echo anyone," he said. "I think it would be good for Athmore if you stayed. It might even be good for Justin."

"How can it possibly be good for Justin when he wants to marry Alicia Daven?" I cried, falling back with a thud into my own deep unhappiness and forgetting everything else.

"Drink your sherry," he said, and came to sit opposite me on the sofa, turning his own glass by the stem, watching the pale amber liquid move from rim to rim.

When I had taken a sip or two he began to speak again, and I listened in surprise, thinking of how little I really knew Nigel Barrow.

"Once before you were offended when I allied myself with you," he reminded me. "And I was wrong that time. I had forgotten how sensitively American an American can be. The English mind criticism of the English less, I think. And—perhaps unfortunately—we accept it less. Feeling more assured, perhaps. But we are still alike in some ways—you and I. You haven't outgrown the need to have someone tell you constantly who you are. While I've never outgrown the need to tell the world constantly who I am. I think mine is the better way to prove myself. It may irritate, but it depends less on others."

I smiled wryly at this unexpected picture of Nigel telling the world. "That's hard to believe about you. I've never heard you brag. I've never heard you tell the world a thing."

With no responsive smile, he set down his glass and held out both hands for me to see. This morning he wore a sleeveless blue sweater over his gray shirt, but at the cuffs of the shirt were the star-sapphire links I had seen him wear so often.

"What else is this?" he asked. "Star sapphires with a sweater? No Athmore man would be caught dead wearing such cuff links. I suppose it's my way of saying, 'What do I care for your traditions?' I never dared say it as a boy because I was too much in awe. But I can say it now. Perhaps that's the very reason I can better respect its traditions now and feel quite comfortable about marrying Maggie."

He spoke with quiet assurance, and I knew he meant every word. But he had learned this assurance through years of proving himself—which was something I had never been able to do.

"It takes a certain amount of persistent obstinacy to stand up to Athmore," he went on, and added with a slight smile, "You have that at least. Behind this house and the people who live in it, behind the portraits on the walls and the very stones of those old ruins in the woods, are hundreds of years of tradition and more or less responsible behavior. All of which provides a certain built-in superiority which those who are born to it take for granted. Yet what can Athmore do in the face of my cuff links but shudder? And shuddering I have never minded. You see, my dear, I have found out who I am.

I need no one to tell me. I can live here now as Maggie's husband without having Athmore destroy me. Can you, as Justin's wife?"

I sipped the last of the sherry and set the glass aside. "I don't know," I admitted. "I only know that I *am* his wife—still."

"And you want to go on being, don't you?"

"Yes—yes, I do! I haven't any pride about that any more. But Justin keeps telling me that he doesn't want me here. So what am I to do?"

Nigel answered me dryly. "You have the usual two choices. You can stay or you can go. If you go—what then?"

"I don't know. How do other people live when they lose everything they care about?"

He regarded me seriously, not smiling now. "You're very young. There will be other men. It's ridiculous to think there won't be. And love always changes. Even with the same two people it can take different forms. I suppose it never stands still, and for that reason it's safer not to count on it."

I had never expected to pour myself out to Nigel Barrow. Somehow he had opened the floodgates that had been closed for a long time, and there was a certain relief in talking like this to someone. His manner, which took me seriously, his uncritical objectivity, made talking to him possible.

But now he had obviously had enough of playing confidant. He stood up and moved toward the door.

"Stay for a while at Athmore," he said. "If you stay, a way may open."

I held out my hand to him. "Thank you, Nigel. Perhaps I owe you that—since it was your suggestion to Maggie that brought me here."

He took my hand briefly, then let it go. He still had not called me Eve. I found myself thinking of Dacia's words—that Maggie would marry Nigel in order to save Marc and Justin and Athmore. If that was true and he really cared for her, then I ought to feel a little sorry for him. Somehow I did not. I had the feeling that Nigel would never do anything blindly. If Maggie married him he would be aware of her terms or he would not take the step. I found myself liking him better than I ever had before—perhaps because I knew him a little better.

When he had gone I left my chair and went to one of the rear windows of the room, where I could look out over the topiary garden. No matter what Maggie or Nigel urged upon me, how could I stay when Justin did not want me? There were limits to foolish hope, limits even to my ability to snatch at straws. Perhaps the only sensible thing to do was pack at once and get myself aboard the next bus to London.

But I did not move. I stayed where I was, staring out the window. When had I ever been sensible when it came to Justin?

VII

From my high place at the rear window the plan of the topiary chessboard lay spread below me, with every piece standing neatly on a square. This was a curious game, since those who had designed the garden so long ago had wanted to keep most of the pieces still in play. I had known nothing about chess until Justin had taught me the game, and even then I lacked the patience to learn it well. But at least I understood what was supposed to be happening down there on the grass chessboard.

Because all the figures were carved from the same dark yew, Daniel had followed the old plan for distinguishing between the opponents. Black was black, but around every "white" piece he had placed a circlet of seashells as an identifying border. Even the grass played its role, with alternate patches clipped short, to form the dark and light squares of a chessboard.

The possible end of a game was represented, rather than the beginning—perhaps because this seemed more dramatic. The black rook was in position to check White's king in the next play, but convention decreed that it was White's turn. If White succeeded in blocking the rook, then the game would continue. But if White was not clever and alert, the game would be over with Black's next move.

One rainy Sunday afternoon Justin had set up a board in the library to match the game in the garden. He had taken White's side, easily blocking my black rook from its move to checkmate. We had gone on from there to the ignoble defeat of my black chessmen. Justin could always beat me and he never hesitated to win impatiently, so that I had liked better to play with Nigel Barrow. Nigel, too, had come late to the game of chess, but he had learned it far more expertly than I, and he was willing to point out strategy, and even help me at times to win against him.

As I looked down upon the garden from Maggie's window, the yew chessmen stood in place with the battle endlessly arrayed, and never a man moving. Only once, thanks to a cruelly mischievous prank, had the black rook moved. That had happened long ago one summer when the boys had been home from school on holiday. Maggie had told me the story a bit ruefully. One morning the family had been wakened by Daniel's cries of outrage. He had not been "Old" Daniel then, but he was as deeply devoted to his topiary masterpiece as he was in later years.

Maggie had rolled out of bed and rushed to the rear window of her sitting room to look down upon a garden that was still wet with early morning dew. Daniel was in a frenzy of rage, dancing about the place where the black rook should have stood ready for its strategic play. Instead, a yawning hole in the turf was all that showed where a rooted yew had once stood. The rook was gone, its roots torn out—and the game on the chessboard meant nothing.

There was a considerable uproar. That summer Marc had been at his irresponsible worst, constantly playing tricks upon Daniel, tormenting him in one way or another. Yet when the gardener had accused him, Marc had simply laughed in his face. The man went into such a fury that it was only Justin's generous act which saved Marc from Daniel's rage. Justin calmly took the blame upon himself and admitted to digging up the rook. It was not Marc at all, he said. He had done it on a bet and he was sorry. He had not expected such a rumpus. He would buy a new yew tree himself and Daniel could transplant it.

Maggie had told me that she believed not a word of Justin's "confession," nor did she think Daniel believed him either. The gardener hadn't it in his heart to be angry with Justin, however, so Marc was let off scot free. It had taken a long while for the new yew to take hold and grow properly so that it would accept the ministrations of Daniel's shears. But with patience this end was achieved and the rook's castle-crowned head once more rose in its ordained place.

Now, as I looked down from the window, the black rook seemed to stand in triumphant readiness, like a hunter ready for the kill, while the old man who had for so long trimmed the garden was dead. I wondered if anyone else had the skill to take over this exacting task, or if anyone could be found who would give it the endless, loving patience Old Daniel had.

"It's the rook's play," he had warned me yesterday. I was to remember, he told me, that Old Daniel had reminded me that it was the rook's play next, and the king had better watch out.

Once before the rook had moved, and it was Marc who moved it. Was this what Old Daniel meant? Had he tried to tell me in a sort of code that Marc was once more to be feared and that the white king—Justin, of course—had better be careful? Perhaps he had meant me to go directly to Justin with the message, but when I tried to tell Justin what the old man had said, he had shrugged the whole thing off. Now Old Daniel was dead, and I was unable to believe that his sudden death had been wholly accident. Someone else must have been there in that place of ruin. Perhaps the snapshot I'd taken recorded the hidden truth, which I had not been able to recognize.

I stared at the dark yew shapes as though they might tell me something, studied the expert carving of a knight's equine head, considered the mitered crown of a bishop—and returned always to that rook which was not black in reality, but dark green, even in the bright sun of noon. The garden was not the shadowy place it could be at dusk, or by moonlight. All stood open and revealed and quiet. Yet when I looked at the topiary forms I felt more uneasy than ever. "Unnatural," Justin had once called them. He liked trees to be trees. He liked the forest and the park about Athmore better than he did the manicured lawns and ordered flowerbeds —or this topiary garden.

Then, quite suddenly, breaking the dreaming spell of quiet, there was movement on the board. A woman in a light dress came running toward the house, darting between the carved chessmen. She was Maggie's secretary, Caryl Davis, and there was a look of alarm upon her face.

The back stairs for this wing opened across from Maggie's rooms, and I ran down one flight to meet her at the back door. She saw me and flew toward me breathlessly.

"Do you know where Mrs. Graham is? Or Mr. North?"

I shook my head. "No, but I can help you look for them. Is it important?"

She gestured behind her. "I was walking in the woods— and I saw a man. Not one of our people. When I came on him he stood and stared at me insolently, and he walked off rudely when I asked him what he wanted. He had very black hair and a strange sort of look in his eyes. With all that's been happening around here, someone ought to discover who he is and what he's doing on Athmore ground. He gave me quite a fright."

She hurried away toward the front of the house and I let her go. If I went with her the intruder would be gone, and I wanted to be useful to Justin for once. I ran through the back door, wound my way through the topiary figures and crossed the lawn to a path leading in among the trees at the rear of the house. But though I looked behind every shrub and tree as I walked, I saw no black-haired man. Instead, I met Maggie Graham coming through the woods toward me, walking fast, so that her face was pink with effort—and agitation.

"That dreadful woman!" she murmured when she saw me. "I suppose it was a mistake to confront her—but I had to try."

I remembered that the path leading off behind Athmore was a shortcut to Grovesend—if you were a walker, as Maggie was. She wore the same gray trousers and sweater she had worn when she came downstairs last night during the fire, and she wore them well, for all that she was a big woman.

"Did you see a man when you came through the woods?" I asked. "Miss Davis has had a fright, running into an insolent stranger."

Maggie nodded carelessly. "Yes, I saw him. It was Leo Casella, down from London. Alicia bought the Club Casella from him, and he still manages it for her. He said she had sent him to Athmore with a message for Justin. Sometimes he comes around, though I don't like him. I suppose Caryl has never seen him before."

That mystery explained, I walked back with Maggie. She turned toward the drive that led behind garages and workshop, seeming far more perturbed than I'd ever seen her, striding beside me, rather aggressively, now and then putting absent hands to her head, rumpling her hair thoroughly in a gesture I had seen only on those rare occasions when something upset her.

"What is it?" I asked. "What has happened?"

She was too indignant for caution. "I went to see Alicia because of Marc. He's been running with a gambling crowd in London that he can't afford And the Club Casella's his fa-

vorite casino. I wanted to have it out with Alicia as to how
much he owes the club by this time, but she wouldn't tell me.
She only smiled in that maddening, superior way of hers when
I asked her to keep him out of the club. She's encouraging
him to gamble—I'm sure of it. And I don't like it one bit."

"Can't you tell Justin?" I asked.

"He believes I'm prejudiced against Alicia—which is perfectly true. Besides, I don't want him worrying about Marc
now. He needs his mind free for his work. Alicia knows I
won't tell him so she feels safe in what she's doing. But why is
she doing it? I can't see that it's to her interest to let Marc go
on like this, yet she won't agree to bar him from the club."

"Isn't it time Marc finds a way to pay his own debts?" I
asked impatiently. "Hasn't there been enough of his leaning
upon other people?"

Maggie was still too upset to be cautious about what she
told me. "I don't believe he can. He's more deeply in debt
than any of us suspected. Justin mustn't know how bad it is
—so don't say anything to him, Eve. I'm worried because I
don't know what Alicia means to do, and I don't trust her."

As we walked along the banked pavement of the test
course, I could sense her tension, her very real concern.
When Maggie's poise was upset, something serious was undoubtedly wrong.

"Dacia says that Alicia's marriage to Justin would bring in
the money to settle Marc's debts," I said. "But surely it can't
be as bad as all that. If it's Alicia Marc owes, then—"

"The problem mustn't be solved that way!" Maggie broke
in. "That's why I want to know the exact sum. I want to tell
Nigel exactly what he might have to take on when he marries
me."

I gave her a quick look. "Maggie, you're not sacrificing
yourself to rescue Marc?"

"Don't be an idiot! Nigel and I are fond of each other. We
respect each other. Neither of us expects romantic love at our
age. It means a great deal to me to have his companionship
and guidance. And it means something to him, I think, to
come to Athmore belonging here, as he never could as a
schoolboy. But I want to play fair with him. I want him to
know just how much trouble Marc is in. *I* must be responsible—not Justin. There's nothing left for Justin to be responsible with, though I know he'd take the thing on in a moment,
no matter how angry with Marc he might be. But let's not

talk about this now. I must stop being furious before I speak to Nigel. So tell me about you, Eve. What have you decided?"

"I don't seem able to decide anything," I said. "Not even to go home today."

She tucked her hand through the crook of my arm companionably. "If you'll just stay from day to day, perhaps we'll still rout Alicia. And by the way—she has some curious notion that she wants to talk to you. She told me she would get in touch with you soon."

Any thought of seeing Alicia dismayed me. "We met briefly this morning and I don't want to see her again."

Maggie shrugged. "It's up to you, of course. But she has something on her mind, and it might be wise to find out what's up. She's the enemy, you know, so it's better to discover what she intends."

We were nearing a place where the road made a wide loop around a clump of trees that obscured our view and added an obstacle to the test course. Suddenly and almost silently, a car came from behind the trees, bearing down upon us. Maggie grasped my arm and we both leaped for the side of the road. Justin was at the wheel and he drove past, braked to a stop, and then backed up to us. The car was not one of those plush models driven by Marc and Dacia, but the long gray one I had glimpsed through a window in the small separate garage. It had a rather strange look because of a bumper that seemed to run all around it, as well as an unusual hood—bonnet, Justin would say—to accommodate the engine.

The moment Justin stopped, Maggie ran to him contritely. "Don't scold," she begged. "Eve couldn't know this was a dangerous spot. I've been careless again!"

The passing glance Justin gave me was chill. "She knows. No one is to walk in the middle of these drives under any circumstances. The test courses are here to service the cars, and for no other reason. There are other footwalks. Neither of you heard me coming, did you?"

"No—which is very clever of your car," Maggie said. "No uproar, no nasty smells. Now do forgive us and take us for a spin. Eve hasn't had a taste of what you're up to yet."

She did not wait for a probable refusal, but opened the door to the front seat, pushing me unceremoniously in beside Justin. Then she got in herself and pulled the door shut.

"Justin, did you see Leo Casella?" she asked. "I met him in

the woods just now and he said he'd come over to give you a message from Alicia."

"Leo?" Justin put the car in gear smoothly. "I've had no message. I didn't know he was around."

"I don't like the sound of this," Maggie said. "I've never cared for the fellow, and apparently he gave Caryl a fright."

"I'll see about it," Justin said, and we went off quickly, with scarcely a purr of sound.

"It's the new fuel that's responsible for the quiet," Maggie informed me. "You've really got it, haven't you, Justin?"

He shook his head. "Only in the crudest possible form. It works quietly enough and it won't burn or explode, but it's nowhere near ready for any sort of mass production. Too impossibly expensive now. The problem is to get on with it before someone else cuts in with the answers. Whoever arrives first will have the world market, and of course they're working on various approaches everywhere."

"You'll get it," Maggie said as we picked up speed. "Nothing must stop you now."

We drove in swift silence after that—down the middle bar of the course and around the outer edge of the loop that encompassed the house. I was more conscious of being close to Justin than I was of the wind roused by our speed, or the smooth banking of the curves, the silence of the engine. I stared at his familiar long-fingered hands on the wheel— strong hands, well in control. The car of course was an English righthand drive, so his bandaged left arm was next to me and I tried not to touch him.

As we rounded the loop and turned toward the house, Maggie stopped him.

"Let me out here, will you, dear? I've played long enough. I must get back and look up Caryl. She's probably frantic by now because she can't find me. No, Eve—stay where you are."

The moment Justin braked to a stop, she was out of the car, slamming the door behind her, running across the grassy verge in the direction of the house.

Justin did not start the car again, but waited for me to follow her. "That was pretty obvious of Maggie. Perhaps you'd like to get out here too?"

I looked at him, seeing the pale silver streak in his hair, the strong shape of his nose, the firm mouth I remembered too well.

"Don't be angry with me," I said. "Tell me what you're doing—tell me about the car. It's been so long—I'm out of touch."

For a moment I thought he might put me relentlessly out on the road and drive off without me. The motor still idled and at length he set the gray car into motion. This time he drove more slowly and after a few minutes he began to talk to me. But instead of the technical detail that would be over my head, he spoke of what this car might mean in a wider sense than concerned his personal fortunes. I listened intently, wanting to understand.

"Whether I succeed with these experiments with fuel or not, there's more to this car. Everyone's been afraid to build for safety in the past because the public has rejected such cars. But the ghastly facts of highway slaughter are beginning to get through the hardest heads and there's a more receptive climate now. What we hope for is a car that will put England into top competition in the world market."

Woods and parklands flowed by without haste, so that one could encompass them visually, instead of losing everything in a blur as we'd done when I drove with Dacia. I listened and Justin talked.

"There was a day when England had command of the world market," he went on. "But countries, like people, grow old and too set in their ways. We began to lose out to young, more aggressive nations. I suppose this is as it should be. Fortunately, nations can be reborn and we're not without recent resurgence. But what we've accomplished in radar, and with the jet plane and a few other things has to be multiplied all across the board."

"There's another rebirth," I said, smiling. "There's a whole fresh, new, young spirit coming to life in England. You have only to think of the Beatles and Mary Quant and the rest— the way they've had London popping these days!"

Justin had relaxed a little as we talked. "I admire these youngsters. They've put a few older industries to shame with their eagerness and hard work. They're doing what they believe in, following their own creativeness, instead of grasping merely for themselves, as too many of their elders are doing. I'd like to think this car of mine may shake things up a bit too—if it gets there in time. Recently these malicious disruptions of my work have set me back. They've got to be stopped—and soon."

He turned the car into the home stretch. His coolness toward me had not really lessened, even though for a little while he had warmed to his subject. Now silence lay between us again and I sought for some way to break it.

"What did you make of that wine bottle and the cigarette packets Marc brought you?" I asked. "What do you think they mean?"

He threw me a startled look. "What bottle? He's brought me nothing."

I tried to explain. "Nigel got suspicious of someone hiding out on the roof and he went up there to search. He found these things and gave them to Marc, who said he'd take them directly to you."

The car picked up speed. We rounded the last curve with the wind in our ears, and drew up before the garage.

"I'll talk to Marc at once," Justin said, and barely waited for me to get out of the car before he hurried toward his workshop.

I climbed the embankment between the row of beech trees and crossed the side lawn. Marc came toward me from the front terrace.

"So you've been out for a ride in Justin's masterpiece?" His eyes were bright with familiar malice.

"He's looking for you now to ask questions about the things Nigel found on the roof," I said.

"I'll talk to him." Marc was curt. "There was something I had to look after first. I've a message for you, by the way. Alicia wants to see you. This evening, if you can make it. Dacia and I will drive you over."

I stared at him, astonished at his calm assurance that I would do as she expected. "Why should I see Alicia?" I demanded.

"Why shouldn't you?"

"What does she want of me?"

"That's up to her, but at least I can tell you one thing. She wants you to bring over the snapshot you caught of Old Daniel yesterday before the accident that killed him."

I gaped. "How does she know there is such a picture?"

"When you tell Dacia, you tell the world," Marc said wryly.

Somehow I did not like this. Alicia's interest in this chance picture gave me an eerie, unsettled feeling in which there was a vague sense of threat.

"Why is Alicia interested in the picture?" I asked. "It's only a blurred snapshot which may or may not be of Old Daniel."

"May not be?" Marc was quick. "What do you mean?"

"I don't mean anything except that it isn't possible to tell who is in the snapshot. In any case, why should Alicia care?"

He shrugged. "She didn't confide in me. Sentimental reasons, perhaps. The old man was devoted to her, you know. She used to flatter him over that topiary monstrosity, and he made no bones about thinking she ought to be mistress of Athmore."

I knew this was true, but I doubted that Alicia possessed much sentiment in her character.

"You'd better see her," Marc said softly.

I thought of the rook's play. My distrust of him was increasing. "Why?" I said again.

Again he made that slight motion of shrugging. "Easier for everyone if you do. And it won't hurt you."

The desire to know what Alicia wanted, to know the reason for her interest in my chance snapshot, was stronger than my reluctance to meet her again. I did not care one way or another whether I eased anything for Marc, but I wanted to know more about her interest in the picture.

"All right, then. I'll see her tonight, if she wishes. And if Dacia is coming with us."

Marc cocked an amused eyebrow at me, but I sensed his relief. For some reason he had been worried lest I refuse.

"At least this will be interesting to watch," he said and went off toward Justin's workshop.

The terrace was empty and I crossed it to the front door. The Hall of Armor stretched bleakly on either hand, far more chill than the sunny air outdoors. I wondered, as I often had, where the Spanish bones lay that these helmets and breastplates once covered.

As I climbed the stairs Mrs. Langley's worldly-wise gray eyes seemed to watch me from her portrait. She had been a far more gifted and imaginative woman than any of her daughters, but she must have been greatly beset by the difficult problems provided by them. I wondered how she had met those problems, what courses of action she had taken. Yet all the while it was my own course that concerned me. As Maggie had said, Alicia was the enemy and it was time to stop running from her and meet her face to face. She must not find me the same easily routed and quickly humiliated girl she had met in the past. This morning she had routed me again. Tonight it must be different.

Halfway up the curving flight the beautiful Cynthia regarded me with a veiled gaze, pouting a little. After Mr. Dunscombe had taken himself conveniently out of the way, Cynthia had become Lady Stanhope and moved away from Athmore for good, which must have given her mother a certain welcome respite. This time as I passed her picture I gave her look for look, as though it were Alicia herself with whom I crossed glances.

From the upper banister a voice came down to me. "That Cynthia was the worst of the lot, wasn't she?" Dacia said. "Looking down her nose and all that. I keep wanting to tell her off properly. Though perhaps that look is only to hide how scared she was. What with all that knocking on her door late at night after her husband was dead. She must have been glad when Sir Gerald came along and took her away. And I'll bet her mum was glad to see her go "

"I was thinking the same thing," I agreed as I climbed the last flight and stood beside Dacia, looking down at the great array of portraits, almost three stories high.

"Wonder if they'll add Alicia to the lot someday," she said slyly: "She's beautiful enough. But she's a phony."

I caught her up at once. "What do you mean by that?"

Dacia could be slippery when she chose, and she wriggled away from the question.

"I'd rather see you up there, if you must know. Are you going to Grovesend tonight?"

"I've told Marc I would," I said. "Providing you'll be there too."

She giggled softly. "I know what you mean. Oh, I'm not jealous, never fear. I know where I stand with old Marc. But he's told me about you and him in the old days."

"If I were you," I said dryly, "I wouldn't believe too much of what Marc tells you about the so-called old days. I was there too, you know, and I was never, as you put it, his girl friend."

For some reason she looked crestfallen. "You mean that part wasn't true at all? Of course I know Marc tells a lot of whoppers but then—so do I."

"That one was certainly a whopper," I agreed.

"Well, it's too bad in a way." She cocked her head on one

side as we walked toward the north wing. "I'd have felt a bit set up, you know, to think he'd settled for me instead of you."

"What on earth do you mean?"

"Oh—that you've got looks and education—and you know how to do the proper thing. Besides, you believe in something. I don't believe in anything except getting Dacia what Dacia wants."

"If you see all that in me, perhaps I'm a phony too," I said ruefully. "But I wish you'd tell me what you meant about Alicia being one. I'd like to be armed with whatever I need to know before I see her tonight."

Dacia wrinkled her snub little nose in scorn. "Well—you know—she has family and loads of good breeding, but all the same, somewhere deep down she's a fake—though I don't know exactly what's wrong. It's just that I can smell that sort of thing a mile. I've had a lot of practice. You're the one who's a lot more real, even though sometimes you haven't much sense. The way you keep cutting off your own nose. But at least you're not pretending anything. But that's enough from me. After all, I have to play Marc's game, don't I?"

"So this is Marc's game too?" I said. "Why? What does he get out of it?"

"Only his life, so to speak," said Dacia airily. "If Alicia decides to turn the screws it'll be all over for Marc."

We reached our corridor and I heard music blaring through the open door of Dacia's room. There was no point in pursuing the subject of Marc, since I would not get very far with Dacia.

"You've a record player?" I asked.

"No—tape recorder. I like to pick up things from the telly, and sometimes from Radio Caroline. The pirate stations aren't as stuffy as B.B.C. When I saw Petula Clark on telly doing that one, I took it off on tape so I could play it again. Do you like the song? It makes me ever so sad—all about tomorrow never coming. It will be that way for us one of these days, won't it—the time when tomorrow never comes?"

"Let's hope not for a while," I said and went on to my room with the music wailing after me, more prophetic than I liked. All my tomorrows were bound up with Justin, and it was likely that they had already been cut off.

It was nearly time for one o'clock luncheon, and as I washed, combed my hair, freshened my lipstick, I thought over the events of the morning. The same troubling questions still nagged at me—whether the man in my snapshot was really Old Daniel, and why Alicia Daven was interested in seeing the picture. Tonight I must discover exactly what Alicia wanted.

I opened the bureau drawer and took out my handbag, felt inside the zippered pocket where I had put the picture. My fingers found nothing. Downstairs the gong that summoned Athmore to meals began to sound, but I paid no attention. I carried my bag to the bed and dumped out its contents.

The picture was not there. Someone must have come into my room to search for it and had taken it away. The theft answered one question that had been haunting me. Old Daniel could not have been the man in the picture, or no one would have cared. What I had snapped mattered to someone. Mattered so much that the picture had been filched from my bag. By someone who did not want me to show Alicia the snapshot when I went to Grovesend tonight? If such a person had reason to fear the existence of a picture, what might he fear from me—since I'd been in the very spot where the picture was taken. This was a new and completely unsettling thought.

Once more I removed my suitcase from the wardrobe closet and looked for the packet of pictures and film Nellie had brought me. This, at least, was where I'd left it. I opened the paper folder and took out the negatives. One by one I held the squares of film up to the light, discarding each until I came to the one that showed me the chapel stones of Athmore Hall arching against the sky, and shrubbery with a human figure fading into it. I would not be able to show Alicia the printed picture tonight, but I still had the negative. Now, more than ever, I wanted the answer to her interest in the picture. I could not believe it stemmed from any sentimental affection she might have felt toward Old Daniel.

This time I put the square of film into a pocket in my billfold, and took my handbag with me. For the moment I would say nothing to anyone about the missing picture. Let the hunter, whoever it was, be left wondering whether I had discovered the theft. A sudden intuitive picture flashed through my mind. I could see the castled green figure of the rook waiting on his square—waiting patiently to make the move which had been denied him for so long. As I went downstairs to join the others for luncheon I found that I was shivering.

VIII

Grovesend was a small but elegant eighteenth-century house tucked away in its own small forest and shielded from the outer driveway by an enormous rhododendron hedge. The family which had commissioned Robert Adam to build it was long gone and its descendants scattered. Late in the last century a branch of the Daven family had purchased it, and it had arrived at last in Alicia's hands. With the inheritance left her some years before, she had renewed the house to something of its original charm and beauty.

I had visited Grovesend several times during those innocent days when I had not known about the past relationship between Alicia and my husband. After I knew, I had stayed away as far as possible.

The night was dark and gusty and the great hedge tossed in the wind as Marc drove the red Mercedes around the barrier it made. We left the car and went up the walk to the lighted foyer. The lines of the house had a delicate splendor, for all its small size, yet it was a hidden house—secretive, I'd always felt—as though Alicia had some need to hide away and draw her surroundings close in about her. Which was a strange thought, considering that she had taken over the public management of the Club Casella in London and, as Maggie had said, was often there in person to play hostess.

Dacia touched my arm impishly as we went up the steps. "Wonder what Alicia's got to hide," she murmured, and once more I felt a kinship with her.

"Maybe there is something, at that," Marc said. "You get the feeling of being tight and snug in her club in London, too. We'll have to take you there one of these nights, Eve. Can't get in without a card, so you'll need an escort."

I hardly listened because of the tension I'd begun to feel. Too often in the past I had accepted the disadvantage to

123

which Alicia put me, but this time I must not let this happen.
I knew the stakes, if not the game she played. Tonight she
must not rout me.

A maid opened the door and we stepped into the small
classic foyer, from which a sitting room opened. Voices came
from the adjoining room and the maid threw an uncertain
glance toward the door as she invited us to remove our
wraps. As we stood there a man's voice reached us, the words
slightly accented, mocking in tone and hardly respectful.

"I'll be leaving when I'm ready. So perhaps you will have
to endure me till then. There is more to be done, as you very
well know."

"Oh-oh!" said Dacia softly. "Trouble!"

The maid darted into the sitting room to announce us, and
if Alicia answered her visitor, we did not hear what she said.
The man came through the door as we hesitated—a black-
haired man with a long, bony face from which dark Spanish
eyes challenged us all with a bold glance.

"How are you, Leo?" Marc said. "Still drinking manzanilla
these days?"

The fellow gave Dacia a stare of appreciation and then
looked at me, awaiting an introduction.

Marc offered none. "Better not leave your bottles around
behind you," he said.

So this was Leo Casella, the man who had frightened Caryl
Davis—and Marc seemed to suspect that it was he who had
left that bottle on the Athmore roof. I wanted to stop the
man, say something to him, but he had already pushed past
Marc with a mocking glance and was gone through the door.

"Does Justin know—?" I began, but Marc gave me a quick
shake of his head. "Not now. Don't stir up matters you don't
understand."

Alicia waited for us near a fireplace where coal burned
briskly in the grate. She was standing, not watching us directly, but through the gilt-framed mirror which hung above
the mantel against a pale gray wall. It seemed to me that she
was, if anything, more beautiful than she had been two years
ago. Tonight her mass of fair hair was piled high upon her
graceful head and she wore a chiffon gown of palest gold that
flowed to the tip of her slippers and left her arms bare. She
looked as ageless as those classic women remembered
through the sculptures of Greece. Her blue eyes, reflected in
the mirror, were bright and her color seemed heightened, as

if from her recent exchange with Leo Casella, who had once owned her club and was now its manager.

All my senses were alert, eager to register anything that would help me, leaving me once more sure that her serenity was a pose and no more than skin deep. This was a woman more disturbed than she wanted us to know, and my confidence rose a little.

She gave me a brief glance in the mirror and then turned cordially to Dacia, letting me know how little I mattered to her.

"It's good to see you, my dear," she said to Dacia. "What a charming dress. It suits you."

Divested of her orange coat, Dacia turned pertly about to display a frock which was half plain, half printed in a wild design of shocking pink triangles appliquéd against violent green. "Charming" was, I thought, a doubtful word, yet it was true that Dacia could carry off such a dress.

Alicia smiled and nodded to Marc. "Thank you," she said, and waved a graceful hand on which a great topaz gleamed, matching her gown. "Do sit down, won't you?"

I remembered that she had always been reluctant to call me by name. To her I was neither Mrs. North nor Eve—and now she merely included me in her general greeting and invitation.

I remembered the room and now, because I felt anything but at ease, I tried to look about me with as casual an air as I could manage. If Alicia could bluff, so could I. I observed the handsome ceiling, with its Adam design of garlands and festoons in low-relief carving, the surfaces delicately touched with color. I studied the rug from China, the satinwood furniture that was typically Adam, and recited to myself the lessons I had been given in such matters by Maggie when I had first come to Athmore, young and ignorant of such things as authentic furniture and architecture.

And while I looked and pretended I was entirely at ease, Marc spoke his mind to Alicia.

"What is Leo up to?" he demanded. "He's been hanging around Athmore a few times lately and Justin is about ready to jump him and put him off the premises for good. Why do you keep him on at the club and stand for his cheekiness?"

Alicia's self-possession did not waver. "If he is useful to me, I shall use him. If he's running about Athmore, perhaps you've some girl there who appeals to him."

Marc stared at her uncertainly, then shrugged. I had a feeling that there had been some meeting of forces between them and that Marc had been faced down and was in retreat. I stole a look at Dacia and saw that she was listening, warily alert, her cropped head atilt, her long legs crossed casually, the better to exhibit them beneath a skirt that came halfway up her thighs. There was something engaging and unself-conscious about slim girls who never tugged at their skirts as our mothers had done.

"Will you have something to drink?" Alicia asked. "Marc, you know where—"

For the first time I found my voice. "Let's not take up your time, Alicia. After all, this isn't a social call. You wanted to see me for some particular reason?"

She considered me remotely, and the faintly pitying manner was there again, though managed so subtly that only I knew what she was about. I had seen her treat me this way before.

"Perhaps this is a difficult matter for an American to understand," she began, "but an old man like Daniel, who has been with one family all his life, may come to hold the deep affection of those he serves."

I said nothing. However frequently she had visited Athmore, Alicia had not lived there, and Old Daniel had never served her or her family, even though he might have wished to see her as Justin's wife instead of me.

"I was deeply shocked to hear what had happened," she went on. "The old man came to see me day before yesterday and brought me flowers from Athmore's gardens. We had quite a chat while he was here."

"About what?" Marc put in abruptly.

Alicia shrugged, but I had a feeling that she was on guard. "About whatever subjects an old man likes to discuss, of course."

Her words implied consideration, yet her eyes watched me without echoing the sympathy in her tone. I did not think she cared at all about Old Daniel. When I still did not speak, she came to the point.

"I understand you took a picture of Daniel yesterday. I'd like very much to have it. You've brought it with you?"

"No," I said, "I haven't brought it."

Marc gave me a quick look and Dacia swiveled her head to stare in my direction.

"I asked Marc to request that you bring the picture with you tonight," Alicia said.

Dacia wriggled in her chair and spoke for the first time. "Why didn't you just have him bring the picture? Why'd you want Evie to bring it?"

Alicia glanced at the girl with a look less approving than before.

"It doesn't matter," I said. "I couldn't bring it because someone went into my room while I was out and removed the snapshot from my handbag. I've searched, but I've not been able to find it."

Alicia looked as if she did not believe a word of my story, while Dacia said, "Gosh!" with an astonishment that seemed real enough. Marc was staring at his hands.

I opened my bag, took out my billfold, unzipping it to remove the negative.

"There's been no time to have another print made," I said, "but at least I've brought the film for you to see."

Marc intercepted it and held it up to the light. "This won't give you much," he said and turned it over to Alicia.

She moved closer to a lamp and held the negative to the light as Marc had done. Then she tipped it back and forth so that light struck across the dull side, exhibiting the picture quite well.

I watched intently, wondering what she saw. The lines of her classic face told me nothing, and long lashes veiled her eyes. Finally she looked meaningfully at Marc.

He seemed to understand. "Come along, Dacia," he said. "Alicia wants our Eve to herself. We can wait in the dining room."

Dacia was less than willing to go, but Marc took her by the elbow, insisting. She flashed me a look that said, "You'll tell me later," and went reluctantly with him from the room.

Alicia set the negative near me on a table as if it were of no further consequence to her, and returned to the fireplace, her gown glinting gold in the flame light. There she stood with her hands to the fire as if she were cold, her head bent so that I could not catch her reflection in the mirror.

"You were right," she said. "The picture is meaningless for me. The focus isn't clear. The picture was only an excuse to bring you here. I wanted to speak with you on other matters."

I held to my silence. My heart was thumping uncomfortably and my face had grown hot because this woman made me think of only one thing. Justin had loved her in the past, and why should he not love her now? She wanted him and she would have him if she could. I was braced to resist whatever she said to me.

After a moment she raised her head to look into the mirror above the mantel and I found her eyes meeting mine in the glass. The subtlety, the pretense, had dropped away now that she had no audience but me.

"Why did you return to Athmore?" she challenged me.

It was strange to speak to her like this—as though we two could not meet face to face, but must see each other only by reflection in a glass.

"The answer to that lies between Justin and me," I said evenly.

Her sculptured face had lost something of its repose and her look grew intent. "Perhaps you'll hurt yourself more painfully than you did before. Isn't it time you learned wisdom? Or are you still too young for that?"

I did not think she had brought me here to repeat words so futile. Her reason was still the picture, however carelessly she dismissed it. But in answer there was only one thing I could say, and I said it quietly.

"I am still Justin's wife."

Her movement as she turned from the glass was without restraint. I was right, I thought triumphantly. All that lovely serenity was a veneer she had perfected because she knew it pleased Justin. Now it cracked across its surface like shattered glass.

"You're his wife for only so long as it will take Justin to be free of you! Do you really think you could keep him permanently? You had your foolish interlude, and you both came to recognize how ridiculous such a marriage was. That will be corrected now. And it will be less painful for you if you return home soon, instead of forcing him to send you away, as he is already anxious to do."

I stood up, fumbling for my purse. I had none of her poise, her assurance, her skill in such dueling, but I had the desperation born of love. I moved toward the door without giving her the satisfaction of an answer.

"Wait a moment," she said. "About that picture—if I were you, I would not make another print. It will be better if you let me have the negative before someone takes it from your room. It isn't wise for you to keep it."

I swung about. "What do you mean?"

"To how many people have you shown that picture?" she asked.

"I've shown it to no one, though apparently several know of its existence."

"Please give it to me." Alicia held out her hand, accustomed to command.

"Why should I?" I asked her bluntly. "If the figure is out of focus, how do you know for sure that it is Old Daniel?"

"I wondered if that had occurred to you." Alicia came toward me across the room. "Are you sure you saw no one there when you snapped the shutter?"

"I saw no one until Old Daniel spoke to me," I said. "But if the figure can't be recognized as the old man, neither does it look like anyone else."

"You're wrong!" Alicia stepped close to me, dropping her voice to speak softly. "I recognized the person in the picture at once."

"Who is it, then?"

There was no serenity in her now. She hesitated, playing nervously with the ring on her hand, finally coming to a decision.

"The person in the picture is not a man," she told me finally. "It is a woman wearing trousers and a jacket and the hunting cap I have seen her wear many times around the stable, when horses were kept at Athmore. The person in your picture is Maggie Graham."

I stared at her in astonishment. "Maggie wasn't in the chapel ruins yesterday! Only a little while afterward I saw her in the topiary garden with Justin."

"And you're sure she was there all along? You're positive she was not in the woods earlier?"

Of course I wasn't positive, but I did not like this fanciful suggestion Alicia had made about Maggie.

"It will be safer if you leave the picture with me," she repeated.

I shook my head. "If what you say is true, Maggie is the one who should have it." I retrieved the negative quickly, lest Alicia should pick it up.

"Do you think Justin will thank you for that? Do you think he will be pleased if you upset Maggie and frighten her?"

"Frighten her? Why should she be frightened? Even if she was there and saw Old Daniel, how can it possibly matter?"

Alicia's smile was tight. "Perhaps you're really not clever enough to see the implications."

"There aren't any complications!" I cried. "If Maggie was there when I met Old Daniel, it can't possibly mean anything. But if there's something to be said, Maggie must be given the chance to say it."

Alicia made a gesture of repudiation and turned her back me, wanting only to be rid of a recalcitrant visitor.

I went into the foyer and called for Marc. He and Dacia joined me at once, looking pleased with each other after their moments alone.

"I'm ready to leave," I said.

Marc gave me a questioning glance and stepped to the sitting-room door. I heard Alicia say, "You'd better go now," and he came to help us with our coats. Alicia did not reappear.

The moment we were in the front seat of Marc's car, Dacia began to prod me.

"What happened? What did she say? Why did she go secretive all at once?"

"She doesn't think it was Daniel in the picture," I said. "She wanted me to leave the negative with her."

Marc said nothing, but Dacia wriggled impatiently. "Who does she think it was? Why should she want it if it wasn't this great old friend of hers?"

"Let's not talk about it," I said shortly. "I'm not sure she's right in what she believes, and it doesn't matter anyway."

Dacia's bump of curiosity was too large to allow her to subside readily, and she would have gone on questioning me if Marc hadn't stopped her abruptly.

"Let it be," he said. "Eve is right. It can't possibly matter now."

In the seat between us Dacia slumped down, pouting a little, and we drove in silence, with the cold wind blowing past and the car's headlights parting the dark countryside ahead. As we followed the road back to Athmore my mind was busy questioning, probing. Another print of the picture must be made soon from this negative. I still did not believe in Alicia's identification of Maggie as the figure in the picture, or why she should say it was not Daniel.

By the time we reached Athmore I was cold clear through, and I jumped out first and ran up the steps and through the front door before Dacia could catch me.

Lights burned in the drawing room, and Maggie heard me

and came to the door. "Has Marc come in? Alicia Daven just phoned. She wants him to call her at Grovesend."

"He's putting the car away," I said and ran for the stairs.

Maggie came after me, catching me by the arm as I started up. "I know where you've been. Marc told me that Alicia wanted to see a snapshot you took in the chapel ruins yesterday. Did you show it to her?"

She grasped me so tightly that her fingers hurt my arm. The urgent need for flight went out of me. I stepped down to her level, trying to read her eyes, her meaning.

"Someone took the picture from my room," I told her. "But I still have the negative, and that is what I showed Alicia."

Maggie must have realized the force of her grasp upon my arm, for she dropped her hand abruptly.

"What did Alicia say when she saw it?" Maggie asked.

"That it wasn't Old Daniel in the picture, after all," I said, not taking my eyes from her face.

"Who does she think it was?"

I hesitated, unsure of my ground. "She wanted me to leave the negative with her, but I wouldn't."

"Who?" Maggie repeated. "Tell me what that woman is up to!"

From outdoors came the sound of Dacia's laughter, of Marc's voice. I bent toward her.

"Alicia says it's you in the picture—because of the cap the figure is wearing."

Maggie was completely still, her gaze never shifting from my face. "What does she mean? Does she think I went out there and pushed that wall over on poor Old Daniel? What an absurd thing to say!"

Somehow I was relieved. Of course it was absurd. It was ridiculous that I had even mentioned it to Maggie. Alicia was engaged in throwing up some sort of smokescreen. A new possibility struck me. What if she knew very well that it was a woman in the picture because it was Alicia whom I had caught with my camera? This would explain her anxiety to have the negative in her possession.

"Perhaps I can guess who is really in the picture," I said. "Though I don't know what to make of it yet."

Dacia had reached the door, and to escape further questioning I fled up the stairs and down the long corridor to my room. Like Alicia, I wanted to pull my surroundings snugly about me. This need for a cave was something one might feel because of fear, because of dangers that prowled the outside world. I wondered what dangers might threaten Alicia, and why she had been so anxious to impress upon me the fact of her long friendship with Old Daniel. Even if I had caught Alicia in my chance picture, I could not see that it would mean anything in particular. Certainly I would have another print made soon so that I could examine it more carefully. Perhaps an enlargement would give me the answer I wanted.

The evening had laid a dark uneasiness upon me. Too much that was out of key seemed to lie beneath the surface, both here and at Grovesend, all adding up to some ominous total that frightened me. If only I could go easily and naturally to Justin and put all the bits and pieces before him, perhaps he would make something of them. But he had no wish to see me, and he would certainly not welcome any questioning of Alicia.

I pulled the draperies tight across my windows, lighted the fire Nellie had laid for me and huddled on the hearthrug before the flames, my woolly blue robe muffled about me and furry slippers on my feet. For a long while I watched the coals lick into flame, burn red and then blacken and fall. I listened to the sound of the wind roaring down my tower.

There seemed just one slight thread of hope in what had happened at Grovesend. If Alicia chose to bother with me to the extent of asking Marc to bring me to Grovesend, she could not be wholly confident of her future with Justin. That was all I could cling to now. And at least I had not crumpled completely in this latest encounter with her. Perhaps I was learning—just a little.

From the direction of the gate I heard a car turn into the drive and wondered who else was out on this dark and windy evening. Turning off my light, I drew the draperies apart a crack at the side window so that I could look out toward workshop and garage. Headlights showed a car turning onto the apron of concrete. The dogs began to bark and then were silent at a command. This was someone who belonged, or the guard would not have let the car past the gate. As I watched, the man who had quieted the dogs stepped from between the beech trees on the embankment and into the beam of light as the car came to a halt. The man was Marc North. I saw him go to the door of the car to speak to the driver, and after a few moments of hushed conversation, he stepped back. The car turned about, flashing white as it caught a ray of light from the garage. The woman at the wheel swung away toward the entrance and sped off.

The driver was Alicia Daven. Their meeting had a swift and secretive air, yet it had not been managed with surreptitiousness. Anyone who looked could see.

I let the curtain fall, but I did not switch on a light again. The fire lent enough radiance to the room as I got into bed. It was not very late, but I felt less accessible between the covers. I had been half-afraid that Dacia, when she parted from Marc, would come running to my room to tease and cajole in an effort to find out what Alicia had said about the picture. If she came now, I would simply call to her that I had gone to bed.

Once between the sheets, with the hot-water bottle at my feet, and a slippery English puff atop the covers, I began to find how weary I was. There had not been enough time to catch up on the change of hours after my flight across the Atlantic, and I had been at high tension most of the day. Perhaps tonight I would sleep straight through and forget about that tower door with the bureau shoved against it, forget about the faithless Cynthia Langley and the unhappy Mr. Dunscombe—even forget the present inhabitants of Athmore, with their equally besetting problems.

I slept indeed, but not through the night. At two o'clock the tapping began. My first nightmare thought was that the green rook was after me. I struggled awake and sat up in bed to listen. Someone or something was rapping on the tower door. The sound was not that of knuckles against wood, and I reached in alarm for the cord of my bed lamp and blinked into the resulting brightness of the room. Everything was quiet. I thought of calling out to Mr. Dunscombe that his Cynthia no longer slept here, no longer awaited her lovers in the blue lady's room, but I thrust the impulse back in time.

There was no further sound. My watch showed me ten minutes past two when I switched out the light and slipped down beneath the covers. Had I dreamed the knocking? What had I been dreaming? Not more than five minutes more passed before the rapping came again, reverberating through the tower. I propelled myself from the bed, still half-asleep, and stumbled to where the bureau blocked the tower entrance.

"Who's there?" I called. "What do you want?"

Except for the wind in the sentry slots high above, there was no sound. I called again, more loudly, but nothing answered me. Yet the moment I started back to bed, the pounding on my door returned, demanding something of me in no uncertain terms. The sound seemed like that of metal against wood, though I did not think poor Mr. Dunscombe went about in clanking chains.

This time I pushed the bureau slightly aside and stood in silence with my hand upon the knob of the door. This knocking was mischievous, meant to alarm me, and I would not endure it the whole night through.

There was a long interval in which I waited motionless beside the door before metal struck sharply upon the wood. I thrust the door open promptly upon tower darkness, mellowed by pale moonlight from above, and by the glow from my room below. There was a flash of something above, and then nothing more to be seen. Nothing crouched in the small space at the foot of stone steps. No one was visible on the steps themselves, although an intruder would have been silhouetted against the door-framed sky above. The opening into the tower stood empty, and the sound of the wind was louder as it came whooping across the rooftops. Some superstitious part of my brain warned me that only Mr. Dunscombe could disappear into thin air so quietly, but I would have none of that. There was an answer to this, and I did not mean to be kept awake all night by such tormenting.

I closed the door and went to my wardrobe. Hurriedly I pulled on warm slacks and stuffed my nightgown into the trouser legs as I put them on. Then came a sweater and my green trench coat. I pulled rainboots on my feet, tied a kerchief over my head. While I dressed, the thumping came again, but I did not answer it, growing increasingly indignant.

Before I opened the tower door again, however, I took the billfold that held my negative from my bag and looked about the room for some safe hiding place. After all, the room had been searched before, and someone might be trying to frighten me out of it now. The coal scuttle offered a good hiding place, providing I retrieved the wallet before Nellie built her fire in the grate. With a poker I knocked a cranny into the coals and thrust the billfold into it, toppling a few black lumps to hide it securely.

Then I picked up my flashlight and was ready for the tower, still far more indignant than frightened. At dinner tonight there had been talk about patrolling the roof, keeping a guard on watch up there all night, so I knew it would not be empty. Though if Leo Casella was behind the mischief which had been taking place around Athmore, Marc's remark about bottles would probably have warned him away. Nevertheless, I would find Marc, or Nigel, or Justin up there on the roof, and if I saw nothing myself, I would simply report this new mischief and go back to bed.

I waited for no more knocking but pulled open the door and turned my flashlight beam upon dark steps. The light made less impression than I'd hoped—being only a small flicker against luminous darkness. Still, it showed me the steps as I followed their turning ascent to the tiny room at the top. Once, during a lull in the wind as I climbed, I thought I heard running on the roof overhead—which might mean that I had frightened off my tormentor.

The tower gave onto the flat roof through a narrow, arched doorway, and as I stepped to the opening I saw my flashlight would not be needed. The full moon shed a pale, intense light upon the rooftops of Athmore. Only when wind-driven clouds blew raggedly across its face did darkness return—to vanish again as clouds shredded past.

Once before I had been up here on the roofs, but then it was by daylight. By night they looked monstrously different and far vaster than before. From where I stood, the rough underfoot surface stretched the full equivalent of the corridor below, parapet-rimmed, and joined at its center by the connecting bar that duplicated the area of the long gallery and reached across to the roof of the south wing. At each of the four outer corners of the H rose a black, slope-roofed tower, and in between were numerous chimney banks which cast long, confusing shadows across my path. Only these shadows, so sharply etched, gave evidence of how strong a light could be cast by the moon. All else was bathed in a luminous radiance that seemed unearthly, unreal. And all across the rooftops nothing moved. If there were watchers they were well hidden, silent and motionless. The chimney shadows looked almost human—like the shadows of tall men, but they too stood a motionless guard, and there was no sound but the wind.

I stepped out from the protection of my tower, suddenly less than confident of my ability to track down the mischief-maker. There were too many places to hide, with all these numerous chimney banks set about. The four towers stood dark, and Justin's guards, if any, were invisible.

Then, as I hesitated, I caught faraway movement. Diagonally across the top of Athmore toward the front of the opposite wing, someone stepped boldly from shadow to bright moonlight, though I could not recognize the moving figure from this distance.

I took another step forward and my foot struck something that clattered with a sound that crashed through the roaring of the wind. I bent to see what I'd stumbled over, but before I could find it, a challenge ran across space: "Who's there?"

I recognized the voice. That was Nigel, patrolling his area, and I stood very still, hoping he would not investigate. My quarry must still be on this side of the house, and I did not want to be delayed by questions and explanations. I had a feeling that whoever had come down my tower steps must have melted into the shadow of some nearby chimney bank, or at least had escaped no farther away than the tower which led to Dacia's room. Had he run across the bar to Nigel's side I would have seen him.

By crouching below parapet level, I found that I could creep along the roof, bent over and uncomfortable, but without betraying myself to Nigel's view. I wished it had been Justin on the roof. Then I might have gone directly to him.

When I neared the first bank of four chimney stacks rising from a wide brick base, I stepped gratefully into their shadow and straightened my body. I had covered nearly half of my wing of the roof and was close to the connecting bar. Cautiously I peered around the chimney base and saw that Nigel had marched to the opening of the bar and stood looking down it in my direction. I kept very still—and if my companion in hiding was on the roof, he was equally quiet. I wanted to see him, make certain of him before I shouted for Nigel.

As I waited, Nigel came partway along the bar and then apparently decided that he must have been mistaken for he swung about and returned to his post in the shadow of the far front tower of the house.

I loped into my crouching run again, crossed the opening to the bar and was into the front portion of my own wing. Once more I stepped into chimney shadow, not at all sure of my invisibility, but at least bringing no further challenge from Nigel, who was himself once more invisible.

Cautiously I looked about me, studying the chimney banks and the shadows they cast upon the roof, and finding nothing irregular except my own shadow which, I suddenly discovered, protruded in a sharply human silhouette among straight chimney stacks. I crouched again, erasing the pattern, and melted into a darkness from which I could peer once more toward Dacia's tower.

This time my watchful gaze was rewarded. From that distant corner I caught a faint flicker of light, quickly extinguished—as though someone had gone down those stairs and stepped into a light room below, quickly closing the door behind him. I was sure now that my tormentor was Marc, and my indignation grew. I ran across the roof, not troubling to crouch this time. If Nigel saw me and came to investigate, it would not matter. I would be close on Marc's heels, and I might even need Nigel's help.

The wind tore at me as I ran, buffeted me, tried to beat me back from the tower as though there were purpose in its thrust. Breathlessly I stepped into the relief of the small room at the top of Dacia's tower stairs, where the wind could claw at me only through sentry slots. There I stood utterly still and listening. There was no pursuit by Nigel from the other part of the roof, no sound at all from below. I did not use my flashlight on the steps, but clung to damp stone walls, my fingers brushing over the rough dust of years as I descended. At the foot of the steps a line of light etched Dacia's door. I pulled it abruptly open, hoping to catch Marc before he escaped.

The room within was bright and empty. I stood blinking in the glare, staring about me at plentiful evidence of Dacia's occupancy. Bright-colored clothing was strewn about, and shoes and boots cluttered the floor—as if she had dropped everything wherever she happened to step out of it. The tape recorder stood open, but for once it was silent. Dacia herself was not to be seen, nor was Marc, if it had been he who had climbed down from the roof.

I crossed the cluttered room, but before I could open the corridor door, Dacia herself came bursting in. She looked as keyed up and excited as I had seen her last night during the fire. Her cropped hair was ruffled out of its chrysanthemum cap, her cheeks were flushed, and her eyes shining as though with high fever. She still wore her half-figured dress and no coat. When she saw me she came to a surprised halt, then closed the door quickly behind her.

"Well!" she said. "Fancy meeting you here! A bit cheeky, aren't you, luv—just walking in and making yourself at home? How did you get here anyway? I was right out in the hall and—"

"I came across the roof," I said. "Someone has been rapping on the door of my tower, and I went up on the roof and followed him across. I saw someone come down your tower, so he must have gone through your room. Was it Marc?"

She stared at me in continued astonishment. "You mean you came across that spooky roof in the pitch dark? You must be crackers!"

"There's bright moonlight," I said.

She glanced at her open window. "So there is. I hadn't noticed."

Her words sounded ingenuous enough, but how could one ever be sure with Dacia?

"If you were out in the corridor you must have seen whoever came through your room," I said. "Who was it?"

"I haven't seen a thing. I only crossed over to the bath," she told me. "It's a bit late and I thought I'd better wind up the day and turn in."

Her words surged out with an excitement which made it clear that something had titillated her to the high pitch she loved.

"I remember," I said dryly. "You like danger, don't you?"

"Of course I do—but I wouldn't go running around those roofs up there—not for nothing. I don't like high places—they scare me in a different way from fast cars. A nasty sort of way."

She meant to tell me nothing useful, and I went to the corridor door and opened it.

"I don't know what you and Marc are up to," I said over my shoulder, "but he'd better watch out on the roof. Justin has his patrols up there tonight, you know."

"Of course I know," said Dacia tartly. "Marc's one of 'em, so you can't pin a thing on him for being up there tonight, now can you?"

I stepped into the corridor and closed the door. The sparse lighting of the hall seemed far dimmer than the moonlight, and somehow more ominous. I had begun to feel uneasy. My room, I thought—I had left it alone too long. Sudden anxiety drove me as I ran down the long corridor and pushed open my door. The light was out, although I was sure I had left it on. I fumbled for the switch and the room sprang to life in all its shocking turmoil—as untidy as Dacia's room, but for a different reason.

Whoever had searched this time had been in a hurry and careless of covering his tracks. My dresses had been pulled from their hangers and left where they fell. My suitcase had been tumbled out and emptied over the floor. The packet of pictures and film Nellie had brought me were strewn about. I turned my back on disorder and knelt by the scuttle, to thrust my fingers down among lumps of coal. The leather wallet was there. I brought it out and unzipped the inner pocket. The negative was safely in place. I thrust it back into hiding amidst the coal and hurried from the room.

Down the corridor I ran, to rap hard on Dacia's door. There was no answer and I tried the knob. She had locked herself in, but unless she had joined Marc on the roof she was there, refusing to respond.

"I want to speak to you," I said. "Let me in!"

Her voice finally answered me, mock-sleepy. "Do give over and stop waffling around, Evie old dear. Go to bed and let me sleep."

I walked back to my room, considering what must have happened. The pattern seemed clear. Alicia could have had second thoughts and phoned asking for Marc. Then, too impatient to wait, she had driven over herself, perhaps not trusting her message to the telephone. I could guess what it must have been: "Get me that negative!" If Marc was so thoroughly in debt to the Club Casella, it was likely that he would do what Alicia wished. Tonight he had undoubtedly connived with Dacia in this prankish effort to recover the scrap of film. It was the sort of trick she would love, and, as she herself had said, she must play Marc's game.

Between the two of them they had played it well, and I had almost stepped into their trap. Almost, but not quite. I had taken care to hide the negative where it would not be found, but I had obligingly got out of the way for one or the other to search my room. Probably it had been Dacia, while Marc had performed his tantalizing knocking and led me a wild goose chase across the roof. So now I must talk to Dacia, get the truth out of her, learn if possible why my negative was of such consequence to Alicia Daven. Anything concerning Alicia might have bearing on my relationship to Justin—whether he liked it or not.

By this time Dacia was uneasy about me, surprised by my willingness to brave the roof, and wanting only to be rid of me. But I knew very well how to reach her. Those tower doors boasted no locks, and her room was as accessible to me as mine had been to her. I need only climb my flight of stone steps and go straight across the roof again.

My hand was on the knob of the tower door before I stopped. Did I want to go up there for a second time? I remembered the roof shadows and I knew the hiding places they might offer. The thought of facing the roof again bred uneasiness in my mind—an uneasiness all too ready to turn to terror.

I tried to remind myself that there was no need for fright. Marc had finished leading me a chase, and with a guard set upon the roof the mischief-maker of the past weeks was not likely to be abroad. There was no sensible reason behind my sudden conviction that the menace on the rooftop was more ominous than it had been before.

Nevertheless, uneasy or not, I had to act. Morning would be too late. I sensed strongly that Dacia was vulnerable now —and that by morning she might not be.

I turned up my coat collar and went up into the blackness of the steep stone steps. The moon had gone behind clouds again, and somewhere I had dropped my flashlight, for it was not in my trench-coat pocket. I reminded myself that Nigel was up there. I had only to call to him for help if I should need it.

At the top I paused in the turret's black shelter, listening to the wind as it hurled itself upon the chimneys of Athmore. In spite of all reason, I was fearful—where I had not been before. A sense of evil seemed loosed upon the night.

The black, windy rooftops stretched ahead of me, and there were no individual shadows. Everything was shadow. I cast a glance at the sky and saw silver etching a cloud— though it would be a minute or two before the moon sailed into the clear. At least, if I could not see, neither could I be seen. Or so I thought.

I stepped into the open and at once my foot struck the clattering object I had stumbled over before, and from which I had been distracted by Nigel's challenge. This time I bent to pick up the heavy thing and found that I held some sort of long shaft with a blade at one end. A lance, perhaps, from the Hall of Armor? But I had no time to puzzle over its presence on the roof.

At least it offered me a weapon of sorts, if that was what I might need. Carrying it with me I started down the long corridor of the north roof, able to make my way through gray shadow, avoiding the denser chimney banks. I never saw the thing that tripped me. I knew only that my foot caught some obstruction and I went flying. My temple struck stone as I fell, and I plunged full-length, my head ringing, bright pain flashing before my eyes. Half-stunned, I lay there, unable to get to my feet. Steps rang through the haze and I felt hands touch me, found myself lifted in arms well able to carry me. Yet I had no sense of rescue, but only a certainty of danger and the need to struggle back to full consciousness. A trace of self-preservation was left to me, and warnings seemed to scream through the enveloping fog. Whoever carried me meant me harm, yet I could do nothing to save myself.

IX

The nightmare was one from which I could not waken. I was caught upon a chessboard, a helpless pawn in a game of life and death, and the green rook was hunting me. That tall rook of green-black yew who had it in his power to destroy the king and end the game.

But this was hallucination and I fought my way back to reality. Hazy consciousness returned, and beneath my back I could feel hard stone. Beyond there was nothing to support me—and only the sky overhead. I knew that I lay upon the narrow ledge of the parapet, with the bricks of a courtyard waiting for me far below. Hands pinned me to the ledge, yet I could not scream, could not free myself of those thrusting hands. Worst of all, a visual haze engulfed me. Nothing was in focus, nothing sharp.

From far away there came a sound of running footsteps coming this way, and I knew helplessly that Nigel must be hurrying to my aid, knew that he would never reach me in time. Then, as my clouded vision began to clear, I looked up into Marc's face, alarmingly close above me, and knew that Marc's were the hands that thrust me toward the parapet's edge and oblivion.

I fought in earnest then, and we struggled together on the rim of danger, Marc thrusting at me while I battled to save myself from going over to certain death far below. Somewhere there was now a high, thin screaming—my own!—and then nothing. Emptiness. Nothing.

Fog swirled about me. Throbbing pain returned. I flung my arms out wildly—and found that it was Justin I fought. The hard parapet was no longer beneath my back. Something soft supported me. All around me swam a cold blue light, and I found that I was looking up into the blue canopy above my bed. I was in my own blue room and Justin was bending

143

over me. When I ceased to struggle and looked at him rationally, he took his hands from my shoulders and stepped back.

"That's better," he said. His face seemed dark with an anger which I comprehended no better than anything else.

Maggie stood at the foot of the bed regarding me sadly, shaking her head. "Oh, Eve—how could you attempt a thing like that? Nothing is worth your life—nothing!"

Justin supplemented her words roughly. "I'd have expected more courage from you!"

I looked from his face to Maggie's, trying to remember, to understand. "I don't know what you're talking about. Marc carried me to the parapet and tried to push me over. I'd fallen and knocked my head and I was too dazed to save myself. Was it you who stopped him, Justin?"

Maggie and Justin looked at each other and I knew they did not believe me.

"It's true!" I cried a little wildly. "Marc tried to fling me over that parapet wall. I don't know what saved me, what kept me from going over."

"Marc kept you from going over, dear," Maggie said, leaning past Justin to pat my hand reassuringly. "It will all clear up in a few minutes. He wasn't trying to *throw* you over. He was trying to keep you from flinging yourself down from the roof."

There was no convincing her, and I spoke to Justin, still trying to rouse myself fully. "Tell me what you think happened."

As he spoke, the note of anger deepened his voice. "I came up on the roof because I heard some sort of rumpus going on. Marc shouted for me to help him, and I called Nigel from his end of the south roof. We both rushed over to your side and found you fighting Marc and screaming your head off. It took the three of us to pull you to safety. You resisted being saved with all your might. Luckily you fainted at the crucial moment and we were able to get you downstairs to your bed. Marc has a scratched face to show for his efforts. You'd better get it clear in your mind that he was trying to save you. Nigel and I were both too far away to be of much use when he found you. If it wasn't for Marc, you'd have gone off the roof. If that's what you wanted, if you're that lacking in courage, you're not the girl I used to know."

"It's not what I wanted!" I moaned. "It's not, it's not!"

Justin looked at me coldly, and I closed my eyes to shut out a face I hated as much as I loved. Beyond him I could hear Maggie moving about, and remembrance crept slowly back.

"Whatever has happened to this room?" Maggie murmured. "Why is everything in a turmoil, Eve?"

My head throbbed and I put up my hand to feel the bruise that was swelling at my temple. So that part was real, at least. I had tripped and fallen, bumped my head. Then Marc had carried me to the parapet. And before that there had been the rapping on my tower door, the effort to coax me from my room. Perhaps they had expected me to go out by the corridor door, and then Marc would have come down from the roof and searched my room himself. But I had stopped him by going up on the roof, so Dacia had come instead. Then I had gone to the roof for a second time. But how was I to explain any of this to the two skeptics who watched me, one in sorrow, the other in angry disgust?

I tried to answer Maggie with a simple statement. "Someone searched my room for the negative of that picture I took in the ruins of Athmore Hall the day Old Daniel died."

"What picture?" Justin demanded. "What are you talking about?"

I told him then. Told him of asking Nellie to have the film developed, of discovering in one of the prints a blurred figure that might or might not be Old Daniel. I did not tell him what Alicia had said about Maggie, nor did I betray my wild notion that it might be Alicia herself.

Justin was impatient, unimpressed. "Why should anyone care about such a picture? Aren't you jumping to far-fetched conclusions?"

Since that was exactly what I'd done, I did not argue. My head hurt and I felt too dizzy to cope with the puzzle of the picture.

"I don't know!" I wailed. "I don't want to think about it now!"

To my surprise, Maggie came to my aid. "Of course you don't, dear. You're upset and confused—and it's not necessary to think of anything except rest and sleep. Come along, Justin. Don't torment her now."

He stood beside my bed and looked at me without sympathy. "Will it be necessary to place a guard at your door to watch you?"

I turned my head from side to side on the pillow and felt warm, self-pitying tears upon my cheeks. Denial was useless. These two had decided against me and they would believe nothing I tried to tell them. So I had better be angry, rather than sorry for myself.

"She'll be all right now, I'm sure," Maggie said, resolutely cheerful again. "I'll go make you a cup of tea, Eve dear. And if you like, I'll give you one of my capsules to help you sleep."

The last thing I wanted was drugged sleep. They were both moving toward the door and I propped myself on one elbow.

"I don't want any tea! But I won't stay in this room alone. There's no bolt on the tower door, and if you leave me I won't stay."

Again they exchanged looks, Maggie despairing, Justin impatient.

"I'll send Deirdre in," Justin said curtly. "She should do well enough as nursemaid, if you must have one."

He went to the door and whistled. A moment later Deirdre came bounding down the corridor and through the door, as though she had been waiting, not far away.

"She doesn't like this room," I said. "I tried to bring her here yesterday, and there was something about it that bothered her, so she wouldn't stay."

But even Deirdre belied my words. Nothing about the room seemed to trouble her now. She came to the bed and put her forepaws upon it, thrusting her head forward to lick at my cheek in tender solicitation.

They left me then, apparently satisfied that I would stop my silly objections to the room, and at the same time be prevented from doing any harm to myself with Deirdre on guard. When the door closed after them I put my cheek against her rough coat and clung to her.

"How can I make them believe me?" I cried. But Deirdre had no answer. She merely licked my cheek again to show that she believed me.

Justin had never been able to abide weaklings, and now he believed that I had done something unutterably weak and unforgivable. The bruise on my temple made my head throb, and after a time I got up and bathed it and took aspirin. The lump was tender, but no longer swelling. When I went back to bed, Deirdre stretched herself on the floor nearby, watching until I fell asleep.

There were only a few hours left till daylight and I slept them through, thoroughly exhausted. When I wakened, Deirdre had been let out, and Nellie was moving about my room, picking up my scattered possessions, putting things to rights. A cheery fire burned in the grate.

A fire in the grate!

I sat up and waved a frantic hand at the coal scuttle. "Nellie—you didn't—?"

"No, Miss Eve, I didn't," she said, coming toward the bed with a troubled smile. "Here you are, then. I found your wallet in the coal scuttle and I didn't think you meant it to be burned."

She produced it from her apron pocket, wiped off coal dust with a cloth and placed it beside me on the coverlet. Nellie had the gift of natural tact and having returned the wallet to me, she went on with her task of putting my room to rights, as though there was nothing remarkable in its state, or in my hiding my wallet in a coal scuttle.

When I had reassured myself as to the presence of the negative in its pocket, I finished the tea Nellie had brought me. Once, as she worked she turned toward the bed, holding something up in both hands.

"Why's this here in your room, Miss Eve?"

The object she held seemed to be a spear or lance, and at sight of it further memory swept back. The weapon had been dropped on the roof near my tower door last night. Twice I had struck it with my foot, and the second time I had picked it up. I must still have been clutching it when Marc carried me to the parapet, and someone must have brought it downstairs and forgotten it in my room.

"It's not mine, Nellie," I said. "I don't go in for jousting."

"Oh, it's not the jousting sort, Miss. You'd never lift one of those. Looks more like a cavalry lance—I've seen some in the weapons collection downstairs."

I could think of no reason for its use on the roof, unless someone had indeed carried it as a weapon.

At least I felt stronger now, and the bruise on my temple did not throb as it had last night.

"Will you do one more thing for me?" I asked Nellie. "Do you suppose your husband could make an enlargement from one of the negatives he developed for me?"

"Sorry, Miss Eve, but he's sold off his enlarging equipment," she reminded me. "If you like, I can take it to the village for you and have an enlargment made."

I handed her the negative. "That's fine, Nellie. It's very important, as you can guess, since I hid it where I did."

"I'm going on an errand for Miss Maggie soon," she said.
"So I can do this at the same time."

"Don't show it to anyone, please," I begged her. "Not even
Miss Maggie. Take care of it yourself, and pick it up for me
when it's ready. Will you do that?"

She wrapped the bit of film in a clean handkerchief and
slipped it into an apron pocket. "I'll see to it myself, Miss.
And I'll tell no one." She did not go back to her work, but
stood beside the bed, her look downcast, her manner hesitant.

"I can't tell you what happened," I said. "I don't think I
can face explanations this morning. I mean about the room
and—and all that."

"You needn't say a word," she told me quickly. "It's just
that I think you should know the talk that's going 'round.
Miss Dacia started it. When I brought her tea this morning
she was already up and dressed—early for her. She seemed
nervous and jumpy as a flea, and she kept bouncing around,
bursting out with all sorts of wild things."

"About me?" I said.

Nellie nodded, flushing. "Miss Eve, I hate to repeat what
she said, but she told me you got so despondent about Mr.
Justin wanting to get a divorce and marry Miss Alicia, you
tried to throw yourself off the rooftop last night. She said it
was just luck that Mr. Marc was on guard up there and he
was able to pull you back in time and call for help when you
fought him."

I closed my eyes, enveloped by an old and familiar sense
of being hunted down by lies, of being chained and made
helpless by plausible untruths until I was a ready target for
the hidden enemy. I had not felt this for a long time, but I
knew the feeling from old nightmare.

Nellie's hand touched mine and I opened my eyes to find
her patting me gently.

"There now, Miss. Don't you look like that. I told Miss
Dacia a thing or two right then and there. Maybe I didn't
mind my manners as I should, but I let her know straight off
that I didn't believe the shocking things she was telling me.
You know what I said? I said, 'Miss Eve is a fighter. She'd
never go for doing a thing like that, and whoever says so is
making up something that's wickedly wrong.'"

I squeezed her hand gratefully. "Thank you for standing
up for me. Was she angry with you?"

"No—that's the funny part. She stopped bouncing around
and got very quiet—like she was thinking about something.

Then she said that was how she felt about you too. She didn't think you were the quitting sort, even when quitting was sensible. And no matter what Mr. Marc said."

I felt a small rush of gratitude toward Dacia. I might have known it was from Marc that this story stemmed. Dacia wasn't to be wholly trusted because she had to look after Dacia first, as she readily admitted. Yet there was a basic honesty about her, even in her self-interest.

"You and Dacia are perfectly right, Nellie," I told her. "I didn't try to throw myself over that parapet last night. Nor did I make a shambles of this room myself. Will you go on believing that, please, until I get all this figured out?"

"Of course, Miss. And if they start talking belowstairs I'll give them a piece of my mind—you can count on that."

I knew I could, and I watched her affectionately as she drew back the draperies upon a gray and rainy sky. When she had given my room a few last touches she returned to my bed.

"Why don't you rest awhile this morning, Miss Eve? There's nothing you need be up and doing in this drizzle. Things will look better for a few more hours of rest. Meanwhile I'll take care of the picture for you. Never fear."

Deirdre slipped through the crack of the door the moment Nellie opened it, and came to my bed to wish me a joyful good morning. Then, finding that I did not mean to get up right away, she stretched herself before the fire, her head upon her paws, her round brown eyes fixed on me unblinkingly. Her presence, at least, gave me a sense of comfort if not safety. The old feeling of being hunted, with my destruction as the inevitable goal, was growing stronger than ever. Its origin lay in the past, but Athmore was making it real.

Until my mother's death the nightmare had never touched me. Even in the following three years until I was ten, I had remained free of it. Lena White had come to cook and keep house and take care of me, and I loved her dearly. Lena's skin was brown and her heart was big enough to ignore and forgive my own pale epidermis. Her prejudices were of a different sort. She hated all forms of dishonesty, and, as she said, she didn't care if it was pink or green or purple.

With Father and Lena and me—so comfortable together —I found it hard to understand that my father might be lonely and that a girl like Janet could offer him nearly all he needed to make his life complete again. Lena tried to make me understand before she left, and so did Father. He had al-

ways believed in calm reason when dealing with a child. So
he explained to me carefully that loving Janet did not mean
that either of us would stop loving my mother. In a lifetime
there were many loves. Like mine for Lena, which I could
easily see took nothing away from love for my mother. Janet
was a new and different love and she would make our lives
happier and richer. I did not see why we needed to be made
happier when we had Lena, but I loved my father a great
deal and I wanted very much to please him. Besides, Janet
was a pretty young thing, very neat and shining, and always
smelling lovely. So I wanted to please her too. Since I did not
have to think of her as a mother, I would not mind doing
that.

I like to believe that I tried. And perhaps Janet tried too,
though I know now that her world was my father and that
she had no room in it for loving another woman's child. Her
prejudices were larger and less noble than Lena's, and I believe she must have harbored a consuming jealousy of my
mother that she could not help.

Somehow things went quickly wrong between us, though
trouble remained beneath the surface for a time, since neither
of us said a word to my father. I had my own solution. I had
not slept with my teddy bear, Jumby, for years, but I dug
him out of the mothballs in my mother's old trunk and began
to take him to bed with me every night.

For some reason the sight of Jumby upset Janet more than
anything else I did. It was true that he had been moth-in-
fested at one time, that he was missing one shoe-button eye,
and had a generally grimy look about him. His rather gray
stuffing was leaking out in several places, and he offended Janet's strict sense of cleanliness. She said he was germy and
unsanitary, and she complained to my father about him. But
not even Father's reasonable remarks about my being too old
for teddy bears moved me to give Jumby up.

Matters dragged along in a more or less uneasy state for
some weeks after I had unearthed my old companion. Then
one day I came home from school and Jumby was gone. He
was not waiting cheerfully for me on my bed, nor was he
under it, or among any of my playthings. I searched for a
long while before I went to Janet. She explained to me with
kind patience that it wasn't possible for me to go on sleeping
with a dirty old thing like that, and he had been carried away
by the rubbish man that morning and could not be retrieved.
The invisible hunter had made his first kill! The scene I

created must have been dreadful. Perhaps pressure had been building up in me for some time and Jumby's horrible fate tore off the lid. I flew at Janet like a demon child. I kicked and scratched and screamed, until she finally got me into my room and locked the door upon me. In my bedroom I laid about me with a will for a few minutes, breaking what came to hand, and kicking things into damaged confusion. This vented my rage, but did not ease my pain. When my father came home I was sodden with weeping, and totally unable to speak coherently or listen to cool reason.

Janet was in tears too. She had dabbed iodine on her scratches, which rather emphasized their appearance, and Father had needed to comfort her for a while before he came to deal with me. He found me sullen and uncooperative. I wanted Jumby back. No other solution was possible. Also I discovered that Janet's account of all that had happened, including her own part in it, took certain liberties with the truth. Liberties that were, of course, in her favor. I did not know how to fight her methods.

During the next few days a falsely contrite Janet brought me a huge new teddy bear, far handsomer than Jumby had ever been. He was a lie too. I put him head down in my wastebasket every day for two weeks, and came home from school each afternoon to find him waiting on my bed in Jumby's place, with an idiot grin on his disgustingly clean face. I behaved so badly over this that Father often ended up comforting Janet for my behavior, and condemning me. Finally I took that white plush beast to the beach with me one day, buried him carefully in the sand where the rising tide would find him, and returned home empty-handed, to announce that he had been washed out to sea.

Janet had to be comforted again. Father spanked me, and I hated them both.

My grandmother, whom I dearly loved, was almost helpless with arthritis by this time, and could not come to my rescue by taking me herself. In the end the only solution was to send me away to school. I went gladly enough. I had lost my father, and Janet was not to be endured, so school could not possibly be worse.

It was really much better in a number of ways. There was always someone in school to whom I could give an all-enveloping love. It might be some teacher who was kind to me, or even some older girl who looked upon me as a little sister. These in turn became the object of my smothering affection.

I tried to absorb each new object with my love, demanding of them an equally blotterlike affection in return. When each abandoned me, it confirmed my secret conviction that no one could really love me because I was, underneath, a kicking, screaming monster who did not deserve to be loved.

Of course I grew up eventually—more or less. I learned to see Janet as she was and I looked back with greater understanding of my own behavior. I learned that I must stop blaming myself and stop making such strenuous demands for reassurance upon those I happened to love. Boys did not care for that sort of thing, I found out quickly, and I managed to work out a near-convincing act for myself. I found I could fling myself emotionally into the pursuit of various causes and occupations. I was bright and busy and my interests were real enough and rather earthshaking—or so it seemed to me. It began to appear that I had stopped falling into hopeless crushes. I carried my bluff along on dates and watched myself sternly.

Then I came to England. I met Justin North—and everything that had gone before paled by contrast. My well-practiced bluff convinced Justin of an Eve who existed only partially, and he had his own self-delusions as well. Once, in the months that followed, I asked Maggie desperately why he had married me, what he could possibly see in me, and she had said something strange: "Perhaps he sees what is really there, Eve, if you'd just give yourself a chance." That had shaken me.

But before then we went on our honeymoon in Greece. Among the moonlit ruins of Delphi I began to realize for the first time that I was truly loved and valued. The small monster seemed lost in the past, and I began to seem a real person, even to myself. A young woman possessed of dignity and self-confidence—all those lovely things I had bluffed about.

Then we came home to Athmore and I discovered that my husband was also in love with a good many things outside myself. Against the competition of his devotion to his work, my new self-confidence began to falter. There was Alicia, besides, whose existence I could not cope with. And there was Marc with his clever little tricks. Since I had a genius for doing the wrong thing under stress, I managed to destroy my chance for happiness much more expertly than anyone else could have done for me. That Marc helped this along was incidental.

The chain of events which had started at Athmore had never stopped moving in the wrong direction. Now that I had returned, they simply picked up their old momentum. But now my conduct must be different. As a young bride I had defended a pride that must be preserved at all costs—even if everything else was shattered. Without pride I was nothing. Or so I had always thought. Now, however late, I was beginning to see how stupid it was to demand that I be loved for myself, exactly as I was, and without any disturbing changes. Of course everyone wanted that. It was always more comfortable to insist on a love that demanded little effort. Being lovable seldom entered into it because that took a great deal of hard work. Besides, I could always point out that Justin was not particularly lovable and that he had no intention of changing.

But I could do nothing about Justin—except love him. I could only manage me.

Deirdre, who had returned to doze on the hearth, yawned widely and opened her eyes, waiting for my summons. I held out my hand and she came at once to nuzzle her long nose against my palm.

"There are things to be done," I said, and tossed back the covers.

Deirdre waited by the fire until I was bathed and dressed. I did not want to be trapped inside by the rain, so I picked up my trench coat, folded a plastic hood into the pocket, and carried the coat with me when I left my room. Deirdre trotted beside me down the long corridor in the pale light of a rainy morning.

We walked through the long gallery and I had only a slight nod for Mr. Dunscombe, who had done no better than I in solving his problems. I went down the stairs, my hand on Deirdre's neck, like some Athmore lady of old walking out of a portrait with her hand on the neck of an Irish wolfhound. The incongruous picture this evoked made me smile and I began to relax a little. I was anything but a proper Athmore lady, and such dramatizing was better left to Alicia Daven. Any changes I managed need not take so theatrical a direction.

One truth which I must face was simple. I was undeniably jealous of Alicia. This was a human enough failing, for which I must forgive myself. But at the same time I had to learn to keep that very jealousy under control. The one primary truth that mattered was that I loved Justin, though

whether he wanted anything I had to offer was still doubtful.
What else was true?

Marc had some reason to want me dead. It was a frightening truth that last night he had tried to kill me. Could this be
because of Old Daniel? What if it was Marc in the snapshot I
had taken? Marc, who had once destroyed the key figure in
Daniel's topiary garden and whom Daniel would ever after
connect with the rook, no matter how often Justin "con-
fessed."

But this was only speculation. It was not necessarily the
truth. Last night had been real and I knew what had happened to me then. Now I must learn why.

There was still one person who might help me. Nigel, too,
had been on the roof last night, and while Nigel was an uncertain quantity, what he could tell me might count for more
than Marc's lies, Maggie's blind devotion, or Justin's scorn.

I let Deirdre out the back way, and hung my green coat on
the rack near the door—a portentous gesture, though I did
not know it at the time. Then I went into the Wedgwood dining room to eat a sketchy breakfast, so preoccupied that not
even the coffee disturbed me. When I had eaten I stood for a
time looking out the long windows which overlooked the garage area. Through the beeches I could see Justin moving
about, wearing a wet gray mac. I moved to the rear windows
that looked out upon the topiary garden.

That fateful phrase kept running through my mind: *Rook's
play.* Last night the rook had moved again—though not to
place the king in check. Not even to attack the opposing
queen. Whatever the game, I was no more than a hunted
pawn, with more powerful pieces moving about me, ready for
the kill. Pawns were easily dispensed with when they got in
the way—the least useful man on the board. That is, unless a
pawn could steal its way to the opposing line and emerge as a
stronger piece—perhaps even as a queen. There was little
hope that it would last the game, if pursued by another piece.

The chessboard imagery was too apt for comfort and I
found the view more depressing than ever. Even the pervad-
ing color of everything outdoors depressed me. There is nothing more green than country England during a springtime
rain. Trees and lawns and shrubbery blurred into an enveloping green aura that was too insistent for comfort. One longed
for a flash of strident color to relieve the green intensity.

Abruptly I had my wish. Dacia's orange coat added a neon
note as she ran among the topiary chessmen and bounced up

the rear terrace in her high boots. She saw me at the dining-room window and waved to me as she ran. A moment later she bounced into the room, slicking down rain-streaked hair, divesting herself of the wet orange coat.

"Are you all right?" she demanded at once.

There was no need for evasion with Dacia. Direct attack might startle her into response.

"As right as I can be, considering that Marc tried to push me over the roof parapet last night," I said.

Dacia's eyes could seem as round and as brown as Deirdre's—and more unblinking in their stare. "So that's your story! You know what Marc claims, don't you?"

"Why does he claim it? Isn't that the point? If I knew why, then perhaps I'd have a clue to go on."

"Perhaps he's claiming the truth. After all, you were off your noggin last night when he found you. So it could be you didn't know what was really going on. Anyway, I have to stand by what he says, don't I? I have to help him, however I can."

"To the extent of searching my room last night?" I said. "It was you, of course. Or Marc."

Dacia stared at me for a moment longer, then whirled to the sideboard and helped herself to a piece of dry toast which she piled with marmalade.

"I didn't need to search," she said. "I would have, but it was already too late. Whoever it was made a bloody mess of your room, didn't he?"

"Then it was Marc," I said flatly.

"He claims not." Dacia seemed uncertain for a moment before she brightened. "But we did work out a lovely scheme, didn't we? At least I thought so, since most of it was my idea. The way poor Mr. Dunscombe is supposed to rap on your tower door at night made me think of it. So Marc got a long lance from the armor collection and then he reached down the stairs in the tower to bang on your door with the heavy end of it. We wanted you to skip out of your room in fright. Only you fooled us and came up to the roof, so that he barely got out of your way. What a carry-on, wasn't it? And after all that, we were too late to do your room because somebody else had beat us to it."

"Who?" I said.

Dacia shrugged. "I'm wondering about that myself. Maybe you'd better figure out who that picture might hurt the worst —and why."

As if I had not been wondering. The why was Old Daniel's death, of course. The old man had been frightened, and because of what had happened to him someone was desperate to hide his identity—or hers. Whoever I'd caught in my picture must have been waiting there, hidden. And Old Daniel knew he waited—and had tried to warn me with a cryptic message that I had not understood at all.

I left Dacia to her nibbling and went upstairs. It was Nigel I must talk to now.

I found him in the library, deep in a red leather armchair beside a fire that burned in a vast stone fireplace. Stretching upward above his head long window panes gave upon green daylight, and rain clattered incessantly against the glass. He saw me coming toward him down the room and closed his book, his expression guarded. He too would know what was being said about me, so perhaps it was hopeless to talk to him. But I had to try.

I dropped into an opposite chair and leaned toward him earnestly. I did not want to be put off.

"You were on the roof last night?" I began without preliminaries.

He set his book aside and nodded gravely.

"Do you believe that I tried to kill myself?"

He continued to study me with that grave, faintly guarded look, not answering.

"Did you see what happened?" I prodded him.

"I saw some of what seemed to be happening," he said.

I took a deep breath. Nigel, at least, was leaving room for doubt.

"Will you tell me about it, please? Tell me, starting with the first out-of-the-ordinary thing you noticed last night."

He considered this for a moment. "The first unusual occurrence was a racket on the roof diagonally opposite from the tower where I was posted," he said. "I believe this happened shortly after Maggie went downstairs."

"Maggie!" I echoed. "Was she up there last night?"

"Only for a short time," he said. "We walked up and down together for a while. It was a spectacular night with the wind blowing clouds across the moon. But Maggie got bored and chilled after an hour or so, and went downstairs."

"Through the tower in your room?" I asked.

He seemed surprised. "No. I suppose she went down through the tower that opens into the green-velvet room—the entrance nearest her part of the house. It was dark and I didn't really note the way she went."

"Go on," I said. "Tell me the rest." Maggie's earlier presence on the roof was surely of no consequence to later events, since she was already downstairs by then.

He went on to tell me how he had heard the clattering sound which I had made the first time I had kicked the lance Marc had left on the roof. But there had been no answer to his shouted challenge. Marc, who was supposed to be on guard in that section of the roof seemed to have disappeared. Nigel had seen off-and-on lights from Dacia's tower, probably due to a door opening below, and had supposed that Marc had gone down there. For a time everything was quiet. Then the clattering sound was repeated, followed a few moments later by the impact of someone falling. Almost at once Marc had shouted for help, Justin had come running up from the green-velvet room to call out in turn, and Nigel had left his tower to join him, running across the rooftop to where Marc was struggling with me at the parapet. They had both helped Marc in pulling me to safety and Justin had carried me downstairs, while Nigel stayed on to guard the roof. The rest of the night had been uneventful, and there had been no trouble on the ground either.

"Tell me what you thought when you saw Marc struggling with me," I said when he finished. "Did you really believe I was trying to fling myself off the roof?"

"You were putting up a fight, let's say."

"A fight for my life! Couldn't you tell it was that?"

He answered me carefully. "Do I know you well enough to judge? Mustn't I take the word of those who know you better?"

I leaned back in my chair. It would be no use to accuse Marc again. Nigel would believe me no more than did the others. Only Marc knew the truth, and he would not even tell Dacia. Why should he want me dead? We might dislike each other, but I was no threat to Marc. What he had attempted seemed too violently extreme for any cause I could guess.

Rain continued to strike the windows of the library with an endless rattling. Nigel and I sat together in the glow of the fire, listening to the sound. Once he reached tentatively toward his book and I roused myself to ask another question.

"Did you know that someone searched my room last night while I was on the roof? This is the second time. A snapshot

I took the other day was stolen first. This time the search must have been for the negative of that picture. But I hid it well enough so it wasn't found. Nigel, have you heard anything? Have you any idea what is going on?"

Again there was hesitation, in which I sensed uneasiness. "Only what I've heard from Maggie," he said at last. "She seems upset about the existence of this picture because someone has hinted that she might be in it. Though why that should matter I can't see."

"That's nonsense, of course," I assured him. "I have a better idea about who my camera may have caught. Nigel, was Old Daniel afraid of someone? Have you any idea why he went to see Alicia Daven the day before he died?"

"Aren't you striking out a bit wildly in all directions?" Nigel asked. "Alicia has always been clever about making friends with Athmore help, and Old Daniel was no exception. There's no reason why he might not go to see her."

"This was more than that," I said. "I really believe it was more. I think she was trying to use him in some way. And of course she's been using Marc too."

"You're beginning to see ghosts around every turn," Nigel told me dryly.

I paid no attention. It wasn't Alicia in the snapshot, I thought. It was not Maggie either—but Marc. Speculation or not, I kept returning to this as the answer.

"Was there a good deal of antagonism between Old Daniel and whoever cut the rook out of the topiary chessboard that time when Marc and Justin were young?" I asked.

Nigel was clearly surprised by this new turn I had taken. "Do you mean Justin? No, of course the old man felt no antagonism toward him. He was devoted to him and forgave him completely."

"But everyone seems to think that no matter what Justin said, Marc was the guilty one. So Old Daniel must have thought that too and disliked him all the more for it."

"Isn't this more wild guesswork?" Nigel said.

It was clear that I would get no more help from him than from anyone else. My speculation was only an effort to throw out different trails in the hope that one of them would lead to real answers. But if the answer to the puzzle was to be found, it was growing increasingly clear that I must find it myself. And until I saw the blow-up of the negative I had entrusted to Nellie, I had nothing to go on. Waiting made me edgy. All of a sudden there seemed to be so little time.

I thanked Nigel and moved away, leaving him to pick up his book, while I wandered the length of the library to where a glass case stood beneath the portrait of Margaret Athmore.

Maggie Graham, I remembered, had been named after Margaret, and I recalled trying to find some resemblance between the two—though Maggie herself said there was none. Perhaps the resemblance was inner. Maggie was possessed of just such courage and of as great a loyalty to Athmore, though she was, I suspected, a less gentle person than Margaret Athmore had been.

Now, however, as I paused before the portrait, I found myself remembering the first time I had stood in this place, before this very lady, moved to tears and revealing what I felt. I had looked into the glass case which held the stained and faded dress Margaret had worn when John Edmond died in her arms, and Justin stood beside me. He had believed in my love for Athmore—and he had kissed me. The trouble was I had believed in it too—thoroughly and romantically. Even now the story was a part of my own heritage because of my grandmother's tales, but it had not carried me through to make Athmore my real home.

I turned from the case, drawn almost without volition to the door that opened from the library into the north-wing corridor. This was a hallway I knew far better than the one above, which I now occupied. The first door across on my left opened into the room Justin and I had once shared. I did not want to set foot in that room again. It was the next door that interested me. With Justin outdoors, I could surely be forgiven for looking into what had once been my small, elegant dressing room.

The knob turned beneath my hand and the door opened upon echoing gloom. I knew where to find the wall switch, and as I touched it two bracket lights near where my dressing table had stood flashed on—to show me utter emptiness.

Nothing remained of the furnishings I had so lovingly chosen. Not a mirror, not a picture, not the chaise longue where I had sometimes napped. The rug had been rolled up and placed against one wall, the draperies removed, with only bare shades left at the windows to shut out the light.

My banishment from Athmore was complete. Why I should have expected anything else I did not know. Of course Justin would free himself of unwanted memories by removing every reminder of me from this room adjacent to his.

I stepped softly across the bare floor, noting that the wall-paper at least was the same. Once its pale yellow had seemed like early spring sunlight, with tiny wildflowers blooming across it. The paper still looked as clean and unmarred as it had when Justin had first approved my choice. I put out my hand where there was nothing to touch. Here against this wall my dressing table had stood with its folding mirrors and glass top. But the wall carried no memory of its being. It had not stood there long enough to leave a shadow. Here where the lovely painting of the Temple of Apollo at Delphi had hung, not a mark remained to tell of it. The picture which Justin had bought for me when we were in Greece had hung here too briefly to be remembered. The room was empty, as my entire being seemed empty. It was a shell without life.

I moved on about the room. Where a closet had been built into one section I opened the door. My suits and dresses had once hung upon this rod and there had been a rack for my shoes, plastic hatboxes on the shelves overhead. Now there was nothing. Nothing except a dark square that leaned against the back wall. I touched it and knew it was a picture. Curiously I drew it out, pulled up a shade and carried the picture into the light.

The glass was intact over a painting that showed the lovely columns and the remaining platform of Apollo's Temple. Behind rose the ruins of Delphi, with great shining cliffs above, and an eagle wheeling high in the clear bright air.

I sat cross-legged on the floor of the empty room and held the picture before me. We had walked up that stone way which curved across the foreground, Justin and I. We had explored these ruins by sunlight and when the moon was bright. We had walked among these very stones hand in hand, with our lives before us, and more happiness in our possession than we had ever dreamed possible. We had talked to each other endlessly, and each had taken time to listen and to care. Perhaps all lovers did that in the beginning. When the stories grew old, it was new and shared experiences they discussed. But our stories had aged, and our shared new life had scarcely begun before it was ended. What was there to talk about after Delphi?

The glass felt cool beneath my fingers, but the colors of the picture glowed warm and clear as the sunlight of Greece, banishing gray stones and green Athmore rain, restoring the past, denying the empty room about me.

I heard footsteps in the corridor and recognized them. Yet I could not move. I could not so much as raise my eyes from the warmth of the picture as Justin came through the door I'd left ajar and walked into the room.

X

He stood behind me, looking down at the picture, and he did not speak. I dared not lift my gaze from the glowing scene. All the emotion that welled up in me was one with the picture.

"Do you remember the olive trees?" he asked after a time.

I nodded. The olive trees were not in the painting, but I would never forget the way they flowed down the gorge far beneath our hotel windows—a solid phalanx of olive trees marching toward the Gulf of Corinth. The stream had narrowed as it entered the gorge, then widened as the silver-gray torrent poured down toward the plain. Once we had seen the trees on a day of storm, with all their silver branches atoss, so that the illusion of flowing seemed real.

Justin dropped to one knee beside me—and was too close. So close that I dared not move. He reached past my shoulder to point out the sacred way that men had climbed through all those centuries since the Oracle had last spoken at Delphi. His finger traced the path, curving back and forth among the ruins, as once our own feet had traced it.

"We climbed to the top," he said in my ear. "Up through the amphitheater, and out into the open where the stadium still stands."

I remembered. It had been early in the morning on a day of wind and sun, with a glorious blue sky overhead and the warmth of Greece wiping England's damp out of our bones. We had been ahead of the tourists and we'd had all that beauty to ourselves as we climbed to a grassy field above the stadium, with only the sky overhead.

My voice was a small thing that seemed to stick in my throat. "Where did it go—what we had then? How did we lose it?"

"It hasn't been lost to memory," he said, quite gently. "It's

still there in time. But we can never again be the two people
we were then."

I laid the picture on the floor and put my face in my
hands. I could not bear it that we could never go back to
Delphi and be once more the lovers we had been.

I felt Justin's hand slip beneath the fall of my hair in the
old way, bridging the column of my neck with his palm. Only
then did I look up at him. I leaned my head against the support of his hand and looked into his eyes. His own seemed to
shine with a dark light and he put his mouth upon mine. It
was a strange kiss—sudden and quick, both fierce and tender
—all in an instant. I could neither respond nor repudiate. His
lips touched mine and were gone.

He stood up and pulled me not ungently to my feet. "Perhaps we can talk a little now," he said. "Perhaps for once we
can use words without quarreling and accusation."

I could not keep from shaking as I followed him into the
next room. I was glad to sit down quickly in a chair near his
desk. Without staring about me, I knew the room had
changed very little since the last time I had seen it—that
desperate, angry time. It was a man's room, done with taste
and restraint in hues of deep brown and burnt umber, with
slashes here and there of scarlet and yellow—in pictures, in
draperies, in the deep warm red of the rug. Justin went to a
window embrasure and stood looking out upon green rain.

"I don't want you to be unhappy," he said. "I don't want
you to be driven to such foolish action as you tried to take
last night. I was furious with you then—that you should be
so stupid as to try such a measure. Now I'm only sorry."

Only sorry, I thought. What a dreadful thing it is when a
man you love is only sorry for you.

"Why do you believe Marc instead of me?" I asked.

He turned from the window. "Eve, you were out of your
head at the time. You couldn't know what you were doing. I
saw you. I saw how you fought to get away from us."

"I was carried to that parapet," I told him. My voice
would not behave, but at least it was not angry or querulous
—just uneven from my quick breathing.

He waved his hands despairingly. "All right. It doesn't
matter now. I'm sure your dream seems real to you. The important thing is where do you go from here?"

"Where do *we* go?" I said.

"We go by separate roads," he told me. "What are the

clichés? Our bridges are burned, the dies are cast. There's no turning back."

I stood up and went slowly toward him. I had to walk around the end of the great carved bed, and I did not want to look at that bed. When I came close to him I stood braced, with my feet apart, and my hands clasped behind my back to hold them still, and I looked up at him without trying to hide what I felt.

"If you're through loving me," I said, "then I'll have to go away. There's nothing else I can do. You needn't worry about what you think happened last night. I'd really never do a thing like that. But first you have to tell me you're through with ever loving me."

He took me by the hand, drew me up steps into the stone embrasure of the window where two cushioned seats faced each other. Gently he thrust me into one seat, and took the other himself. We sat with our knees nearly touching—yet did not touch each other at all.

"What happened to us was complete insanity, Eve. We both threw good sense to the winds and tried for the impossible. We believed in something that was never real. It didn't work out and it would not again. I am no more the husband for you than you are the wife for me. Surely neither of us wants to repeat what happened before. I could never give you what you need, never fulfill the demands you must always make upon a man. I understand why you make such demands, and so do you. But that doesn't make them easy to live with. What's more, there are needs of mine that you never wanted to fulfill. You never wanted to be a wife for Athmore. Now I'm committed elsewhere—to a woman whom I did not treat very well when you burst into my life. It's not in me to let her down twice."

I could not bear the way his eyes searched my face. I could not endure knowing there was kindness in him toward me—and nothing else. I would almost rather have him angry, hating me. But anger was the old way, the wrong way. Had I grown up a little, or had I not?

"Once Maggie told me that you and Alicia never meant to marry," I said. "She told me Alicia was irresponsible and reckless and that you never quite trusted her."

There was a pause before he answered, and I knew he was restraining an impulse to quick temper. "And did you prove that you could be trusted?" he asked coldly. "Alicia has matured, changed, but I wonder if you have? I wonder if you've

any idea how much Alicia would bring to Athmore as a wife
—that you could not?"

The words were cruel—and honest.

"I know," I said helplessly. "I really do know all the ways
in which I failed us both and how little I brought to Athmore. I'm only beginning to find out who I am, and what I'd
like to be."

"Eve—Eve!" His eyes were kind again—and too pitying.
"It's not like you to be humble. Don't play a new role that
may not fit you either." He reached for my hand and held it
tightly in reproach. "A good deal of what happened was my
fault. There's no need for you to take all the blame. I've
never been a patient man and I should have known better
than to attempt the impossible. But there is no going back for
either of us, whatever our faults or virtues. What is past is
past. There's time ahead for you to make a new life. We
can't go back to—to—" He broke off and his grip on my
hand tightened.

"To the olive trees?" I said.

"Exactly. Or to anything else we had for a little while in
the beginning. Unfortunately, I wasn't wise enough to stop
what was happening before it ran away with us."

"And this time you are." Having stated a fact, I took my
hand from him gently, without snatching. There was no
anger left in me.

For a few moments longer I sat looking out the window.
The view from this part of Justin's room was over the front
terrace and driveways. I saw the white car as it came around
the curve to stop before the house. Alicia wore a shiny vinyl
raincoat that matched her car and she made a flash of brilliant white against green shrubbery as she ran toward the
front door.

I looked at Justin. He was watching me rather warily and
had not seen the approaching car. Far be it from me to tell
him he had a visitor. I slipped down from the embrasure and
left him there as I walked out of the room. There was more
which needed to be said, but I knew I would never say it. If
I tried I would break down, and that I would not have. Especially not with Alicia Daven on her way into the house. The
house that could have been mine.

In order to avoid her I followed the corridor to the rear
stairs and went down to the ground floor. My green trench
coat was not where I had left it on the rack by the back
door. Instead, Dacia had hung her wet orange coat there, ap-

parently preferring my dry one. Escape from the house was
what I wanted and I put on her coat and my own rainboots,
found a kerchief in her pocket and tied it over my head.

Outside, the topiary garden seemed oppressively green
amid an overwhelmingly green and drizzling world. I went
around the side of the house, past tall drawing-room windows. At one of these I caught a gleam of white and knew
that Alicia stood watching. At once I turned my back on the
house and hurried toward the path that led through rainy
woods in the direction of the ruins.

I wanted only to get off by myself—yet I felt uneasy as the
woods closed about me, somberly green and awhisper with
the sound of rain. English rain is seldom drenching and I
slowed to a stroll, unmindful of the wet, though Dacia's coat
was shorter than I liked. It was not about Alicia, or the eerie
feeling of rainy woods that I wanted to think. Justin had convinced me of several things. He believed in his debt to Alicia
because he had hurt her badly in the past, and he believed
that she had changed and matured. He believed that the
course he meant to take was right and just. But he had not
yet convinced me that what had existed between us was hopelessly lost.

"Dogged," my father had once called me. Very well—I
would be dogged! Prejudiced I certainly was. I could not believe that it was either right or just for Justin to marry Alicia.
Even if he never looked at me again, she was not worth his
loving. Once I had thought her everything an Englishwoman
should be—everything I was not. I had accepted her baiting
helplessly, not recognizing it for what it was, not seeing how
cleverly she concealed what she was doing from Justin. Now
I knew better. I saw through the sham, and I knew that Maggie did too, and that Justin must eventually. But if there was
to be disillusionment for him, it might come too late as far as
I was concerned.

Somewhere in the distance I heard the sound of a car. It
came from across Athmore land and I could not tell whether
it traveled some outside road, or followed the test course
within. Probably it was the former. This was no day for testing a car.

It was drizzling harder than before, and I began to hurry
through the woods. The sound of the car was quickly lost in
the nearer sounds of rain as it dripped about me from every
tree branch and leaf. The woods were too wet by this time to
offer shelter and I hurried toward the arches and walls of the

old ruins. There I would find some stony nook in which to be
quiet and think. Far away from the house, where I could balance one thing against another and gain some sort of perspective. Balance Justin's kiss against all else. That, at least, had
been unplanned. There was in him still the wild, unruly impulses of the young man I'd known. Impulses that were still
at war with more sober reason, for all that he wore his self-
control like armor these days.

There was a sudden explosion of sound, as of a car accel-
erating sharply not far away. Who could be out on a day like
this? I began to run toward the place where the woods
opened upon the course, but by the time I reached the road
whatever car had passed was gone. I heard it roaring away,
the sound diminishing for a moment or two, and then breaking off completely—which was strange in itself.

The eerie quality of the forest on either hand, silent now,
except for the dripping, increased my sense of uneasiness. I
stepped out upon a shiny wet pavement, ducking my head
against the rain, stamping mud from my boots as I hurried
along the open stretch of road. The curve lay ahead that sep-
arated me from the path. There was no longer any sound of
a car, but I did not want to linger in the open. Once more I
began to run, as though it were suddenly a matter of life or
death to escape from the road before something dreadful
happened. This was the way I had felt last night when I
climbed to the roof for the second time, and I was beginning
to believe in my own sense of premonition. This road was
too far from the house, and far more open than I liked.

As I ran along the pavement's edge I brushed past wet
shrubbery that slapped at me, weighted by the rain, and almost fell as I stumbled over something which lay across the
roadway at my feet. Something which lay face down and un-
moving, clad in a green trench coat, with a plastic hood covering the head. A coat of hunter's green, streaked by scarlet
threads that ran in the rivulets of rain.

I stood staring down at the still figure for a moment of almost supernatural horror. It was as though I had come upon
a visualization of my own death, as though I could not move
because I was no longer alive. Then I dropped to my knees
beside the figure, knowing very well who it must be. The
plastic hood almost covered her face, and as I moved it ap-
prehensively I saw the blood from some dreadful wounding
of her head. Dacia's eyes were closed, her face empty of life.
As I stared in that instant of frozen horror I seemed to hear

her own words echoing through my mind about tomorrow never coming—that it would be like that for us one of these days. Dacia who had been so full of life—

I found my voice then and began to call for help. It was Justin I shouted for, my voice rising above the rain sounds with the wind helping me as it blew toward the house. Justin heard me and shouted an answer that came to me distantly, faintly. Long before he reached me I could hear him crashing through the woods in my direction. There were others as well, running behind him. I could hear the thud of feet, the thrashing of wet brush, and I stopped screaming to listen again for any sound of the car that had hunted Dacia down and had not stopped to help her. There was nothing to be heard except the rain and the sound of running. I knew without doubt what had happened and that evil was intended. There was nothing to do but stumble to my feet and wait at the side of the road, huddled in Dacia's orange coat, while she lay dead in mine. A pawn's death had been intended. I was the pawn, not Dacia. She had been mistaken for me.

Justin gave me scarcely a glance as he came around the curve and crossed the road. All his attention was for the girl in green—green with that dreadful scarlet trim.

"Eve!" he cried as he bent over her. "Eve, my darling!" He picked her up in his arms and blood streaked the plastic hood as it fell across her face, washing away in the rain. The truth was in his eyes, his voice, his words. Never again would I doubt that he loved me—but this was too tragic a price to pay for the knowledge.

Marc and Nigel came into view beyond and Justin carried Dacia toward them. I hurried beside him, choked with emotion—for him, for Dacia, unable to speak. Finally he looked at me—looked past the orange coat and into my eyes, then at the face of the girl he carried.

"A car struck her down," I told him breathlessly. "A car struck her and didn't stop!"

For the space of an instant I saw his stark relief and my heart leaped exultantly. The feeling was no more than a flash between us because all concern must be for Dacia.

Marc recognized me at once and made no mistake about the coat I wore. He knew it was Dacia whom Justin carried.

"Give her to me," he said. There was bitterness in him as he took the slight figure into his arms and looked past her at me. I knew very well that he would prefer me dead, if that would bring Dacia back to life. Here and there on his face scratches flamed red—marks which my own fingernails had left.

Already Justin was hurrying ahead. He did not see his brother's look or hear his words.

"You changed coats with Dacia and this happened," Marc said and the accusation was clear. As though I had done this to harm Dacia and save myself.

I walked behind him on the path, possessed by such horror as I had never felt before. Horror for Dacia—horror for me. Yet no matter how disturbing was my fear, there was something else as well—something to comfort me. I need no longer doubt that Justin loved me.

Nigel fell quietly into step beside me. He had heard Marc's words, if Justin had not. At least Nigel would listen, and I found myself trying to explain.

"Dacia's coat was wet, so she took mine and left her own behind. I had nothing else to wear, so I put hers on. I didn't know she had come this way too. I heard a car, and I ran toward the road and found her lying there."

"Who would have a car out on the course on a day like this?" Nigel said.

I could only shake my head. We had reached the place where the path opened upon Athmore lawns, and as though in answer to his question a white figure came running toward us—not from the direction of the house, but from the topiary garden behind. It was Alicia Daven in her shiny wet coat.

"What has happened?" she cried to Marc. "Has Eve been hurt? I heard shouting and I came this way."

Vaguely I wondered why she was outdoors at all, when I had last seen her standing at a drawing-room window. Some question must have crossed Nigel's mind too, and I knew by the look he gave her that he did not like or trust this woman.

Marc told her coldly what had happened as he walked ahead of us carrying Dacia, and she listened with an air of anxiety that did not seem altogether real. She was anxious enough, but I sensed that it was for another cause.

The scene in the Hall of Armor almost repeated the night of the fire, except that now there was no excited Dacia dancing about, and Maggie was not there either. Someone went to look for her, and after a delay she came into the hall to take quiet, efficient charge.

"I stopped upstairs to ring the doctor," she said to Marc. "He'll take care of getting an ambulance here."

"It's too late," Marc said savagely and laid his burden upon a couch. As he leaned above Dacia I thought I had never seen so grieving a look upon his face. It seemed that Marc could care genuinely about someone, after all.

Justin reached past his brother to take Dacia's wrist between his fingers. After a moment he shook his head. Maggie gave him a small pocket mirror and he held it to the girl's parted lips. We all stood motionless, bound by a common dread. Slowly a faint mist clouded the glass. A spark of life still flickered in Dacia's young body. Marc sat beside her holding her hand, whispering to her softly, trying to coax back her fighting spirit.

Through all this Alicia stood a little apart, quiet and hardly noticed, her hands thrust deep into the slash pockets of her coat. Only I found myself looking repeatedly her way, wondering what it was I sensed in her that made me distrustful and uneasy.

Once Nigel, watching at a front window, turned to look at her speculatively. "Where did you leave your car, Alicia?" he asked.

I heard her quick intake of breath. She did not answer him directly, but turned to Justin. "I left it at the front door. I waited in the drawing room for you. When you didn't come, I went to the front windows and looked out—and found my car gone. That's why I went outdoors. It wasn't in the garage area and I was trying to find out who had taken it, where it had gone."

Marc did not speak, or raise his gaze from Dacia's face, but I saw the quick turning of Maggie's head as she stared at Alicia.

The woman appeared not to see her look. "We must find my car," she said.

Justin gave quick orders and the search was on.

Shortly after, the ambulance arrived, and the doctor. The police followed, since Justin had phoned for them. Marc went off with Dacia to the hospital and no one made any effort to prevent his leaving. I felt a further twinge of uneasiness as he walked out the door. Maggie watched him, and I knew she was uneasy too.

The constable questioned Justin, and then the rest of us, and we all answered as best we could. What seemed to emerge was the picture of a hit-and-run accident. Someone had struck Dacia down, then panicked and fled. The police

were quietly purposeful. This sort of thing was not new to
them. I wondered what they thought of two accidents so
close together at Athmore.

No one mentioned the switch in coats, or any possible intent to kill: Yet Marc had believed in this, and so did I. In
fact, I might have blurted everything out if it had not been
for Maggie. She came to sit beside me and once she put a
hand upon my arm. "Wait—don't judge," she seemed to
warn me, as plainly as though she had spoken. So I was silent, for the moment at least.

Eventually someone came to report finding Alicia's car on
the test course, not far from where Dacia had been struck
down. The front fender was dented and a headlight bore the
marks of a severe impact. The girl must have been struck and
flung to the side of the road while the white car was going at
high speed. Whoever had driven it had abandoned it just
around the next curve, and fled on foot through the rain.

Fled where? Back to the house? Back to where he could
come out with the others when my shouting had summoned
help? The constable asked a good many questions, but did
not speculate aloud about what might have happened. It
seemed that everyone except Dacia and Alicia and me had
been indoors out of the rain. But while each one accounted
for his own presence in the house, each had been alone and
lacked other corroboration. Maggie was in her sitting room,
Nigel had returned to the library. Justin was still in his bedroom. No one seemed to know where Marc had been, though
Maggie admitted that he had looked in on her some time earlier to ask if she knew Dacia's whereabouts. She did not, and
presumably he had gone looking for her. Whether outside, or
inside, no one knew.

To me it began to seem that almost anyone might have
looked out a window and seen a girl in a green coat walking
toward the path that led to the ruins—a path that must inevitably follow the test course for a short distance. But if anyone had seen her, he made no admission of the fact.

Alicia, of course, was questioned carefully, but she seemed
to give a straightforward account, apparently horrified at the
use to which her car had been put. She had left it standing in
front of the door, she repeated, the keys in the ignition. She
had not given it another thought until, while waiting for Justin to come downstairs, she had wandered to the front windows of the drawing room and looked out, to discover the

car gone. She had thereupon gone out in the rain to find where it had been put.

"Didn't you take it for granted that it had been moved to the garage, and let it go at that?" the constable asked her.

Alicia shrugged. "I chose to look myself. I like my property to remain where I leave it. And of course when I found that it had not been put into the garage I was annoyed. I started around the back of the house to find someone to question, and heard Mrs. North calling for help. The moment I saw what had happened, I began to worry if it was really my car which had struck Dacia down."

In the end the servants were better able to vouch for each other's activities than were those within the house. No strangers seemed to have been noticed around the place, and the mysterious Leo Casella was supposed to be back in London.

The police left to turn in their report and Maggie went at once to ring up the hospital for word of Dacia. I managed to slip away unnoticed and climbed the stairs to my room. A deep trembling reaction was taking place in me. I was the only one of them—except Marc—who was convinced that it was my death which had been intended, and not poor Dacia's. It was a miracle that I could walk upstairs on legs that were slightly rubbery, but still sound, that I could reach out with a hand that was whole and open the door of my room. I was alive only because Dacia had been sacrificed, and that was a dreadful thing to be grateful for.

I closed my door behind me and stood in the center of the shabby blue rug, looking vaguely about me. At least there had been no further searching of my room. But how was I to remain in this house when I knew without doubt that someone wanted me dead? Yet if I went to Justin or Maggie with this story, I knew very well the reception I would receive. They had not believed me last night, nor would they now. Athmore blood was thicker than any ties of marriage. They would stand together and protect one another against an intruder like me. And because they stood together, I would still be in danger, with no one to believe in that danger and help me. Yet I would stay. I had seen Justin's face when he thought me dead. I had heard him call me his darling. I had something real to fight for now.

This was the time to make myself a promise. I went to my dressing table to stare into the mirror. My face was pale, my hair tangled, my eyes dark with shock—yet there was something different about the face that looked out at me. Not mere stubbornness or the ability to endure. This was an Eve who knew she was loved, knew she must have the courage to set herself against whatever evil force had struck Dacia down. This was the promise I must give myself.

In one corner of the mirror a square of white caught my eye and I stared at it, startled. A small envelope had been thrust into a corner of the glass, with my name written across its face. I picked it up and tore it open, looking first for the name that signed the few lines of handwriting.

At the bottom of the notepaper, written in a rather scrawled young hand, was the signature: "Dacia."

XI

My gaze darted to the beginning of the note and I read it through. Then read it again.

Eve:
I must talk to you alone. We'd better meet away from the house. I can't find you, so I'll leave this note and hope that you'll look for me out near the ruins where there's a bit of shelter. You often go there, so no one will give it a thought. But—and this is important—don't tell Marc you're meeting me. In fact, it's better if you don't tell anyone.

Dacia

I had not found the note in time. I had not met her after all, and now I might never know what she had to tell me. *Don't tell Marc,* she had written. If she had not made that whimsical switch to a dryer coat than her own, she might still be unhurt and as lively as ever, while I—going out to her rendezvous—might be dead.

Could it be that the note was a trap and that Marc had persuaded her to write it? There was never any telling when Dacia spoke the truth, or when she would turn facts to her own advantage. But I could not condemn her now, no matter what she might have done. The memory of her white face streaked with a scarlet that washed away in the rain was too clear.

A sudden knock at my door made me fold the note and slip it into a drawer before I called, "Come in."

Maggie walked into the room and closed the door behind her, stood with her back against it. For a strange, arrested moment we regarded each other in wary suspicion. The smell of doubt, of distrust, was in the air. This was the hostile woman I had known before I'd left Athmore that other time.

It was not the Maggie who had counseled me as Justin's wife, or who had wanted me to stay when I met her in the topiary garden on my arrival this time.

She wore her roughest country clothes. Her leather jacket was rubbed and old, the trousers worn at the knees where she had knelt at her gardening. Even her shirt had a button missing. It was as though she had snatched at whatever she could find to put on, uncaring.

"What do you hear from the hospital?" I asked.

She raised her shoulders slightly. "They're giving out no information and I couldn't get hold of Marc."

"Dacia's a fighter," I said. "If she has a chance, she'll pull through."

"She must pull through!" Maggie's concern was real, but it seemed more for Justin and Marc than for Dacia. "It's bad enough the way things are," she went on. "But if Dacia dies—"

I found my old resentment rising against Maggie's blind devotion.

"Nothing is worth Dacia's life," I said. "Or mine, for that matter. You know about the switch in coats, don't you?"

She moved away from the door and crossed to the blue chaise longue, dropping into it as though her legs were as uncertain as mine.

"Sit down, do!" she said impatiently. "Whether we like it or not, there's something we need to have out between us."

So she would not talk about the coat. I seated myself on the padded bench before the dressing table and clasped my hands together tightly.

"The matter of Marc?" I asked.

She nodded fiercely. "Yes! I'm grateful at least that you did no foolish blurting out to the police about that affair on the roof last night. And that you attempted no further accusations against Marc today."

"Why did you think I might?"

"Why wouldn't I? The beastly way you feel about him is written in your face for anyone to see."

"It would be dreadful, wouldn't it, if he caused Dacia's death, when it was mine he intended?"

"Stop that!" She spoke so sharply that I stared at her.

"You really are worried about Marc, aren't you?" I said.

"Stop it, stop it," she repeated. "Oh, you don't know Marc. You've never known him. He's capable of pranks, but not of murder." She sprang to her feet and went to a side window, flung it open upon the clatter of rain on thick vines.

"Haven't you always deceived yourself about him?" I pressed her quietly. "Isn't it time for you to face the facts about your cousin Marc?"

For a few moments she was silent, her face lifted to the spatter of rain that came through the window, as though she needed its cooling touch. When she spoke it was without turning to look at me.

"The facts, as you call them, are something I faced long ago. This makes no difference in the way I feel about him. I'm only a few years older than Justin, but I'm more than ten years older than Marc. When I used to come here on visits as a young girl he was the baby I adored. And he liked me better than any nurse or governess. I was the one who taught him games to play, and got him onto his first pony. A good thing it was I taught him to ride, as it developed, even though he never really cared for riding. When he was fourteen, he saved me from serious injury. I've not often had a horse run away with me, but we had a bad-tempered filly in those days—a proper rogue. She got out of my control and headed for the woods one morning, where she'd certainly have smashed me against the close-set trees. Marc saw us go and he came after me on his own mare and made a dramatic rescue, scooping me onto his own horse. It wasn't very gracefully managed, because in the end we both fell off and sat on the grass hugging each other and laughing, just to be alive and unhurt. He was too old to be my son, but truly he's the only son I've ever had. Or wanted."

Her story touched me, warmed me. Warmed me toward Maggie, if not toward Marc. He had never lacked courage or the ability to perform spectacular acts. But this did not make him trustworthy. I put my hand to the bruise on my temple, touching the hurt of it gingerly. I had that to remind me of what Marc was really like.

"He changed as he grew up," Maggie said sorrowfully, as if in answer to my thoughts. "Justin was always too impatient with him, too intolerant. He needed a father's hand, instead of a young cousin's. I failed him, Eve. I know I failed him. I owe him my life, yet I haven't been able to help him as I always wanted to. Whatever I try to do for him fails."

She was silent for a moment, reaching her hands into the rain, placing their cool wetness against her cheeks. There was nothing I could say. She was either trying to make me understand something, or she was trying to becloud the issue.

"Marc needs me," she went on. "He has always needed me. Perhaps that's the greatest hold he's had on me. There was no one else who did. I'd lost my husband, and I had no children. Even as a boy Justin was independent and never one to lean. Marc is the only person I've ever known who has needed me so desperately—and still does. More, perhaps, than he realizes."

"What about Nigel?" I said. "Haven't you someone new to need you now?"

Her laugh was a little too careless for my liking. "In a different way perhaps. Not that Nigel and I don't have a need and affection for each other. And we're wonderfully good friends. After all, we've known each other for a long time and we've both been lonely. Besides, he can help Marc."

Always the twisted force of her love for this only "son" she would ever have came sharply through. This was a primary drive with her. She could not help herself. I knew now that she would sacrifice Justin, and Athmore too, in order to assure her darling's safety. In this respect she could not be trusted at all. Of the words she had spoken about her relationship with Nigel, only the last had an honest ring. Nigel would be able to rescue Marc—that was what mattered. Perhaps not even Nigel, for all his quiet awareness, truly understood how she would use him to help Marc.

She went on again quite brightly, unaware of how thoroughly she betrayed her single-minded obsession. "Of course Nigel would help us now, if Justin would let him. But Justin won't have that. Once we're married, this will change. Nigel will settle enough in my name and I have my ways of making it easier for Justin to use some of what will then be my money. There will be no need for him to marry Alicia. He can't do that—he can't! It would be horrible if she came here to live. If she were mistress of Athmore, I would have to move away, and I couldn't bear that. This is my home, too. I've earned the right to live here for the rest of my life, and I won't have Alicia spoiling everything!"

Her outburst was so impassioned that I felt increasingly disturbed. Her antipathy toward Alicia seemed neurotically extreme, and the discovery that the poised, usually self-possessed Maggie Graham hid a volcano beneath that controlled exterior, made me feel a little ill. I did not need to look far for the reason.

"Alicia is using Marc!" Maggie blurted out. "She means to bludgeon Justin through him if it becomes necessary. She'll stop at nothing."

"Do you think Justin would be easily bludgeoned?" I asked.

She shrugged my words aside and turned on me. "What a fool I was to welcome your return! It was stupid of Nigel to think you might help. He believed that you could turn Justin your way as you did once before. But all you've done is stir up dreadful trouble. You've enraged Justin and you've tried to injure Marc. We were wrong about you—altogether wrong!"

She rushed across the room toward me with a suddenness that startled me, and caught up both my hands, turning them palm up so that she could pore over them. Her grasp was that of a woman who could hold a spirited horse in check, and I did not try to twist away.

"Justin hates palm reading," she said. "He would never let me look at your hands in the old days. So let me see them now. Come here to the light where I can look at them."

She frightened me a little, but I went with her to the window, rather than struggle, and held out my hands reluctantly, so that she could study the palms. I remembered this as an amusing party trick she had sometimes produced in the year I had lived at Athmore. Now she seemed in deadly earnest.

Whatever she saw she did not like. She told me to flex my fingers, relax my right hand. Then, cradling it lightly in one of hers, she traced a line with a finger, pointed to a mark across it.

"This comes while you are still young. I don't like it at all. It spells something dreadful, something—destructive. Either to you or to someone close by because of you." She looked at me intently. "Do you know what you are to Athmore? You're a lighted fuse. That mark is the explosion. Perhaps it won't happen if you go somewhere else. Consider that, Eve. How much harm are you willing to bring down on our heads? How much risk for yourself are you willing to run?"

She dropped my hand and I put it behind my back. "Palm reading doesn't convince me," I said. "But what happened last night on the roof, and what nearly happened to me today, tells me a great deal. Who else but Marc can be behind these attempts on my life?"

"Attempts on your life!" The words were scathing, but the tide of bright color that rushed to her face alarmed me further. It was fortunate that Nellie appeared in the doorway just then and caused her to check herself.

Mr. Marc was ringing from the hospital, Nellie said.

Maggie hurried off to take the call and left me alone with Nellie.

"I fetched your negative into town," the girl told me. "Enlargements take longer, but you should have it in a week. I'll pick it up when it's ready." She studied me anxiously. "You're all right, Miss Eve?"

"Not exactly," I said. "We've had a shock over what has happened to Miss Dacia."

Nellie nodded vigorously. "A hit-and-run! It's plain horrible. And right on our own premises. Of course we don't believe anyone in this house would do such a thing."

I wished I could take comfort from her words, but there was no comfort for me anywhere, except in the knowledge of Justin's love.

During the following days it was this I clung to. No matter how guarded he was with me, the truth was there to warm me and I could not be wholly despondent. There had to be a way out.

Marc was in London much of the time and he did not return for the sad occasion of Old Daniel's funeral. The rest of us went to the cemetery in a small group, and the funeral brought back to me vivid reminders of the beginning of this time of terror. Fear walked with me night and day, and was all the greater because Justin still did not believe in any real cause for the way I felt. I knew now that it had begun when I met Old Daniel in the woods. The accidental falling of a wall no longer convinced me. The old man had been hunted too.

Every night I slept with Deirdre beside my bed, and during the day I hurried through my empty wing with the dog always near me. She was my guardian and protector, my friend.

What the police believed by this time was evident. They thought that someone at Athmore had struck Dacia down by accident and panicked, and that the family had closed its ranks to protect the driver of the car. If Dacia died there would be an inquest and further investigation, but as things stood, pursuit of an answer seemed futile, and no charges were being brought. Thus we were not harassed to the extent we might have been. *Should* have been!

Dacia was moved to a London hospital at her mother's insistence, and Marc had gone to the city to stay as near her as possible. The time of her mending was uncertain, but as the days slipped by, her condition improved and we all breathed more easily. I could not believe that anyone at Athmore meant to harm Dacia.

Since her talk with me, Maggie seemed to have had second thoughts. But even as she made more friendly overtures toward me, she did not seem herself, and I had the growing feeling that something was happening beneath the surface as far as Maggie was concerned. Something not even Justin was aware of. I was paying her enough attention to note her plotting look.

As reports of Dacia's improvement came through, I began a plot of my own. I knew that I must get to London and pay her a visit. There was still the matter of her note to be considered—as soon as she was well enough to talk to me. Justin himself played into my hands. He had to go up to London himself on business, and on the morning he planned to leave, I packed my suitcase with overnight things and put it in the back of his car. Then I got into the front seat and waited for him. I said nothing to anyone. Later I would phone, but for the moment I wanted no one alerted.

When Justin came out and discovered me he put his own bag into the car and started to take mine out.

"Please!" I begged him. "I need to go to London to shop. Maggie has loaned me a coat, but I must buy one of my own. I can't go on wearing that orange thing of Dacia's. Besides, I'd like to look in on her at the hospital."

My purpose must have seemed innocent and reasonable enough. He put back my bag and got behind the wheel, wearing his most unattractive scowl. I said nothing more until we were on our way, with Athmore well behind us. I took care to sit close to the door and I kept my eyes ahead upon the road. We drove for a half hour of scowling silence on his part before I spoke.

"I do need to talk to you," I said. "Some other time, if not now. Because of what happened to Dacia, you'll have to hear me out eventually. But can't we call a truce for today and pretend we're friends instead of enemies? We can always go back to being angry with each other later."

His scowl did not fade at once, but it smoothed out gradually. The day was beautiful and I watched the hawthorn hedges run by, and delighted in glimpses of hill and meadow country, all abloom with that wonderful lushness of springtime in England. On a sunny day the green had a touch of gold to it and was never oppressive.

By the time we stopped for lunch at a wayside inn which had several hundred years of history behind its wavering floors and low, beamed ceilings, Justin's mood had turned almost agreeable. I tried not to irritate him. I stayed away from all dangerous subjects. He had the matter of his work very close to him and he was ready enough to talk about that. A breakthrough had come, he felt sure. Because of this, he must see some of the men in his company and talk over his progress. Even though he was now working for himself, the company would be behind him when it came to final production. Several of the safety features of his car were ready to be tested, and there must be no more delay.

When he spoke of his work his interest was electric and I listened with my mind, as I had never listened before. What Justin did, what he cared about, meant everything to me now.

We talked at leisure over English roast beef and Yorkshire pudding, unimaginative, but good. I ate the savory and did not turn my nose up at trifle, as once I had done. I found that this time around I was neither idealizing all that was English, nor flying to the opposite extreme of decrying it vigorously, as I had when I left. I could live with England more comfortably now, and perhaps the English could live more comfortably with me—if ever I had the chance to try again.

After lunch we did not return to the car at once. Justin knew this inn and wanted to show me about. A stream meandered pleasantly out behind, with a rustic bridge that took us across to a garden abounding in trellises and leafy arbors. The azaleas were in bloom and it was a lovely place, empty at the moment except for us. We walked in the sun and I needed no coat in this welcome warmth. I lived for the moment only, hoping that this unexpected gift would not end and drop me into emptiness again. Somehow, briefly, we were friends, if not lovers, and while this was hardly enough, I accepted the gift of the moment. In the past we had loved too recklessly without being friends.

We found smooth grass to sit upon near the edge of the stream. A great lilac bush, heavy with purple blooms, shielded us from view of the inn and shed its sweetness around us. We tossed pebbles and twigs absently into the water, and for a long while we said nothing and were strangely content. Then Justin broke the quiet spell with words which once more brought pain.

"The other day," he said, "when I saw Dacia lying on the road in your green coat, I thought it was you. I thought you were dead."

"I know," I told him.

"I felt as though half of myself had been cut away." He spoke almost wonderingly.

"You called me your darling," I reminded him.

He did not scowl or turn away from me. "And so you were to me—my very dear, lost darling."

"Yet not if I'm alive? Not at any other time?"

"Too often you are still my darling," he said gently. "Come here to me, Eve."

The way he put his arms about me told me all the truth. Yet his kiss frightened me. He did not kiss me angrily, but with tenderness, almost sadly. As if he were saying farewell.

"How can we ever work this out?" he murmured against my hair. "How can I love you, knowing how hopelessly we failed at marriage? How can I want you near me when I know what I must do to save us all—you and me and Alicia? I am to blame for the harm that has been done to both of you. I must not worsen everything now."

"But you love me and I love you!" I cried, close to tears at his gentleness. "So why must we pretend anything else?"

"Unfortunately, everything in life can't be divided as easily between the true and the false as you want it to be, my darling. There's a good deal of shading in between."

"Is it still what happened with Marc before I left Athmore that you hold against me? There were shadings there, too."

"I know," he said.

"You mean Marc told you what he did?" I asked in surprise.

Justin shook his head. "No one has told me anything. I'm past needing to be told. I know you better now. You may behave badly, foolishly, when you're angry, but I think you'd never let me down. If the outcome rested only on what you are to me, I'd have no worry. But it doesn't."

"Because you had an affair with Alicia? But that's in the past? Why must it matter now, if—"

He almost smiled as he interrupted me. "I seem to remember that Alicia mattered a great deal to you once."

"She still does," I said. "I won't pretend she doesn't. But I can live with what's past if I know it isn't the present."

"She will always matter to me," he said more gravely. "She

doesn't deserve unkindness from me, and I can't shrug her off brutally."

I was growing impatient again. "While you try to decide what you must do, how am I to stay alive? That may be more difficult than anything else."

He turned to stare at me. "What are you talking about?"

"I'm talking about something you've closed your eyes to because it concerns your brother," I said. "I'm talking about what nearly happened to me the other night on the roof, and again when Alicia's car struck Dacia. I'm not supposed to be alive. Can't you see the truth of that? Next time it may be the end of me."

Still he would not accept what I claimed. "Maggie has told me about these notions of yours. I'm sure you believe in them. This second thing coming so fast on the heels of your nightmare experience on the roof must seem to you indisputable proof. But Eve, darling, this sort of terror isn't real. Why would anyone at Athmore mean you harm?"

"Because someone is afraid I know who killed Old Daniel," I said bluntly. "How can you be sure he was killed by an accidentally falling wall? What if he was struck unconscious and then dragged over to where the wall could be pushed down on him?"

I had his full, serious attention now, though I knew I had not convinced him. Such a statement, made so abruptly, must seem altogether wild to him.

"Is it because you can't bear the thought of what Marc might be trying to do that you won't believe me?" I demanded.

"Marc saved your life that night on the roof. You could thank him for that."

We were back on the old treadmill. Our pleasant day was slipping hopelessly away while hostility and disbelief grew between us. I took Dacia's letter from my handbag and gave it to him.

"This was left in my room. I found it after Dacia went off to the hospital. I didn't read it in time to meet her as she wished. My going out there was pure chance. Someone saw her through the rain and thought it was me because she was wearing my coat. If not Marc—who? Alicia perhaps? She is the one who most wants me gone, and she knew the car was there, waiting. When she joined us she was outdoors and wet from the rain she'd been running about in. Do you believe her story?"

He must have questioned it, because he did not fly at once to her defense. Nor did he dismiss my words with his usual anger.

"I don't know," he said at length. "Something is troubling Alicia. She has been hurt by your coming, and frightened, I think. Now I must hurt her more."

I held my breath in an effort to bite back the words that wanted to pour out. If he meant what I hoped he meant, then life might begin all over again for me—for us. And this time I must deal with it more wisely. Yet what I had told Justin was true—my first purpose now was to stay alive until we could live as husband and wife again. If only I could be in Justin's arms for good, nothing could touch me.

He cast his last pebble into the stream and sprang up to pull me to my feet. Then he put both hands on my shoulders and looked at me long and quite lovingly. I let him read my eyes. I had nothing to hide from him any more. He would work this out somehow. I did not think he would let me go again.

Nevertheless, we walked to the car without touching each other, and the specter of Alicia Daven walked between us.

Once we were on our way, he said, "I'll take you to the hospital first, so you can see Dacia. You mean to ask her about the note, of course?"

I nodded. "If I can see her alone, and if she's strong enough to talk to me."

"I'll wait for you," he said shortly. "I'll want to know what she says."

For the rest of the drive to London I relaxed almost completely. For the moment I was safe. Danger had remained behind at Athmore, and I had a feeling that the burden was being taken from me. There was nothing to fear on this sunny day. Not even London traffic appalled me, as it had once done. There was no fear in me as we walked through the hospital door together and Justin spoke with authority to the woman at the reception desk.

At the door of Dacia's private room we met Marc coming out. He glanced at Justin and then regarded me in open dislike.

"What a surprise," he said. "Do you plan to go in there, Eve, and tell Dacia that I rode her down thinking it was you?"

"I'm not going to tell her anything," I said. "There are some things she wants to tell me."

He hesitated as though he would have liked to prevent me from entering, but realized there was nothing he could do to stop me. Not with Justin there. He would have gone past us down the hall without another word if Justin had not stopped him.

"Eve's staying overnight in London," he said. "I'll be at my club. Will you join us for dinner, Marc?"

He shook his head. "Sorry. I've an engagement of my own tonight. At the Club Casella. If you like, I can tell Alicia that you two are in town—together."

Justin's jaw tightened. Marc had always been able to flick him on the raw, but he did not lose his temper.

"Perhaps we'll look in and tell her ourselves," he said.

Marc went off down the hall and I spoke my alarm. "You don't really mean that!"

"Perhaps I do," he said. "We'll talk about it later."

A nurse came out of Dacia's room, and stopped to speak to us. When she stepped aside, I went in and Justin entered with me long enough to speak to the girl in the bed and give her the flowers we had picked up at a nearby stall.

The room was already bright with blooms. In London Dacia had no lack of friends and admirers, and they had evidently rallied to bring her as much cheer as they could. Her face looked strange against the white pillow. Beneath yellowing bruises it seemed paler than usual, and her eyes, without all the artificial enhancement she painted around them, looked round and dark and very young. A bandage hid most of her head and one arm was encased to the shoulder. Yet her smile was as bright and brave as ever.

I bent to kiss her cheek, and she gave a small cockney yelp and grinned at me.

"Aren't I a fright? They still won't give me a mirror, and that's probably a good thing. When I look cross-eyed I can see that my nose is changing from blue to yellow. Do you suppose blue and yellow noses could be trendy?"

"You could start a trend for anything you choose," Justin told her. He leaned to pat her hand on the coverlet, said he would wait for me downstairs and went off.

"The nose will fade," I said to Dacia. "How do you feel otherwise?"

She gave me a knowing look. "Up to talking. If they don't rush in to stick a thermometer in my mouth, or stab me with a needle. Pull up that chair, Eve. You found my note, didn't you?"

There was something so conspiratorial about her tone that I found myself lowering my own voice, as though eavesdroppers might hover outside the door.

"I found the note," I admitted, "but too late to meet you. It was only by chance that I went through the woods in that direction and stumbled over you lying in the road."

"And thanks for that! If I hadn't snatched up that coat of yours perhaps I'd still be all right. But then where would you be?"

"So you know that what happened was intended for me?"

She tried to nod, said, "Ow!" and closed her eyes for a moment against the pain. Then she opened them and went on. "Marc says you think it was him driving that car. But I don't. He's got his bad points, but he'd not do that. He's a layabout sometimes and he likes to play. But believe me, Evie, he's not up to murder—oh, he's not!"

I hoped for her sake that she was right, but she seemed to protest a little too fervently and I said nothing.

"Funny how I decided it was a good joke on you to leave you my grotty old coat and come out all nice and dry in yours," she mused. "While still making you curious enough so that you'd have to wear mine and come after me. I've been too full of plots, haven't I? Fun and games! But I got what was coming to me for that, didn't I?"

I inched my chair nearer to the bed. "You didn't see who was driving the car—not even a glimpse?"

"Not a thing!" Dacia was emphatic. "I heard a car earlier, far off, but what with the rain I didn't know it was near till the last minute. I can't even remember being hit. The next I knew I woke up in the hospital with a nurse jabbing something in my arm. But let's not waste time, Evie. It's other things I wanted to tell you. I thought they might be useful in some way. Marc's no good at holding out on me. I wangled everything out of him that I could. About that awful Leo Casella and the tricks he's been playing around Justin's workshop. It's true that Leo could get in through the back door and he hid on the roof, or in the towers, or whatever tower room was empty. You almost caught him once, I guess. He would come down at night, and then go straight back up before anyone was onto him. From the roof he could watch his chance. Though Old Daniel nearly caught him too."

"If Marc knows this and hasn't told Justin, that's pretty awful, isn't it?"

"Marc didn't know for sure. He suspected somebody was using the roof, because of the smoking in the tower rooms and all. He was trying to catch him on his own. Then when Nigel found those things up there and Leo was seen around, Marc went off to talk to Alicia. She wouldn't tell him a thing, and she made him shut up about it besides."

"But what was Leo trying to do?" I pressed her. "Why hasn't he been arrested?"

"He was paid to upset things as much as he could, and Marc knows Alicia was behind what happened. Maybe that's why Justin hasn't had Leo picked up by the police—because of what might come out in any sort of investigation."

I could only shake my head in bewilderment. "Whatever Alicia wants, it's surely not interference with Justin's work."

"Why not?" Dacia's brown eyes were unblinking, knowledgeable. "Couldn't it be this is the way to make Justin need her money even more? After all, it was only mischief—no real harm done. Not even with that fire. And now Leo's been sent back to London, so there'll be no more trouble."

"Marc ought to go to Justin with this whole story."

Dacia tried to shake her head and winced again. "Not when all Alicia has to do is point a finger and ask payment of the money that's dribbled through Marc's hands at her gambling tables. She's let him have his head, you know, and he's used no sense at all. He's got gambler's fever. Alicia has it too, but in a different way. It's like dope. He always believes the next time round will bring him a winner, and he'll get everything back. If ever I marry him—which isn't likely—I'll not let him keep a farthing in his pocket. Of course if Justin's experiments work out, then Justin might make enough money so that he could pick up the ticket without any trouble. And then Alicia'd have no more hold over Marc, or over Justin either. But if Marc tries anything now, his house of cards will tumble around his ears, and he knows it. He's running scared, Evie. I'm worried about him. It might be better if he'd tell Justin everything, but neither he nor Maggie wants to do that. Maggie especially—she wants to protect Marc at all costs, and goodness knows what Justin might do. So Alicia has Marc just where she wants him."

"She'd never have that sort of hold over Justin," I said. "It's not Alicia's money he'd marry her for."

Dacia wriggled about to the accompaniment of a few more "Ows," and gave me a long stare. Then she changed the subject abruptly.

"Justin brought you to London today, didn't he? How are you doing with him, Evie?"

This was not what I could talk about, and I shook my head in warning.

"Is this everything you wanted to tell me?" I asked.

"It's all I have to tell. What I wanted was to have you say what I'd better do with it. Go to Justin, or what? But that doesn't matter any more. Not with what's happened to me. All that matters to me now is getting well, getting back to my job. I've *had* it at Athmore. That's no life for me—or for Marc either."

Somehow I had to give Marc his due. "I think he's genuinely in love with you," I said. "What happened to you has upset him badly."

"Sure, I know. But he'll get over it. He's got a roving eye. I know that too. I guess it was the idea of *me*—Dacia Keane! —visiting at Athmore, running around with Marc North and all his swell friends that went to my silly head."

"It's not such a silly head," I told her. "But you'd better keep it quiet for a while and stay out of trouble. After I found you I kept remembering what you said about tomorrow never coming. It was an especially awful feeling—being to blame for what happened to you."

She held out her good hand. "I like you, Evie. I hope your tomorrow will be a fine one. But take care, do you hear? It's better if you don't go back to Athmore. There's something desperate going on."

Desperate or not, I knew very well that Athmore would call me back until, in one way or another, everything was settled between Justin and me. Nothing would make me give up now.

A nurse came in, and I left Dacia and went downstairs where Justin waited for me. We said nothing until we were in his car, moving into the stream of London traffic.

"Can you tell me about it?" he asked.

On the way down from Dacia's room I had decided what to do. There had been too much holding back of the truth from Justin. He must be told about Marc, and about Maggie's notions and strange behavior. Even about Alicia— though it might set him against me again if I went into that.

"Let's go where we can talk," I said.

He left his car at a garage and we walked across busy London streets toward the river. The Victoria Embankment looked all too familiar. Justin and I had walked there before.

The tall iron lampposts cast shadows across the cobblestones and the plane trees fluttered their leaves above us. We sat on the low wall and watched the barge traffic on the river. Justin waited, not prodding me, but I found it hard to begin. Across the bend of the Thames the Houses of Parliament and the tower that housed Big Ben stood out bold and warm in the afternoon sun. I let my eyes and my thoughts be distracted.

"You'd better tell me," Justin said at last.

There was no way in which to put any of this gently. Besides, it was all hearsay, as I tried to make clear to him. Perhaps he could sort truth from lies, reality from Dacia's imaginative approach. I mentioned Marc's grave debts and how Alicia had apparently been carrying him for a long while. I told him what I knew of Maggie's concerns and fears, and her conviction that she could save everything by marrying Nigel.

Passersby gave us hardly a glance as they hurried along the embankment. London was like New York in that. Strangers were no curiosity here, and though Americans could usually be picked out with ease, no one troubled to stare at me. I talked and Justin listened, making only a slight movement of impatience or disbelief now and then. I had so few facts to give him, but adding up the words of other people still presented a thoroughly disturbing picture. He said nothing, even when I was through.

My story done, we walked toward Piccadilly and Half Moon Street. Justin took me to the same small hotel where we'd stayed after we were married, and checked me in. He had appointments this afternoon, he told me, and he would be busy at dinnertime. But this evening he would call for me, and I would go with him to the Club Casella.

We stood in the dim lobby of the hotel, while an elderly bellboy waited to take me to my room.

"Why?" I asked him. "Why do you want me to go with you to the club?"

The look in his eyes gave me new hope. "Perhaps there's something to be smoked out," he said. "If Marc is to be there tonight, I want to be there too. And you with me. After all, you've made some serious accusations."

"But Alicia—" I began.

He said curtly, "I'll call for you at ten o'clock. The casino doesn't open till then," and went off across the lobby.

I signaled the waiting bellboy and took the lift upstairs to my room.

The time before ten o'clock seemed to stretch ahead endlessly, though not because I dreaded to see the hour come. In fact, I was eager for it now. I was no longer afraid of Alicia.

During the afternoon I mapped my campaign of feminine strategy. I cashed some traveler's checks and went shopping. First I bought a lightweight coat—popcorn, stitched with black wool, and as smart as today's London. Then I hunted for a dress to wear to the Club Casella. It took me awhile, but I found what I wanted at last in a little shop in Knightsbridge.

When I had made my purchases, from sandals to evening pouch, I brought the packages back to my room and scattered them across the bed. These were my armor for whatever lay ahead. That anything might defeat me tonight was a possibility I would not accept.

Since I did not want to dine out alone in London, I had a tray sent to my room. Afterward I could only wait while the minutes ticked along toward ten o'clock. Of course I started dressing long before then, and took my time.

When I was ready I studied myself in the full-length mirror on the bathroom door, and found the dress right for me. The soft, light crepe draped to a cowl neckline, with a deep V at the back. In front it went winging out from a high inverted pleat that fell to the toes of my sandals. There were no sleeves and the color was a marvelous lime. Without being strident, it was a dress of the moment—not for Dacia, not for Alicia, but for me. When I moved before the mirror the gown stirred sweetly about me, soft as springtime music. I felt like moonlight in it—an enchanted, singing moonlight!

There was no need to pile my hair on top of my head. I brushed it to a sable gloss and let it fall to my shoulders in the fashion Justin liked best. I had brought no jewelry with me and I wore none. The dress and I complemented each other, were meant to be. Only another woman could understand that feeling of being armed in beauty, and know how important it was for any encounter.

In the mirror my very face seemed different. I wore only a touch of lipstick, but my look was bright, unshadowed by self-doubting. I knew my direction now and I did not mean to be stopped from my course. Tonight I too must be a gambler—for the highest of stakes.

When the telephone rang I lifted the receiver and heard Dacia's voice. She was calling from the hospital, and there was relief in her tone as I answered.

"Evie! It's jolly lucky I caught you! Marc says you may be going to the club with Justin tonight."

"I am going," I told her. "He's picking me up in a little while."

"That's fine! But I've just learned something from Marc and I think you ought to know before you go there tonight —that Alicia has lost the Club Casella."

Her words were hard to believe. "What do you mean— lost?"

"It's been taken away from her. Apparently her management has been bad in a business sense and her share of it is gone. There's a new owner. Not only that, but she may be in a bad way all around. Marc is scared, Evie. He doesn't know who has taken over the club, or what will happen if his debts are called in."

"I've told Justin everything," I said. "He knows about Marc's debts and whatever else I could tell him."

She was silent for a moment. "I expect that's for the best. All this had to tumble down for Marc sometime. But Justin doesn't know about this change of hands at the club. He'll go there tonight believing that Alicia is still in charge. She hasn't had time to move out yet, you know. She'll be there, Marc says. Had you better warn Justin?"

"I don't know," I said. "I'll have to think about this."

I could almost see Dacia nodding her bandaged head and wincing at the movement. "Yes. It's best to take one step at a time. And—Evie—"

"I'm here," I said.

"Evie—maybe this is big game you'll be trying for tonight. I just wanted you to know that I'm betting on you to win out."

I smiled at the telephone. "If you're going to bet, bet high, Dacia. You should see my new dress!"

She laughed softly. "Good for you! But take care, Evie."

She rang off and I stood with my hand on the telephone, thinking of what she had told me. If Alicia no longer owned the Club Casella, and Justin did not yet know about this, there were ramifications that had alarming possibilities. I couldn't know what effect this might have upon Justin, and the fact made me uneasier than ever. A strong enemy might be fought boldly and the matter of mercy need not enter in. But how would Justin react to an Alicia who was going down to destruction—if matters had indeed gone that far?

The phone rang again, startling me, and as I picked up the

receiver, I knew what I must do. Justin must of course be warned about what had happened. He must have time to think about his own course of action, whatever it might be. I spoke into the receiver.

Justin was waiting for me downstairs. I put on my coat and picked up my purse, gave myself a last look in the mirror before I walked toward the lift—not hurrying, not flying toward a love I needed to support me, but accepting with a new assurance that he was indeed my love and that whatever happened I must support him. Knowing as well that I had no other hand to play except that which I dealt myself.

XII

In the cab on the way to the club I told Justin the bare facts of Dacia's phone call, and found him less surprised than I'd expected.

"I know Alicia's been worried about something lately," he said. "But she would neither tell me what it is, nor let me help. She's always been proud and self-reliant."

There was nothing I could safely say, and we were silent for the rest of the ride. Justin's manner toward me was curiously blank, as though he too was taking one careful step at a time and meant to commit himself to nothing.

The Mayfair townhouse which the Club Casella occupied was discreetly residential in appearance. One rang the doorbell and waited for admission. Since Justin was known, we were invited into a small Georgian anteroom with classic pillars and a marble floor. There an attractive girl took our wraps, and as I slipped from my coat Justin really looked at me for the first time that evening.

"You're beautiful tonight," he said, and his eyes were softly tender.

He had given me the compliment every woman wants to earn. He had not said my dress was beautiful—I already knew that. He had added up the total and given me what I longed to hear.

We went through double doors into the main gaming room. Other rooms appeared to lead off it, each given over to different play. At the back a graceful stairway curved upward to open upon an oval gallery overlooking the gaming tables below.

The impact of sound was immediate, in spite of an apparent effort to contain the noise by means of draperies and soft carpets. Around the tables for roulette, chemin-de-fer— "chemmy," as Dacia called it—blackjack and other games,

Alicia's elegantly dressed clientele played with the casual air of well-mannered people. Those of London's swinging social set who frequented the better casinos were well-to-do, and not especially young. Gambling at such places was not for the impecunious. The croupiers were properly suave, their calls low-voiced, their manners impeccable.

A great deal of richly elegant red and deep gold had been used about this lower room, abetted by the clever use of mirrors. Nothing was strident in the manner of Las Vegas, and this seemed, on the surface at least, a totally different world. Even the lighting, focused effectively above the tables where it mattered most, carried a pinkish tinge that was flattering to the women.

Several attendants and some of the guests spoke to Justin, and where it was necessary, he presented me as Mrs. North. For the moment I was his wife, yet I did not know where we were going, or what he might intend. I took each step with care and asked no questions.

As we made our way through the room toward the stairway at the rear I looked about for Marc, but did not see him in the main room. We stopped at none of the gaming tables but went immediately upstairs. While the club served no suppers, since Mayfair was filled with fine restaurants, there were small tables scattered about this upper room, where guests might sit and order something to drink. Again, deep crimson had been used lavishly in walls and floor coverings, with the white of table linen furnishing an accent of contrast. In the center of the room the open oval, railed in red velvet, overlooked the gaming area below. Here tables stood close to the rail, where one might look down through the opening at the play and players beneath.

Justin moved toward a particular table, and I saw that Alicia and Marc sat opposite each other next to the rail, apparently engaged in tense conversation. Tonight she made a striking figure with her high-piled golden hair threaded with silver ribbon. The silver-satin sheath she wore beneath cloud-gray chiffon was slashed down the front with a vivid zigzag of pink-and-yellow lightning in a mod design. Her bare white shoulders were rounded as the contours of Grecian marble and she looked altogether beautiful, but for once I attempted no comparison between Alicia and me. Whatever I was must be a compound of my own faults and virtues, my own style and manner—even my own ability to grow.

As Marc bent toward Alicia, I saw that his face was

flushed, his eyes a bright blue, and I knew he must have been
drinking for some time. He saw us before she did and stared
with a look which bore me nothing but animosity. In Alicia's
face there was obvious strain, a tightening about her eyes and
mouth which she tried to erase when she looked up and saw
Justin. For me—though my presence there must have
disturbed her—she had only a stiff smile. I felt quite calm
and ready for the subtly scathing little remarks at which she
was so adept.

She held out her hand to Justin and tried to draw him into
a chair beside her, but he would not sit down.

"I'd like to talk with you," he said, sounding formal and
stiff.

She rose at once and her alarm was evident. "Of course,"
she said in her light, English voice. "In my office, if you
like."

There would be no encounter between us after all. This
was a frightened woman, a woman disarmed, and therefore
all the more dangerous. Open conflict would be easier to
face. I seated myself at the table across from Marc feeling
like a warrior who has just been told there will be no battle
and he can go home to bed. Or was it only that styles of warfare changed and the battle would now continue in a different
way and on different grounds, leaving me still unprepared?

Marc ordered the vermouth I asked for, but I hardly
spoke to him. I leaned an arm on the velvet rail and watched
the animated scene below. All of me was waiting—arrested
until Justin finished his talk with Alicia and I could know the
outcome. From where I sat I was able to see the door
through which they had disappeared, and little else interested
me.

Marc was more voluble as he regarded the gaming tables
below us with unconcealed resentment.

"They've barred me from the play downstairs," he said,
disbelief in his voice. "I'm not to be allowed at the tables tonight!"

I brought myself back from breathless waiting. "Isn't that
natural with a new owner? Considering what you owe the
club?"

He gave me a surprised look. "What have you heard? Do
you know who has bought the club?"

I shook my head. I had no intention of betraying Dacia as
my source of information.

"You might as well know," I went on, "that I've told Justin how serious your debts are. He should have been informed before this. There's been too much held back that is really his concern."

Marc's flush faded to a sickly pallor. "What an absolute fool you are! Are you trying to destroy him?"

"Aren't you doing pretty well at that? Perhaps he needs to be put in a better position to defend himself."

"Justin always comes out on top," Marc said. "He always has. So far."

I did not like the sound of that. Our drinks came, but we did not toast each other. I tasted my vermouth and thought about Justin. One step at a time, as Dacia had said. I must hold to that.

The intensity of Marc's dislike for me was almost tangible tonight. It made me remember the roughness of his hands that night on the roof. But nothing could happen to me in this place. It was only necessary not to be alone with him when others were not around.

"It was clever of you," he said without warning, "to have an enlargement made of that picture you took near the old ruins."

I must have gaped at him, for he recovered himself enough to smile with something of his old mockery.

"What luck for me that I happened on Nellie when she went to fetch it for you," he said. "Though you mustn't blame Nellie. She didn't want to give it up to me. I'm afraid I annexed it, rather. Interesting, that picture. Odd that you should have happened on the fellow so close to the time when that wall toppled over on poor Old Daniel."

This was a thoroughly disturbing turn of events.

"Then you know who is in the picture?" I asked.

He shook his head. "Couldn't make a thing of it—what with that smudge of bushes hiding the outline. But I turned it over to Alicia tonight, since she's been dying to get her hands on it. She claims to know who it is and she seems excited about it—though she won't tell me why."

"She insisted to me that it was Maggie I'd caught in the picture," I said.

"Oh, did she? In that case I'll need to have another talk with her. Come to think of it, she didn't mention whether the person you snapped was male or female. At least I can say what I like to her now—with the club out of her hands. Perhaps there are a few old scores to pay up with Alicia Daven."

Nevertheless, I could see that my words had worried him.

Perhaps he was mentally trying out the image of Maggie in his memory of the enlargement, testing whether she might fit the picture. Would he consider it convenient for him if she did?

I let him speculate and after another glance at the closed door of Alicia's office, gave my attention to the scene directly below the place where I sat. Lights fell upon a roulette table and upon the heads of men and women awaiting the turn of the wheel. A mingling of perfume and cigarette smoke drifted up to me, with the volume of sound increasing as the evening picked up momentum.

In spite of well-mannered, elegantly dressed guests, in spite of the pretense that losing a good deal of money did not matter, the room seemed pervaded by that curious excitement which hangs upon the turn of a wheel, the flip of a card. One caught it in the brightness of a fixed gaze, the reaching movement of a hand, the tensely expelled breath.

Beyond the bright circle of lights about the table I could glimpse the entryway, where double doors opened upon the foyer, and as I glanced in that direction the doors parted and a woman came through and stood gazing about.

I gasped and touched Marc's arm. "Look. It's Maggie!"

He turned toward the rail and stared down at the woman in black who stood regarding the room with her usual air of assurance. But this was a Maggie I hardly knew. Her short hair had been brushed expertly into a lacquered, silver-streaked mound, and her tailored clothes had been changed for something more glamorously feminine. Her black crepe dress was long and hid her sturdy, sportswoman's legs, and for once she was wearing high-heeled black satin sandals. Around her throat and at her ears the Athmore pearls glowed softly rich.

"Good Lord!" Marc said softly, "Maggie has got herself up to the nines. I wonder what's up? She never comes here. Hates the place."

She seemed to be unescorted, but clearly the fact did not embarrass her. With the same quiet air of assurance she took a few steps into the room and waited for an attendant to come to her.

"I didn't know she was in London," I said.

Marc answered shortly. "I brought her with me when I came up today. I thought she needed a bit of a rest from old Nigel, and she wanted a look at Dacia for herself."

I had not known he'd been home, not having seen him around, and I wondered where he had stayed.

As we watched, the attendant reached her and she spoke to him, then continued into the room with an air of interest which did not seem in the least self-conscious. But then—Maggie would be at home anywhere. I had always known that. Only in the last week had I seen her façade of self-possession begin to crack under strain.

"Let's go rescue her," Marc said. "In spite of the way she looks, she's a fish out of water."

As I went downstairs with him I wondered how well Marc, or any of us knew Maggie. I had not felt easy about her since our encounter in the blue lady's room.

She had stopped near one of the roulette tables looking on at the game with more interest than I'd have expected, considering her often expressed distaste for all forms of gambling. The wheel whirred, the ball rolled and came to rest on red. Maggie nodded to someone at the table and glanced toward the stairs. Noting our descent, she came toward us without hurry.

"Hello, Eve. Hello, Marc darling," she said, her manner so high-spirited that I felt more at a loss than ever. She might be a fish out of water, but it seemed she would enjoy learning how to conduct herself in this new element.

Marc kissed her cheek. "So you've finally decided on the primrose path? You look marvelous. Will you come upstairs and have a drink to hasten your descent?"

"I might, at that," she told him cheerfully. "Do you mean you aren't playing tonight, Marc?"

He had brightened momentarily at the sight of her, but now gloomy resentment returned. "I've been barred from play. Wait till you hear! Somebody's bought Alicia out and orders have been given to keep me away from the tables."

Maggie smiled at him brightly. "Good! I'm glad my directions have been carried out. How do you like me as the new owner of Club Casella?"

We both stared at her. Marc recovered first and as we reached the foot of the stairs he put an arm about her, laughing and more than a little drunk. Quite evidently Maggie's news had relieved his anxiety.

"Maggie! Angel! Why, didn't you tell me on the way to London today? You can't imagine how I've been suffering over who might take over when Alicia stepped out. I've been having foreclosure nightmares ever since I heard, and Alicia wouldn't tell me a word."

Quietly Maggie extricated herself from his clasp. "Those were my orders too, since I wanted to tell you myself. Because now, my dear, you're going to pay up. Every last farthing, Marc! And without recourse to Justin. In the meantime you'll do no playing at the tables."

As I had always known, there was a toughness in Maggie when the chips were down. She might be soft of heart and yielding toward those she loved, but once her mind was made up and a direction chosen, she had all the determination of a true Athmore.

If Marc had sudden misgivings, he did not show them. "Come along and tell me all about it." He took her arm and urged her up the stairs, bantering and merry, still congratulating both himself and Maggie. All his life he had been getting around her, and he had no reason to think it would be any different now, no matter what she said.

She turned back to me when Marc would have ignored me, and held out her hand so that we could go together up the stairs. It was not so much a friendly gesture as it was one of natural courtesy.

Alicia's table was still empty. The conference between her and Justin seemed to be going on for a very long while, I thought uneasily. Maggie and I sat next the rail and Maggie leaned upon it with a proprietary air, as though fully enjoying this new and intoxicating role of power.

Marc sat between us. "Now, then—tell all!" he said. "Where did you find the coin of the realm, Maggie dear? This was Nigel's doing, I suppose?"

Maggie regarded him a bit distantly, as though she sensed the need for remaining on guard and not being beguiled by him.

"Of course," she agreed. "We're going to be married soon, and I asked for a wedding gift ahead of time. I think I rather bowled him over when I asked him to buy the Club Casella for me—but he came through nobly. He has managed all the negotiations, though he has warned me straight through that I am not getting a very good bargain. Alicia hasn't been clever about money, it seems. For some time now she's lived off her dwindling capital, and fooled us all about the wealth she would bring to Athmore. I don't like that, Marc. I don't like it at all."

"*You* don't like it!" Marc said a bit wildly.

"Besides this, she's been carrying your debts at the club to a ridiculous degree. Why, Marc—why? What have you been doing for her that she's had to buy you this way?"

Marc seemed to be struggling with his own rising fury, and I wished Maggie would stop baiting him while he was the worse for the liquor he had been drinking.

"Now there'll be no more piling up of debts," she went on, paying no attention to signs of warning. "Nor will Justin now have to take on your debts, as he would surely have done if I hadn't interfered to prevent it."

"I haven't asked him to take them on!" Marc snapped.

She went on gently, maddeningly reasonable. "Sometimes a foster mother makes mistakes in the giving of her affection. Sometimes she indulges foolishly and for too long—perhaps trying to buy affection in return. Which is always a mistake —as she may realize too late."

Marc glared at her. "If that's the way you feel, I'm sorry for Nigel. Because he's making the same error, isn't he? Paying a high price for which he may not get good measure— trying to buy *your* affection!"

For once Maggie's control wavered, and I knew that Marc had cut her to the quick. With Maggie, those who belonged to Athmore came first, and their welfare was worth whatever price she might have to pay. Even if the man she married was short-changed. But she would not like to have this pointed out.

Part of my attention was still upon the door of Alicia's office, so that I noticed the moment it opened. Justin and Alicia came out and walked around the end of the oval. She did not come with Justin to our table, but parted from him at the head of the stairs. Her fair, handsomely coiffed head was held carefully high as she went down to the lower room. If the groove along Justin's left cheek had deepened, he showed no other display of emotion as he watched her go.

He came to our table, apparently unsurprised to find Maggie there, and kissed her cheek. Then he drew up another chair.

"How do you like owning this den of iniquity?" he asked.

So Alicia had told him. He knew it all now.

"I rather like it," Maggie said, and glanced affectionately at Marc, who merely glared at them both.

"You know, of course," Justin said quietly, "that you've

bought the entire weight of Marc's indebtedness and that it must be paid off."

She nodded, still confident and quite aware that she was giving generously. "Of course. I've just told Marc so. He'll have to pay up the whole thing. I shall expect to get every pound back from him. He's been very naughty indeed for much too long a time, and now he must pay the piper—me."

"Plus interest?" Justin said, and Marc scowled at his brother.

"Oh, no! I shall waive that, of course. Nigel doesn't mind. He's being very good to me." She glanced reproachfully at Marc. "And I do mean to make him a good wife."

"I suppose you'll carry off whatever you set out to do," Justin told her evenly. "Even to trying your hand at running the Club Casella. But you must know that it would take Marc years to pay back what he now owes, if indeed he could ever manage it—which I doubt. And you're unlikely to make a success of the club without Alicia's personal touch to carry it off with the clientele. So there'll be little income here."

"That doesn't matter," Maggie said. "I probably shan't keep it anyway. Nigel knows exactly how I feel about all this."

"Perhaps the thing none of you grasps is how I feel," Justin said. "If you're making some sort of grand sacrifice for Marc's sake, Maggie, you needn't. Because I shall of course see that you and Nigel are paid back myself. And as promptly as possible. With proper interest."

Maggie stared at him, obviously shaken. Marc looked both angry and shocked, suddenly realizing where Justin was heading.

"My dear—no!" Maggie cried.

"The answer is yes," Justin said. "If my current efforts work out as I hope, then this may not be impossible. If they don't, then we must sell Athmore. There could be worse solutions than that."

Abruptly Marc pushed back his chair and stood up. "If you'll excuse me, I want a talk with Alicia myself."

"Wait—" Maggie began, "—Marc, do be careful. Don't do anything reckless!"

Marc was already running down the stairs. We watched over the rail, saw him emerge below and stand looking about the lower room. He was more than a little drunk, and furiously angry.

From our vantage point we could see Alicia before he did, as she moved among her guests, speaking a word here, shaking hands there. Heads turned to watch her, and there was a whispering as she moved on. The news must have sped around the room as she came among her friends saying goodby. When she moved, the great zigzag of lightning down the front of her dress flashed beneath the gray clouds of chiffon, seeming to signal coming storm. I had the troubled feeling that in defeat Alicia Daven might be a more effective foe than ever and I turned my gaze back to Justin's face.

He was watching her too, though I could not read his look, and when he spoke to Maggie the deadly chill I remembered was back in his voice.

"I think we both know why this was done," he said. "We are both aware of the subtle possibilities in punishment and revenge. Though I'd not have expected you to be so bitter, Maggie."

She turned her back on the rail with its view of the crowd below, her eyes dark with alarm. "But Justin—Justin dear!—this was for you and Marc! That's all I ever intended—to help you out of a serious jam."

"There is also the destruction of a woman to be considered," Justin said, his tone so cold that my heart turned over at the sound of it. "Alicia told me a great deal tonight. The Club Casella has been slipping from her hands for some time. Leo, its former owner, has not, apparently, been trustworthy. And she has lost seriously on other investments as well. Now she loses hope as well as everything else. You understand this, don't you, Maggie? It's what you intend, isn't it? To punish Alicia. That's really your aim."

Maggie's gaze fell. "I—I don't know much about the business side of this. I only know that she was never worth your interest in her. As a wife her presence at Athmore would be intolerable."

"You'd prefer Eve as my wife?" Justin said. "Is that what you mean? Is that why you brought her back? Because you believe that Eve and I could never make it together and eventually there would be a divorce? Is that what you hope for? Then everything could go on as before, with you the chatelaine of Athmore for the rest of your life, even though you have to marry Nigel to accomplish this. Of course it would be insufferable for you if I brought Alicia there to live. And we both know why."

"Justin—you don't understand!" Maggie cried. "I've thought only of your welfare, and Marc's, all along. I've thought only—"

"I don't care about welfare purchased by arrangements which manipulate my life and injure others," Justin said. "Now, because such arrangements have been made, I'm committed more than ever to the course you meant to block."

I sat very still, trying to understand—sure only that the outcome of this duel meant the difference between life and death for me.

Justin must have seen my face, for he reached across the table to cover my hand. "I love you," he said quietly. "Yet this has changed everything. There's too much that I'm to blame for in the past. Old debts have multiplied. Prior debts. And I'm not talking about money."

I knew very well what he meant. Alicia. She was the debt he must honor. Now that Maggie had successfully ruined her, Justin would be committed to her all the more. I did not question his love for me, but without my lifting a finger I had been disarmed and left helpless.

Numbly I looked over the railing, seeking for the woman who had always been my rival, and who had now won, with Maggie's unintended help. I glimpsed pink lightning and gray chiffon, and saw Marc come up to her, take her rather roughly by the arm. She did not resist him and they moved together toward the door, disappearing through it.

Justin and Maggie had not noticed. Maggie was closer to crumpling than I had ever seen her, defeated by Justin's words, by the result of her own scheming. The temptation to say nothing of what I had seen was strong. Marc was in a rage, and if anything happened to Alicia—

I put my hand on Justin's arm. "Alicia has just left the club with Marc. I think he forced her to go with him."

Justin sprang up and hurried toward the stairs. When Maggie caught my arm and would have held me in my chair, I pulled away.

"Let him go," she said. "There's nothing more to be done."

But I was coming to life again. I could not sit by and remain helpless.

"There's a great deal to be done!" I cried and knew as I hurried toward the stairs that I had spoken those words before. I did not look back, or know that Maggie followed until she came through the double doors into the foyer. Justin was there talking to Leo Casella. When Leo saw Maggie he touched a finger to his forelock and grinned at her impudently, his dark eyes flashing mockery.

" 'Evening, Boss," he said.

There was something about his impudence that jarred me. It was as though he occupied a place of privilege and knew very well that she would not reprove him. But I had no time to think about that now.

Justin pushed past the fellow, and Maggie and I followed him to the street. On the sidewalk Justin explained briefly.

"Leo tells me that Marc and Alicia have started back to Athmore in Marc's car. I'm going after them. I don't know what Marc intends, but he's drunk and I don't trust him. You two can come with me, if you want to."

"I'll come," I said without hesitation.

Justin held out his hand to me, and his clasp was strong and sure. Behind us, as we ran toward a taxi, Maggie stumbled in her high heels, but she came too. Somehow she had roused herself and there seemed a new urgency in her. That meant she had thought of something—and I did not trust her when she was driven by secret purpose.

When we reached Justin's garage, it was nearly twelve o'clock. It would take nearly four hours to reach Athmore, and Marc and Alicia had a good headstart.

XIII

Once the environs of London were left behind, the night was dark and sometimes a little misty. Most of the time I could see no stars. The headlights of the car rushed ahead cleaving the blackness, seeming to cut a swath through hedgerows and trees and fields. Eventually there were hills, and the roads grew even more winding. Sometimes we caught the shine of water as we swept past ponds or lakes. When we could we skirted the larger towns, and slowed for crooked village streets.

For a while we drove in silence and Justin held the wheel as though he would urge his own desire for speed upon the car. He drove well and never recklessly, but we were pushing to the limit of what these winding English roads would take. I did not know what it was he so feared that lay ahead. There was no chance of our overhauling Marc, who always drove as though he bore a charmed life—and tonight was in no condition for such driving. In the back seat Maggie hardly stirred, and I did not look at her during that first hour.

But we could not go on like that, endlessly bound by tension. We could not, by hurling ourselves at the road, stop whatever might be happening on ahead. Unexpectedly, it was Maggie who broke the strain of that long silence.

"Isn't it time you stopped feeling guilty about Alicia?" she asked Justin. "You've held yourself responsible for steps she has taken deliberately with her eyes open."

"I am responsible," Justin said. "I made what has happened possible."

"Nonsense!" Maggie cried. "It's the chess game all over again—your taking the blame when the rook was destroyed, though you weren't at fault and we all guessed as much."

"Marc has always been too much protected," I put in bitterly.

207

"Marc? Who's talking about Marc?" Maggie challenged.

"But it was Marc who destroyed the rook, and—"

"Of course it wasn't!" Justin snapped.

I moved my hands despairingly. "Why can't you say what you mean? Why can't we speak the truth for once—all of us?"

Justin reached out to clasp his hand about my own tense fingers. "Hush, darling. Not now. Be patient for a little while longer, Eve. The game isn't over and I'm worried about the next play."

After that there was silence again, with only the wind rushing past through the night. Sometimes the stars came from behind the clouds, but there was no moon. Neither Justin nor I spoke again. It was Maggie who once more broke the silence, miles later.

"Why are you in such a desperate hurry, Justin? What does it matter now if Marc and Alicia have gone home? What are you worried about?"

He answered her coolly. "I'm concerned about two things. One of them is leaving Alicia with Marc. He'll undoubtedly blame her for what happened to the club. The other is my concern for my car and my workshop back at Athmore, if Marc gets home ahead of me, as he's certain to—"

Maggie laughed unpleasantly. "You've never been fair to Marc. Do you really think he'd touch your car?"

"I don't know," said Justin, his tone grim.

I remembered Marc's words—that Justin had always won, so far.

After a while the headlights and the rushing wind made me sleepy and I tried to curl sideways with my cheek against the back of the seat so I might doze a little. But every now and then I'd jerk awake and find that I'd been drowsing with my head against Justin's arm. I wanted to stay that way and I knew he wanted me there. But I could not stay—not yet. After a while I sat up very straight, making myself as uncomfortable as I could in order to keep starkly awake. But that was even worse because of the turns and twists my thoughts could take, the unanswerable questions that kept rising in my mind.

Alicia, wealthy and secure, able to fend for herself, was one thing. Alicia, cheated of all she had, or losing it disastrously, was something else. Justin would not walk out completely on an Alicia who needed him in her desperation, and somehow I would not have loved him as much if he had been willing to. But how far must he go in helping her—how far?

Once we stopped at a hotel in a good-sized town and found someone to make us tea, bring us a bit of stale cake, permit us to break the strain of urgent night driving. But even then we drank quickly, scalding our throats, choking on dry crumbs—and were back in the car as quickly as possible.

At least we were awake now, and Maggie was talking again, harking back to what Justin had said at the club.

"Whatever happens, you can't lose Athmore, Justin. You can't go down such a foolish road!"

"Athmore won't be lost," Justin said. "The house is a piece of England. It will go on for a long while, in any case. Does it matter, really, who lives there now?"

I heard my own voice, objecting. "It matters to you!"

Justin kept his eyes on the road. "Who am I? How long does any one man last? I'm already older than John Edmond Athmore was when he died, and his death had no effect on Athmore Hall. It did not burn down till long after, and out of the ashes sprang the present Athmore."

Maggie answered him quietly. "If this house ends, no one will build it up again. Those times are gone forever."

"I know," Justin said, and we drove on in silence.

He was Athmore now. No one else would preserve it with such love and care. But this talk of burning houses disturbed me, made me anxious and uneasy. There were often flames when I dreamed of Athmore.

I began to strain my eyes to watch for the place from which we could see the house long before it was reached.

A lopsided moon was up by this time, and it appeared intermittently through scattered clouds. The roads grew more familiar. We could see out across fields, and there was no glow of anything burning. At last the distant outlines of Athmore rose in a dark hump on the horizon, briefly glimpsed before woods closed about it. The house was there and I breathed more easily. One dread could be dismissed.

To my surprise, Justin did not turn down the road that led toward the house. Instead he chose a side road that wound off in another direction. In a moment I realized that our detour would take us to Grovesend.

Maggie stirred in the back seat and sat up to look around She must have noted our change of course, but she said nothing. Her angry impulse to prick at Justin and make him

equally angry had died away. Once when I looked back at
her I saw her face, white and strained in the moonlight, and
knew that she was now every bit as tense as Justin. It was not
a burning of the house either of them feared, but something
more ominous, and even more dreadful because it concerned
someone near to them both. Marc, who was brother and foster son.

Alicia's woods and rhododendron hedges grew high, blocking out any sight of her house from afar. We were upon it
suddenly and Justin drove around the end of the hedge and
stopped before her door. Marc's car stood at the curb and
lights glowed at lower windows.

Justin got out at once. "Take it," he said to me. "Drive
back to Athmore with Maggie."

I did not want him to go into that house. All my doubts of
Marc, and of Alicia too, rose up to shatter my control.

"No, please!" I begged him. "If you must go in there, let
us wait for you here."

"I don't want you to wait," he said flatly. "I can get home
on foot if I have to. I'll watch you out of sight, but don't
come back—either of you."

"Do as he says," Maggie ordered me.

We were out of sight of the small hidden house all too
quickly. There was no use in looking back. The car was unfamiliar to me and I drove slowly, unused to the righthand
drive. Behind me Maggie said nothing at all. Raw nerves had
been exposed between us, and we could not pretend to be at
ease with each other.

Like Grovesend, Athmore was lighted, despite the hour.
The outdoor dogs came barking, and we saw that the windows of the Hall of Armor were bright, though it was nearly
four in the morning. More lights burned above in the great
library, but the wings were dark except for the usual dim hall
lights. No lamp burned in Justin's room, or in Dacia's above.

I braked the car beside the garage and saw with relief the
guard posted on duty. While Maggie quieted the dogs,
I jumped out and spoke to the man. He told me that there had
been no disturbances, that all was well. I had to see Justin's
special car for myself. The small garage was locked, but the
guard had a key and I asked him to open the door and turn
on a light inside. The gray car stood untouched and safe, as
Justin had left it. No one had meddled with it tonight while
he was away. Or perhaps that was only because Marc had

not reached home as yet. He had stopped first at Alicia's, not knowing that we would follow soon after.

"Come along, Eve," Maggie said wearily, all her animosity gone. "Let's go inside. I want to talk to Nigel. He must be reading in the library. Justin's no use to us now."

We left the guard to put the car we'd arrived in away, and went toward the house. Morton met us at the door, looking sleepy, as though he had been napping on a couch downstairs.

"You've been up all night?" Maggie asked, considerate as always of those who worked for her.

"I thought it best, Mrs. Graham," he said. "Mr. Barrow is also waiting up in the library. Mr. Marc phoned on his way home, but he has not appeared."

She thanked him and went toward the stairs. I came with her, having no desire to go off alone to my cold, dark room. I would wait up until Justin returned from Grovesend. I cared about nothing else.

In the library Nigel sat before a table, amusing himself with a game of solitaire. He looked up as Maggie and I hurried in, and she went toward him at once—though not into his arms as a woman might, returning to the man she loved. He rose to greet her, nodded to me, and watched as she dropped into a chair.

Her blurted account of what had happened at the club seemed almost incoherent, and when Nigel turned to me in bewilderment, I supplemented her story. He heard us out, and when Maggie came to a faltering halt he chided her gently.

"What has upset you so? How is anything different from what it was before? Of course it's quixotic of Justin to take on Marc's debts under the changed circumstances, but fairly typical, wouldn't you say? What is worrying you, Maggie?"

"I'm not sure," Maggie admitted. "Marc came back to Grovesend with Alicia, and I don't know what he means to do. He's been drinking and—and—" She broke off, distraught and unlike herself.

Nigel remained unperturbed. "Look, my dear, you've been up all night and you're weary to the point of making no sense. I'm fagged too. That telephone call of Marc's sounded a bit reckless, so I stayed up. But since he's made it home safely, I think we can all turn in."

"No, no! You don't understand!" Maggie grew frantic

again. "I'm afraid of what Alicia may incite him to do. Everything has gone against her and she'll place the blame wildly. I've seen in the past how she can stir Marc up when she chooses. You don't know him as I do, Nigel. He can take terrible chances! He can be dangerous when he's angry."

"Dangerous to whom?" Nigel asked, still quiet and reasonable.

Maggie almost snapped at him. "To Justin, of course. Marc is going to blame what has happened on Justin. He has always been jealous of his brother, and if Alicia suspects that Justin still loves Eve in spite of everything, she may—"

Nigel threw a quietly amused look in my direction. "Do you mean that our plan to bring Eve back and recall Justin to his senses is working out?"

"Nigel, be serious!" Maggie cried. "You should have seen Justin's face tonight whenever he looked at Eve. I'll never again doubt his feeling for her. But he's still driven by this sense of responsibility toward Alicia."

"That's ridiculous," Nigel said.

"Of course it's ridiculous. But I can't expect you to understand how Justin feels."

"Thank you," Nigel said dryly. "I fancy Justin can take care of himself and of Marc as well. Though I believe you're right to distrust Alicia. In any event, there's absolutely nothing we can do at the moment. Aren't you willing to grant that, at least?"

Maggie moaned and twisted her hands together, and I stared at her in growing dismay. What she had said made increasing sense to me. Nigel might be calm about this, since it was not really his affair. Now he was the outsider—while I was not. I was involved all the way down the line as far as Justin was concerned. I belonged to Athmore. And I could see what Alicia might do with Marc.

In that moment of helpless silence we heard the approach of a car, heard the dogs barking again.

"There's Justin now!" I cried and ran toward the north wing where I could find a window.

Nigel and Maggie came after me as I hurried through the door of Justin's room and toward a side window, flinging the draperies apart to look out upon the garage area.

A car drove onto the concrete apron and switched off its headlights. The dogs stopped barking at a word from the driver, but this was Marc's red Mercedes, and Marc was alone in the car. Maggie leaned on the windowsill beside me, with Nigel just behind us, and as we watched, Marc got out and spoke to the guard. The man came with him to the small garage, and opened it for him just as he had done for me. I told myself that all Marc wanted was to see that Justin's car was safe, but I watched tensely and I heard Maggie's quiet intake of breath as she saw what he was about.

Marc disappeared into the garage and the guard returned to his post. A moment later Justin's gray car backed out upon the apron. There was no engine roar and its brakes did not squeal. Nevertheless, Marc was backing, stopping, turning at a furious rate. The guard swung about and shouted something at him, but Marc paid no attention. He pointed the car in the direction he wanted and picked up speed so swiftly that he was off along the test course before we knew what he was about.

Maggie spoke desperately in my ear. "That's the direction of the quarry! I was right. He's going to smash up Justin's car."

What anyone said after that, I don't know. I simply started running. I tore down the stairs, holding onto the banister, taking several steps at a time. As I crossed the hall below, Deirdre bounded toward me, came with me as I went out the front door. Together we dashed for the embankment, and down it to the garage area. The startled guard said something to me, but I paid no attention. I climbed into Marc's red car and Deirdre jumped in beside me in the front seat. For a moment I was afraid the unfamiliar dashboard would defeat me, but I had ridden in this car with Dacia and I managed to start the motor and switch on the headlights.

I did not attempt the turns Marc had made. Instead, I drove straight off across Athmore's wide lawns, past the topiary garden, bumping over the turf, heading for the place on the test road where I knew I could cut Marc off. If anyone shouted behind me, I caught no more than a whisper on the wind that whipped my hair into a flowing mass behind my head. Deirdre had caught my urgency, and she sat beside me on the slippery seat, whimpering her excitement. I was glad of her company. I might need her now.

The test road cut suddenly across between me and the woods. I turned the wheel hard left and drove the car at a diagonal across the road, blocking the way. At some distance beyond, the dirt road to the quarry began, but in this narrow place, there was no way for Marc to get past. He could turn around and reach the quarry by a roundabout course, but by that time someone else would surely stop him.

Almost at once I saw the lights of his car coming around a curve, slashing yellow into the straightaway as he headed toward me. I opened the car door and pushed Deirdre out. She would be of no use to me against Marc, but she might be able to bring help.

"Go get Justin!" I ordered. She pricked up her ears and looked at me questioningly. "Go, Deirdre!" I shouted to her, and then paid her no more attention.

I did not think Marc would crash into the Mercedes which he prized so highly, but I did not want him to find me here alone. Trusting my own headlights to blind him, I let myself out on the side of the woods and pressed myself against the remnants of an old stone wall.

Marc came on in Justin's car, his lights striking the Mercedes to a blaze of red. To my dismay, there seemed no break in the wall bordering the edge of the road, no way to let myself through to a safe hiding place in the woods. I must cross the road somehow and run for the immediate grounds behind Athmore.

Justin's gray car slammed to a stop as Marc put on the brakes. I crept behind the Mercedes and peered out behind its far side under cover of my own flaring headlights. I could hear Marc get out of the car though I could not see him, blinded by the duel of lights. I could hear him coming toward me through the brush at the side of the road, and I ran across an edging of lawn and flung myself into the shadow of a huge bush, fearfully conscious of my light-colored coat, and hampered by my long dress. From this new shelter I looked back at the two cars—the Mercedes placed at a diagonal, with Justin's car only a foot or two from it, the headlight beams of the two crossing and entangled.

I could see Marc now. He stood at the side of the road, looking about him. His right hand moved, and in the glare of light before he sprang aside into darkness, I saw the gleam of a gun barrel. Marc had a revolver in his hand. He was searching for me with a gun.

There was an open space across which I must run. I had no other choice. I bent low and dashed across the space. If he could not see me from where he stood, he must have heard me, for he shouted for me to stop. Again I crouched low and ran, grateful for clouds across the moon, and for the black shapes of the topiary garden rising between me and Athmore. In a moment I was in the garden, darting behind the black queen on the edge of the vast chessboard.

I could hear Marc running across the road, and then silence as turf hid the sound of his steps. Swiftly I darted behind another chessman, and then another, until I had run across the intervening space between the opposing lines and could crouch behind the figure of a knight on the far side of the board. Behind me the narrow, sloping lawn led upward to the house.

But now Marc too had reached the chessboard, and it was as if we were engaged in a dreadful game of our own. I could no longer be sure of anything. Each eerie figure of yew menaced me, and I no longer knew whether Marc was between me and the house—or from which side he threatened me. He had not shouted again. He moved silently now, stalking me, with his gun ready, and only an occasional rustle of sound to betray his presence.

Sudden movement near by startled me, and I almost gasped aloud in fright. A dark figure dived from behind a bishop and crouched beside me. Nigel's voice said, "Get down! Get down!"

The sound of the shot from Marc's gun was deafening. The bullet clipped the very nose of my sheltering knight, but his horse's body hid us and Nigel and I huddled low behind the yew.

"Marc means to kill me!" I mouthed the words to Nigel.

"Keep down," he whispered, "and I'll get you out of this."

I crouched on my hands and knees, noting with dread that the moon had begun to emerge from behind a cloud. I was reminded frighteningly of that night of moonlight and shadow on the roofs of Athmore. But this was far worse. Now I knew my enemy. Now I knew for certain who it was that stalked me.

Nigel pressed my arm to indicate that I was to stay where I was, and crept away, to rise in the shadow of a nearby rook. I dared not look for Marc, and I watched the dark shape that was Nigel instead. He had put on a dark-green jacket and a cap that blended into the darkness and made him far less a target than I in my lime-colored dress. The moon came slowly from behind a gilt-edged cloud, and the garden was eerily quiet. Where Marc was I did not know, but

I sensed that Nigel had him in view between his own conceal-
ing yew branches. In the brightening moonlight only Nigel's
face and hands were visible to me.

"Come," he whispered urgently. "Come here! Marc can see
you there."

I moved toward him keeping close to the earth, creeping
into the shelter of the tall green rook. Marc did not fire
again. Nigel reached out to pull me to the safety of black
shadow and I crouched behind him, shielded by his body.
When I looked up he smiled grimly and nodded to me.

"The rook has been useful again," he whispered. "This is
the very one that replaced the rook that was destroyed years
ago."

My mouth was dry, my hands clammy with fear. I could
just make out the peak of his hunting cap as I stared up at
him. The silhouette was frighteningly familiar. This was the
outline that had begun to haunt my dreams. I had seen it in a
snapshot—a figure in hunting cap and jacket, who watched
from a shelter of shrubbery—watched a man who stood beside a crumbling wall.

As I stared up at him in dawning horror, Nigel raised one
hand and I saw that he too held a gun. He was taking careful
aim. Somehow I found my voice.

"Marc!" I shouted. "Marc, take care!"

The second shot crashed across the garden and Marc
cried out. I heard the thud of his fall. There were other
sounds now—sounds from the house. But when I would have
flung myself into the open to run toward Marc, Nigel caught
me by the arm.

"That was very foolish of you," he said softly. "Now you'll
have to come with me."

I could feel the hard nose of the gun in my side, and Nigel's fingers pressing cruelly into my arm. The face of the
enemy had changed so swiftly that I could not right my
thinking in this weird game, but I knew the rook was moving
to checkmate.

We went together, running behind the bushes, while I
prayed for the moon to stay out, so they could see us from
the house and come after us quickly. But this was a night of
uncertainty, of rolling clouds and fitful moonlight. Even as
we ran, darkness swept the garden again. Under its cover we
crossed the open stretch of lawn, returned to the road. Once I
stumbled and almost fell, but Nigel pulled me up and
dragged me with him. He pushed me into the front seat of

Marc's open car, making it very clear that he would not hesitate to shoot if I tried to get away. Then he backed the Mercedes from the vicinity of Justin's gray car, turned it around and set off along the road, driving quietly, without acceleration.

Behind us in the topiary garden I heard someone shout and knew that Marc had been found. But all that was receding into the background. Already house and garden seemed remote and far in the past. As he drove Nigel rested his automatic on the wheel and I knew he watched me sidelong, so that I dared not move.

I expected him to head for the highway in an effort to escape, but when we came to the bumpy, winding course that led to the quarry he turned the car onto it, driving easily and without haste. I did not like our taking this road. They would not reach us quickly now.

"This is a dead end," I said. "The road doesn't go anywhere." He knew that well enough, but I had to learn what he meant to do.

"Yes, the road is exactly that," he said dryly, "though I'm sure I meant no pun."

I shivered at the ugly joke. "I can't believe——" I began.

He stopped me with a sound of irritation. "Believe——believe! What could you expect when you told Maggie you knew who was in that picture, and then later told me the same thing? Didn't you guess you were playing with fire to taunt me like that? You had to be stopped from further chatter. I managed to get the print out of your handbag when I heard that it existed, but I couldn't find the negative. What did you do with it? I tore your room apart that second time, looking for it."

"How could you, when you were on the far side of the roof——?" I broke off, knowing that it would have been simple enough for him to come down through his own tower and search my room while I was away from it. But why? Why?

"Dacia almost caught me," he remembered grimly.

"So it wasn't Marc who carried me to the parapet, after all?" I said. "You went up there again when you finished with my room."

"Do you think I'd miss the opportunity you offered me?" He spoke carelessly, as though it no longer mattered what he said. "It was good luck for me when you tripped over a guy wire and knocked yourself out. Then Marc had to spoil it when he kept you from rolling off that ledge. When you

woke up you were fighting Marc, though he'd saved your life.
Which of course only meant I had to try again."

Nothing, I realized, had occurred as quickly as Nigel had
originally claimed.

His manner now was quiet, almost conversational, as if we
discussed a trifling matter. He was giving me the true answers
only because there was nowhere I could go with them.

"Marc believed it was you he was shooting at—not me," I
said. "But why has all this happened? You had everything to
lose and nothing to gain."

He laughed and the sound was chilling. "I'll still gain what
I want most. Of course it was Alicia who sent Marc after me
tonight. Maggie often wears blinkers. She thought Marc
meant to injure Justin. I knew better. I should have known
from the first that Alicia would try something of the sort,
once she was cornered."

I shook my head, still bewildered, and he went on in that
even, deadly tone.

"I was useful to Alicia after you went away, and Justin behaved so despondently that she thought she had lost him for
good. She came out to the Bahamas, knowing very well how
I had felt about her in the old days at Athmore. She thought
she was too good for me then. This time I found her less un-
touchable. This time she was ready to bargain. I put the Club
Casella in her hands—for goods delivered, as you might say.
But I wanted to marry her, while Justin didn't."

His voice hardened and he breathed more heavily as he
went on. "At the end of a year she returned to England, sup-
posedly for a brief visit to look after her interests at the club.
A visit which dragged on in time. I had Leo Casella working
there, reporting to me. Leo used to be with me and he owes
me a lot. So I knew what she was up to and that she was
after Justin again. I suppose it frightened her badly when I
returned knowing all about her plans with Justin."

So it had been Alicia he had wanted. This was why he'd
induced Maggie to send for me.

"What about Maggie?" I said. "How could you treat her
so—"

He broke in sharply. "Maggie was trying to use me—you
know that perfectly well. So I had no hesitation in using her
to lull Alicia's suspicions until I had her where I wanted her.
Had them all, by that time!"

"How could you—when Justin and Marc and Maggie were

good to you when you were young! Giving you a home, making you welcome! When Justin—"

He would not let me continue. "Never mind all that. You don't know what it was like. Being a zero—a nothing. Being patronized and lifted up from what they regarded as dirt. When all along I knew I was superior in brains to any of them! But I'd have let them alone if it hadn't been for Alicia and her cunning little tricks. Now they've all ranged themselves into one target so I can bring the lot of them down with one blow!" He turned his head to look at me. "Once I hoped to show up Justin through my hold over Alicia, but now I've found it was only you he cares about. So you go with me, Eve."

I sat silent as we continued to follow the bumpy road without urgency on Nigel's part. This in itself was frightening. I knew now that he would never let me go. I was the weapon he held over them all—especially over Justin, whom he hated.

About us the night seemed filled with blowing winds and intermittent moonlight, and the scent of blossoms was sweet on the air. Unbearably sweet, since I might never smell that scent again. Our headlights cut the dark road as it curved into a steeper grade, dipping toward the quarry.

"It's a pity, in a way," he said conversational again and as reasonable as ever. "You know, Eve, I rather liked you. You weren't one of them. You were a nobody—like me. I had hoped we were two of a kind. But you began to make me too much trouble. I'd have succeeded in bringing them all down and getting Athmore for myself—if it hadn't been for you."

"And Old Daniel?" I said bitterly. "What happened to him was your doing too?"

He slowed the car still more, the better to talk. "It's more accurate to say it was Alicia's doing. She set the old man to spy on me. She suspected I was behind the tricks that were being played to delay Justin's work. Naturally I didn't want these efforts of Justin's to pay off before I had him where I wanted him. Leo served me well enough, until he got a bit careless."

"Why didn't Alicia go to Justin with what she suspected?" I cried.

"And have him find out about her little idyl with me in the islands? Find out how she came by the Club Casella? Oh no —that wasn't likely. So she set Old Daniel watching me and reporting to her. I didn't intend what happened. The old fool was onto the glass-smashing Leo did in Justin's workshop, and he met me out there in the ruins for a talk to pin everything down. But he found out soon enough that he was trapped and that I didn't mean to let him go. When you walked onstage he tried to give you a signal—about the rook's play. Only you didn't catch on, did you? I had to take care of him—shut him up for good. Then you came up with that beastly picture and threw the odds against me. If Alicia recognized me in that snapshot, she'd have proof that I'd fixed the old man and she could have turned matters her way by threatening to expose me."

"You'll never have Athmore now," I said, snatching at any straw, "but you still have your life."

He flashed me a look of triumph. "I'll have something even better—the winning shot. There's one big mistake I've made in all this. I never truly believed that Justin could prefer you to Alicia. I thought you might come back and fight the divorce, prove yourself one more thorn in his side. That was my mistake; to believe that what he felt for you was an infatuation which had died out long ago. In a way you've been the worst nuisance of all. Even to tricking me that day when you let poor little Dacia take your coat. You don't think I meant to harm her, do you? It was your silly American chatter that had to be stopped. Now the whole thing will come out— everything. And I don't mean to be around for it. Tonight Maggie gave me the answer and put the best weapon of all in my hands—you! I know now that the best way to destroy Justin is through you. Don't worry—our trip will be over soon."

Terror is a strange thing. Once it is yours there is a point above which it can rise no higher. The mind flings about wildly, seeking an escape, while the deadly goal draws steadily closer. The heart pounds, the eyes stare, and breathing turns labored. Yet if there is time, a plateau is reached where terror can rise no higher. I suppose that is what was happening to me as I faced the fact of my ultimate end. Having faced it, nothing else remained, so that a deathly calm descended upon me. The calm of the hopeless.

With a curious, automatic action I slowly buckled the seat belt around me. Nigel saw me and chuckled wryly.

"You don't think that will help you with a drop to the bottom of the quarry, down—close to a hundred feet! Hold tight now, Justin's darling—" he mocked, "—here we go!"

Our headlights picked up the bluebells blowing in the wind. The lights rose and dipped, dipped again—and fell upon an obstruction which slanted suddenly across the road ahead of us.

It was Justin's gray car, with Justin at the wheel. I screamed—a high, thin sound lost on the wind. I saw Justin's staring face in the glare of our headlights and knew that the lip of the quarry lay only a little way beyond.

This was not what Nigel planned, but he accepted what was there. He pressed his foot upon the gas pedal, and the red Mercedes leaped ahead like a rocket toward the gray obstacle in its path. I flung my arms over my face and prayed with all my might.

I can remember the terrible impact of the crash, the jerk of the seat belt, the rending explosion of sound—and nothing more.

A distant roaring awakened me. My eyes opened to a darkness that was slashed with flame. I must be lying very close to the fire because warmth from the flames burned my face. A dark figure moved in the flickering light. With one hand I felt about me and found grassy earth. Consciousness swept back as something wet licked at my face. Deirdre was there.

I remembered now. It was Marc's red car that was burning! And what had happened to Justin—to Justin's car after being struck broadside?

I found I could move my legs, my arms. I could even stumble shakily to my feet. The tall figure silhouetted against the flames knelt beside something on the grass, then straightened and looked toward me.

"Justin?" I said in disbelief.

A car door slammed and I heard someone shout, heard Justin call an answer. Then he came to me quickly.

"You're all right, Eve? I got you out split seconds before the car caught fire. Then I went back for Nigel."

I could not speak my question—I only looked at him.

"He went through the windshield," Justin said. "He's dead."

I clung to him. "That's what he wanted. But he meant to take me with him."

"Deirdre met me in the woods on my way back from Alicia's and let me know by her frantic manner that something was wrong. I got to Marc in the garden after Maggie found him, and he told me Nigel had you. When I found the Mer-

cedes gone, I took my own car and came after you. I could
see your headlights now and then and guessed where you
were heading. So I cut through the woods by way of the path
—it was just wide enough—and I barely made it ahead of
you."

People from the house had arrived in Maggie's car. Suddenly Marc was there, his arm in a crude sling. Maggie got
out last and stood staring at the burning wreckage, a tall
woman in her black dress and evening wrap, the Athmore
pearls white about her throat. Justin spoke to her gently. She
turned from the dark shape on the grass and came to stand
beside me, her face pale in the flaring light.

"It's better this way," she said tonelessly. "Marc would
have killed him tonight. Alicia did everything I feared,
though it wasn't Justin she wanted to pay off, but Nigel. She
had guessed that he was the one who took her car when
Dacia was struck down. And he'd ruined her through the
club. I've been stupid all along. I truly believed Nigel was
fond of me and that he would help me get Marc out of trouble. I never knew it was Alicia he cared about all along—or
how he hated Justin. Marc has told me everything. Marc has
been their captive, but tonight he meant to free himself."

I put my hand upon her arm to stop her painfully blurted
words. There was nothing I could say in answer. One day
perhaps we would be friends again.

Marc came over to us. "Thank you, Evie," he said, calling
me by Dacia's name. "If you hadn't shouted I'd have bought
it. As it was, I ducked in time and only got winged. I'd taken
Justin's car out to hide it from Nigel because Alicia said he
meant to destroy it tonight. I wanted it at a safe distance
from the house before I settled with him. When I saw my car
blocking the road I thought it was Nigel who had come to
stop me. With those headlights blazing I couldn't see you.
Not till later in the topiary garden."

He bent and kissed me lightly on the cheek. "That's from
Dacia. I don't think I can fit her into Athmore, but I mean to
fit her into my life—my own life away from here."

He turned to Maggie, drew her toward her waiting car,
while I stayed behind.

After a time Justin left one of the men from the house to
guard the burning Mercedes and came to me. The flames had
dropped to smoldering spurts, and beyond I saw Justin's gray
car where it had rolled, almost to the edge of the quarry. The

sight seemed to rouse me as nothing else had done. All the years of work he had spent on this car—and now this!

"Is it hopelessly damaged?" I asked.

He shook his head. "Not essentially. The car bounced away from the impact as it was meant to do. Its inner padding protected me, and the new fuel doesn't explode, of course, or cause a car to burn. I'd not have chosen this way to test it, but the car came through! Are you able to walk now, Eve?"

My knees were still rubbery, but I could manage. We went together, but not along the road the others had followed. We found the path through the woods along which Justin had come on his wild ride, barely scraping between the trees in some places, leaving the marks of his passage in others. The moon had gone behind another cloud, yet the sky was not dark as it had been.

Among the stones of Athmore Hall the grass was wet and my slippers were quickly damp with dew. I did not care. I went to stand before the arch of the chapel window, afraid to look at Justin, afraid to be too close to him. I could not ask about Alicia, though her name burned in my mind.

He answered without my asking.

"Alicia gave Marc the gun he would have killed Nigel with. That's what he wanted. Then she held me at Grovesend talking—held me there deliberately, so Marc would get away before I could stop him. She was too angry to care about caution and she told me everything. About her affair with Nigel and what he'd done for her, what he was up to now. If Marc had killed Nigel, it would have been as though she pulled the trigger."

There was a sickness of disillusionment, of shock in his words. He had lost his belief in her forever tonight, and in Nigel he had lost someone he had believed his friend.

We stood in troubled silence, and I knew that the echoes of what had happened would sound down all the years ahead of us.

Through the arch of the great window pale rose stained the morning, and I moved to where I could look through and watch dawn light the sky. There was hope in light. Tomorrow did come—for some of us.

"Let's go home," Justin said.

Through the woods we walked together—back to Athmore.

Fawcett Crest Bestsellers